For the first time in her life, DeShea felt connected, a part of something.

Cradled against Nick, she savored the feeling of wholeness, of belonging. Somewhere in the back of her mind, a small ray of hope was born. But she reminded herself that this was only a brief respite from the real world.

Nick rolled onto his side and gazed into her eyes. "I've never known anyone like you before, Shea. You're like a small sun trapped in a block of ice. On the outside, you look crystal clear, unblemished and cool to the touch." His hand trailed up her arm slowly. "But on the inside, you're hot, dazzling, a beam of sunshine that's so intense, it frightens me."

She looked away, uncertain if he was bestowing a compliment or expressing his disapproval of her sexual abandon. His strong fingers gently urged her face toward him again.

"Who are you, DeShea? And what's going on in that head of yours?"

Dear Reader:

Romance readers have been enthusiastic about the Silhouette Special Editions for years. And that's not by accident: Special Editions were the first of their kind and continue to feature realistic stories with heightened romantic tension.

The longer stories, sophisticated style, greater sensual detail and variety that made Special Editions popular are the same elements that will make you want to read book after book.

We hope that you enjoy this Special Edition today, and will enjoy many more.

Please write to us:

Jane Nicholls
Silhouette Books
PO Box 236
Thornton Road
Croydon
Surrey
CR9 3RU

LORRAINE CARROLL

The Ice Princess

Silhouette Special Edition

Originally Published by Silhouette Books
a division of
Harlequin Enterprises Ltd.

First published in Great Britain in 1992
by Silhouette Books, Eton House, 18-24 Paradise Road,
Richmond, Surrey TW9 1SR

© Lorraine Beatty 1991

Silhouette, Silhouette Special Edition and Colophon are
Trade Marks of Harlequin Enterprises B.V.

ISBN 0 373 58381 8

23-9203

Made and printed in Great Britain

LORRAINE CARROLL

traces her dream of becoming a novelist back to her
schooldays, when she penned a teenage
romance/action adventure story for a writing
assignment. To the teacher who had unknowingly
planted the seeds of commitment in her, Lorraine
gives thanks.

Lorraine has moved around a bit – from Columbus,
Ohio, where she was born and raised, to Germany,
Connecticut, Louisiana and Mississippi, where she
currently resides. She has been married over twenty
years to the "world's most perfect husband," and has
two sons. When she finds time, she plays the piano
and sews.

Another Silhouette Book by Lorraine Carroll

Silhouette Special Edition

Lead with Your Heart

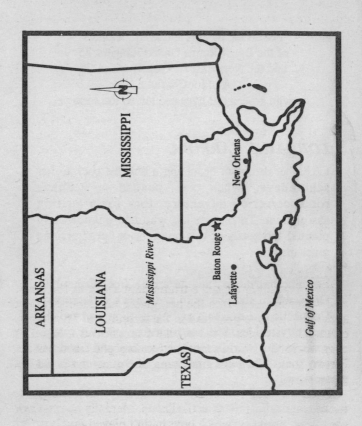

Chapter One

"Cross it. Cross it! Yeah!"

Nick Couvillion let out a triumphant shout as the black-and-white ball shot into the net, giving his under-fourteen soccer team a two-goal lead in the scrimmage. They'd executed the play exactly the way he'd taught them. His dark eyes warmed as he watched his young players celebrate. Maybe they were getting the hang of this after all. But the game wasn't over yet.

There were still twenty-five minutes left, and he needed to make some adjustments in the lineup. Mentally he ran down the roster, assessing which boys hadn't played much, which ones were having a good day, the few that weren't. Hands on hips, he turned and surveyed the players on the bench. One was missing.

"Thompson!" he shouted. Where had the boy gotten to? He'd have to speak with him about staying on the sidelines with the other members of the team. The kid was new, just moved to town three weeks ago. His eyes scanned the small group of parents gathered to watch the game, but there was no sign of the new boy.

"Joe," he called to his assistant coach. "Where's Thompson?" The older man pointed down the line, and Nick spotted the wayward player at the opposite end of the field. With an exaggerated gesture, Nick motioned the lad to his side and was rewarded with a sheepish grin as Thompson hurriedly jogged back to midfield. Nick shook his head and smiled, a message of understanding passing between him and his assistant. The mind of a thirteen-year-old was sometimes a mysterious place indeed.

His team once more assembled, Nick was about to turn his attention back to the game when his gaze fell upon a woman standing just inside the chain-link fence that surrounded the soccer field. For a moment his heart nearly stopped beating. The woman he was looking at was dead—had been for nearly eight months. His brain refused to accept what his eyes were seeing. The face was familiar, painfully so, and he felt grief twist in his gut. Marette was dead. This had to be a ghost, a dream. Either that or he was losing his mind.

"Coach Couvillion? Ya gonna put me in?"

Brad Thompson's voice pierced Nick's dazed state of mind. "It's Coo-vee-ohn," he corrected absently, forcing himself to look down at the boy. Instantly he saw he'd embarrassed him by giving the proper pronunciation of his name. "Don't worry, kiddo. You'll get the hang of the names down here after a while. And yes, I'm going to put you in. I want you to go for Breaux at left wing."

Brad made a sour grimace. "In St. Louis, I always played defense."

"Well, in Baton Rouge we need you to play offense." Nick smiled, but his voice was firm. When the ball rolled over the touchline a few minutes later, Nick shouted out to the referee, "Sub, ref!"

As Brad trotted onto the pitch, Nick turned back to the fence, his mouth set in a firm line. But the woman was gone, and he felt an overwhelming sense of relief. It must have been a passerby, a parent from the opposing team who had merely reminded him of Danny's mother. Shaking his head, he turned back to the game just in time to see the Lafayette Raiders drive the ball into the net. Nick cursed under his breath and called up two more players from the bench, his mind totally focused on the game now and the strategy needed to win. The mysterious woman was forgotten.

The taxi pulled up at the LaFleur Middle School and DeShea Ballard stepped gracefully from the back. Her violet eyes were anxious and searching, but her heart was hopeful. Perhaps her long journey was at an end at last. She'd found the house with little difficulty. Number 505 Suntree Place. Home of René Couvillion and family. But a kindly neighbor had told her they were up the street at the school, watching a soccer game. Acting on impulse she had directed the cabdriver to bring her here.

It wasn't until she stepped around the chain-link fence that the impact of her decision hit her. After seventeen years, she wasn't even sure she'd recognize Marette. Her sister had been eighteen when she left home. She would be nearly thirty-five now. A woman could change a great deal in that length of time. Her second thought was that if Marette and her husband were here, then that could mean they had a son who played on the team. From what she could tell, the only people here were the two teams on the field and the parents. DeShea felt her heart warm at the thought and bit her lip in anticipation. She'd wondered about it often since leaving New York. Marette had always wanted children. Lots of them. Did she have boys, girls? Several of each? Finding her sister after all this time was exciting enough. A brother-in-law and maybe nephews and nieces went beyond her highest expectations.

But as she stood at the fence, her initial excitement began to wane. She realized she couldn't just start tapping people on the shoulder and say, "Excuse me, but are you my

long-lost sister?'' That wouldn't be fair to Marette or her
family. No. This reunion was best done in private, quietly
and gently. There was so much to say, to explain. It would
be better to return to the house, and not attempt a meeting
in the middle of a schoolyard. She'd waited seventeen years;
she could wait a few hours more.

Her decision reached, DeShea took one last glance around
the field, only to find herself locked in a firm gaze with a
pair of deep brown eyes. She watched with interest as the
man's eyes widened, then narrowed. She thought she read
recognition in the dark pools, then shock, then something
else. But the contact was broken when he turned and spoke
to a young player at his side. DeShea found herself still
watching the man with interest. He was tall, with thick, dark
hair that had been mussed by the breeze and dampened by
exertion. A royal blue knit shirt was stretched across the
broad shoulders, hugging the contour of his back before
tapering sharply into white soccer shorts. Narrow hips gave
way to powerful thighs and legs that announced athletic
prowess as the muscles rippled with each shift in his stance.
She saw him grin at the young player at his side, then rest a
hand on the boy's shoulder.

He was one of the most attractive men DeShea had seen
in a long while, and it occurred to her that perhaps this was
her brother-in-law. Marette had always admired the tall,
dark and handsome type. With a firm mental shake she reminded herself that all her questions would be answered
soon enough. But back at the house, not here.

When the cab parked in front of the Acadian-style Couvillion residence once more, DeShea realized she faced yet
another quandary. Perhaps she shouldn't just appear on the
doorstep. Maybe she should find a hotel room and call first.
Just what was proper etiquette for reuniting sisters separated by seventeen years of silence?

Quickly she ran through the list of options again, all too
aware of both the driver's mounting impatience and the
butterflies that were restaging the Civil War in her stom-

ach. Finally she asked herself the question that had become almost her mantra over the past few months. What did *she* want to do? A smile curved her delicate mouth, and she lifted her head confidently. Dismissing the white car, De-Shea walked firmly up onto the wide front porch that ran the length of the house. After a slight hesitation, she turned toward the left and sat down in one of the wicker chairs to wait.

It was a beautiful, clear Sunday afternoon. The late-afternoon sun was sinking low in the sky, and a gentle, fragrant breeze swirled around her, easing her tension and boosting her resolve. As she grew calmer, she took in her surroundings, from the well-kept white and cream porch with its lush hanging baskets to the neatly clipped yard and flower beds. Across the street was a small park with picnic tables and large trees draped with Spanish moss. She could easily see Marette living here. It seemed in keeping with her sister's romantic nature. That is, Marette had been romantic as a child. What was she like now? Did she still like butter-pecan ice cream and old movies? Did she still have a voracious appetite for books? Had she ever learned to play the piano? What kind of man had she married?

DeShea's excitement was tempered with a large amount of apprehension. Would Marette recognize her? Would she be glad to see her or angry at the unannounced appearance? Could they bridge the gap of years and misunderstandings? Could the sins of their mother be set aside, or would they only deepen the distance between them?

The persistent queasiness in her stomach made her wish she'd thought all this through before coming to Baton Rouge. Finding Marette's name and address had felt like an omen slashed across the wall. It had shaken her out of her apathy of the past two months. Since her mother's death, DeShea had felt as if the world was falling apart around her. She was being buried under a mountain of decisions and looking at a future that was vague.

Then she'd been given the letters. Three short missives, spanning seventeen years, still unopened and unread. Letters to Natalie Ballard, the mother who had turned her back on her older daughter, refusing to acknowledge her existence. DeShea had felt a war of emotions exploding within her as she'd held the small envelopes that day: fury at the callousness of her mother for never even opening Marette's mail, sympathy for a sister whose attempts at reconciliation had been cruelly ignored and profound gratitude to a compassionate secretary who had quietly disobeyed orders to destroy all letters from Marette and instead had filed them away in vain hope of future understanding.

The letters had given DeShea purpose, a direction. Since her divorce, she had stagnated. Her self-esteem had deteriorated. She realized at that moment she had used the management of Clotilles, her mother's exclusive health spas, as a barricade against reality. She'd felt like a failure both as a woman and a person, so she'd clung to the only constant in her life. Work. Not because it was satisfying but because it was all she knew.

Suddenly she felt angry—at her mother, at Eric, at life. But mostly at herself for wasting three years of her life, standing in her mother's shadow. That was something she had vowed never to do again. Eric had taught her how to be herself. But the shock and the pain of the divorce had blinded her to those important lessons. She realized then that she had a choice. She could either cave in to the massive burden of a failing business or turn her life around and strike out on her own. For the first time in thirty years, she was master of her own fate. And her first goal would be to find Marette, reclaim the only family she had, start life anew. On her terms, with her desires and needs, not those of a domineering mother.

Within a week, DeShea had delegated much of the responsibility of her mother's company to a trusted subordinate and boarded a plane for Baton Rouge.

Now, sitting on Marette's cozy porch, watching twilight approach, she was having doubts about her hasty departure. Her decision to appear without warning on her sister's doorstep was a rash one. She had no guarantee that her reception would be warm.

Welcome or not, the moment was suddenly at hand when a silver minivan pulled into the drive. Glancing at her watch, she saw it was nearly seven. DeShea felt a fist of fear form in her stomach. Her mind racing over the many scenarios she'd envisioned, she tried to find words that would be appropriate to the occasion. For eight years she'd been second in command of a worldwide company, negotiating financial deals and business contracts, but finding the words to greet her sister seemed an insurmountable obstacle.

Nearly frozen with fear and anticipation, DeShea remained seated in the wicker chair as she watched a man emerge from the van. She recognized him immediately as the one who had locked eyes with her at the field. He walked to the back of the van and lifted the gate, pulling out a blue sport bag and slinging it carelessly over his shoulder. Then he leaned back into the car and removed a large white net filled with balls, which he dropped on the ground and dragged along behind him.

DeShea couldn't help but see that he was even more attractive than she'd first thought. Lean and hard-muscled, he moved with an easy, languid stride that signaled confidence and purpose. His features were strong and distinctive, his chin shadowed with a faint growth of stubble.

Realizing she was admiring a man who was probably her sister's husband, she glanced away, catching sight of a boy who had just then appeared at the back of the van. He wore a red, white and blue uniform with blue sandals and blue socks that were bunched around his ankles. He also pulled out a bag and slung it over his shoulder with the same gesture of nonchalance that his father had used. The boy was small and slender with short brown hair that was shoved back from his face. His eyes were incredibly large and dark.

In build, he was a miniature version of the man, right down to the thighs that hinted at the burgeoning strength. Shutting the tailgate, he dropped a ball on the ground and began to kick it expertly in front of him as he approached the house.

"Did you get your water jug, Dan?" the man asked as he climbed the steps.

"No, sir," the boy answered, kicking the ball up onto the planked floor with one sharp tap of his foot. "I'll get it later."

"Don't leave it in the van. I don't want it leaking all over the carpet," the man said, letting the bag of balls drop and inserting a key in the door.

DeShea had watched them approach across the lawn and sidewalk and up the steps, trying to absorb the fact that this was her sister's husband and son. But where was Marette? Her heart ached at the thought of having to wait even longer to see her.

The man and boy were reaching for the doorknob when DeShea finally set herself in motion. Rising from the chair, she walked toward them, feeling as if she were in a dream. The boy was the first to see her. His eyes widened with alarm, and he jerked backward against his parent. The man straightened, and as their eyes collided, DeShea read again the same emotion in the dark eyes. Only this time, she saw a look of anger as well.

"Excuse me, but are you Mr. Couvillion?" she asked.

Nick stared at the woman before him. This was no ghost. It was the same woman he'd seen at the field. Up close, he could see she didn't look as much like Marette as he'd imagined. Her features were more delicate, her eyes more violet, not blue, and her hair was lighter, more flaxen, and braided expertly along the back of her head. Nick felt Danny back against him farther, as if trying to get away, and he rested his hands on the slender shoulders in reassurance. He knew what was coming and there was nothing he could do about it. Damn the woman.

"Yes, I am," he finally answered.

DeShea took a deep breath. "I'm DeShea Ballard, Marette's sister," she said, her calm manner hiding her emotion. "You must be René." Holding out her hand, she added, "I hope Marette will be home soon."

A strangled moan burst from the boy, and he lunged for the door, disappearing into the house.

Habit made DeShea carefully mask her surprise. She'd learned at an early age to shield her emotions. It prevented all sorts of unpleasant repercussions. At least, it had until this moment. She had no idea what she'd said or done to upset the boy.

"Danny!" Nick called after the boy, but he remained in the doorway. He had something to settle first. He should have guessed who the woman was when he first saw her. He'd just never expected to meet her face-to-face. "What do you want here?" he asked, watching as her violet eyes widened slightly. She hadn't flinched when Danny ran inside, hadn't looked the least bit concerned. Apparently she didn't understand what effect her sudden appearance had had on him; either that or she was being deliberately cruel.

"I'm here to see my sister."

Her voice was calm and even, and Nick felt himself growing angrier. What sort of game was she playing? "Well, you're too late. The funeral was last August."

His words stunned her momentarily. Then the realization exploded in her mind like a charge of dynamite. A wave of nausea and light-headedness drove through her, and for a moment she feared she might pass out.

"Marette's dead?" It took all her remaining strength to force the words from between her lips. "I didn't know." Outwardly, the only sign of her shocked state was a deepening of the violet eyes to a dark purple.

Nick's barely controlled anger spilled over. "Like hell, lady!" he shouted. "I sent you a telegram the day she died." Did the violet eyes seem darker now, or was he just imagining it? If she really didn't know about Marette, then she sure was taking the news calmly. He looked at her intently, searching for some sign that there were feelings behind her cool, perfect exterior. Nothing. Not one indication that the news about her sister had affected her in the slightest.

DeShea looked away. She knew her mother, knew her unforgiving position toward Marette. It wasn't difficult to see what had happened. She didn't want Marette's husband to know that. He didn't need to be reminded of the heartless mother-in-law who'd disowned his wife. "I never saw it. I didn't know."

Nick attempted to control his anger. "What do you want here? Why didn't you call first? I assume they have telephones at Clotilles or wherever you came from." He expected her to reply to his taunt with some finely honed verbal barb. She looked the type who could cut out a person's heart and leave them bleeding on the floor, then walk away without a second glance. He'd heard all about little sister from Marette. She was a chip off the old block, as hard-boiled and unemotional as they came. He was unprepared for her calm, quiet, almost apologetic response.

"I was in a hurry to see her. I needed to find her," DeShea answered honestly. Her simple, straightforward statement warned her just how upset she really was. The shock had allowed her guard to slip, had punctured her control. She'd spoken reflexively before she'd carefully analyzed her response. "I didn't think."

"That's for damned sure," Nick barked. "If you had, Daniel wouldn't have been hit with the sight of a woman who looks like his mother. It was a pretty heartless thing to do, lady."

Still existing in a daze, only one fact penetrated her emotional state. "Then he *is* Marette's son?" she asked softly.

Nick frowned. Marette had sent her mother a telegram after the birth. Whatever kind of sick game was being played, he wanted no part of it. "You catch on quick," he said sarcastically.

"I wasn't sure," DeShea replied, her voice almost a whisper. "I hoped, but I had no way of knowing for certain." She struggled to form a coherent thought. "I only knew Marettè was married." It was all she could do to stand still and keep breathing, to act normal. She wouldn't worsen the situation by fainting, or something equally embarrassing. Her shock was a direct result of her impulsive, thoughtless actions, and she would just have to bear up as best she could.

Planting his fists on his hips, Nick glanced off into the distance briefly before answering. "To my brother. And since you seem to be way behind on family news, René died two years ago." Even this blunt announcement failed to evoke a flicker of emotion in the sleek package that called itself DeShea.

With a silent curse, Nick dismissed her. He needed to be with Danny now, not standing on the porch talking to a mannequin who hadn't bothered to contact her sister until it was too late. Running a hand sharply through his hair, he set his jaw. "I've got to check on Dan." He turned toward the door, then stopped and gave DeShea a cold stare. "You'd better come in. You owe Daniel an explanation." Stepping over the threshold, he left DeShea to follow on her own.

Slowly she put a hand to her mouth, feeling the quivering of her lips against her fingertips. Or maybe it was her fingers that were shaking. She couldn't tell. She fought down the nausea that threatened to fill her throat. Marette was gone, her husband dead, her only son an orphan. This was some horrible nightmare, a bad dream. Daniel. Danny was her last living relative, and she'd been unbelievably cruel to him, dropping into his life without warning, dredging up memories and grief still so fresh and painful. How could she have been so selfish, so thoughtless, to the child?

Numbly, she entered the house and stopped in the wide foyer. After closing the door, she moved into the large living room. Danny and his uncle were nowhere to be seen, so she seated herself in the large wing chair near the fireplace and rested her head against the high back.

Here she sat, in her sister's home, surrounded by her things, but it wasn't at all like her fantasies. In her mind, she'd pictured a joyous, tearful reunion, fierce hugs and happy tears, words and laughter mingling incoherently as they tried to close the gap of seventeen years. She'd imagined a handsome husband sitting in the background, his face reflecting his delight in his wife's happiness. They would sit in the kitchen, hands clasped across the table, while Marette's children hung over their shoulders listening to stories about their childhood. Never, never had she expected to arrive and find Marette and her husband gone and their child in the care of an uncle.

Her teeth pushed into her lower lip as she thought of the boy. She hadn't meant to shock him and she would never forgive herself if she'd hurt Danny unnecessarily. The uncle's comment about her looking like the boy's mother came back to her then. Did she? If so, was the resemblance a strong one? Danny's reaction suggested that she and Marette favored each other a great deal.

Slowly she rose and walked to the mirror that hung over the mantel, gazing at her reflection, trying to remember Marette the last time she'd seen her. At eighteen and thirteen, their resemblance had been slight, although their coloring had been similar. Perhaps maturity had changed that. But the face that looked back at her now seemed pale and drawn and, somehow, unreal. She could see no trace of her sister reflected there, no hint of the smiling Marette who had left for college and never returned. With a grimace, De-Shea turned away and looked around the room. Suddenly it all seemed too much to deal with. To be standing here, so close to her sister, yet so very, very far away.

Brushing moisture from her eyes, she retreated to the chair. Losing her composure now, in front of Danny and the uncle, would be disastrous. Later, when she was alone, she could let go. But now she needed to be strong, to face the boy and the consequences of her impulsive actions. She needed to learn the facts and decide what to do in the future, to make... Voices, faint and from overhead, drew her attention, and she tensed as she heard the shuffle of feet on the carpeted stairs.

Nick guided his young nephew down the stairs and into the living room. He had found Danny lying across his bed, silently staring into space. He'd hoped the boy would be crying, finally releasing the dam of grief he'd built up during the past months. But even the strong physical resemblance between his aunt and his mother had failed to make him let go. They had talked quietly, calmly, for a few minutes, then Danny had decided to go back down and talk to his long-lost relative. There didn't seem to be any bitterness in the boy, no anger, merely surprise and a slight withdrawal that only Nick could sense. All in all, Nick was proud of the way Danny had handled the situation.

He wished he could deal with it with equal maturity. But unfortunately, he couldn't seem to shake the resentment that coursed through him whenever he thought of Marette's family. They had abandoned her, denied her very existence. Now, when it was too late, they dropped into Danny's life to open up old wounds and renew a grief that was still painfully fresh. His nephew might be forgiving, but Nick doubted if he could be so generous.

When he stepped into the living room, his convictions were further strengthened by the sight of DeShea seated elegantly in the chair by the stone fireplace. For a brief second he thought he detected a hint of tears, but then the violet eyes were masked behind long lashes and he dismissed his absurd notion. Women like her didn't cry.

She rose to her feet, slowly, coolly, as if commanding his attention. He took a quick inventory that did little to alter his earlier assessment. She was impeccably groomed, from her Italian leather pumps to her flawless complexion. A perfectly tailored light blue suit skimmed her slim figure, calling attention to the startling color of her eyes. But her expression was composed, unreadable, and if he hadn't seen the faint flutter of the silk collar at her throat each time she breathed, he'd have sworn she was a sculpture. A statue in blue ice with amethyst eyes.

That she could be the sister of the vivacious and unaffected Marette was beyond his ability to comprehend.

DeShea saw the displeasure in the uncle's eyes the moment he stepped into the room. He didn't want her here, didn't want her in Danny's life. She could hardly blame him. She'd handled the whole thing badly. Her only recourse now was to face the consequences. Slowly she rose to her feet, steeling herself for the confrontation that was sure to come. With clenched jaw, she lifted her eyes and looked into his hard cold ones. The room was thick with tension.

Danny was the first to break the uncomfortable silence. "Are you really my mom's little sister?"

DeShea's voice seemed to lodge in her throat, but she forced out the answer. "Yes."

"You look a lot like her," he said, looking at her closely. "Except she was prettier."

Danny's love for his mother sent a stab of pain lancing along DeShea's every nerve, setting loose a barrage of powerful emotions—grief, remorse and bitter sadness. It took all her will to keep from caving in under the burden.

Nick nearly bit through the inside of his mouth in an effort to keep from cursing at her. What was wrong with this woman? Was she really made of ice? Was there no heart beneath the expensive clothes? Couldn't she see that Dan was having trouble just looking at her? No, she didn't have a clue. Her face had remained a mask. Apparently nothing could penetrate that cool marble exterior of hers.

Nearly a full minute passed before DeShea could find her voice again. She looked at Danny and tried to smile. "I'm very sorry if I upset you, Danny. I'm sure it was a shock finding me on your doorstep."

The apology jerked Nick's eyes to the woman in surprise.

Danny shrugged. "That's okay. I knew about you. I'd just forgotten. I mean . . ." He glanced quickly at his uncle. "I knew my mom had a sister, but I'd never seen you, ya know, not really." He sighed. "It was just sort of weird, ya know. Like seeing a ghost."

DeShea struggled to find something appropriate to say to make everything all right again. She'd never been around children, didn't know how to talk to them. And the persistent glare from the uncle was further disrupting her composure. But she had to say something. She couldn't stand here silent and staring like an idiot. "It's all right, Danny. I understand. We're both in a similar position. You see, I didn't know about you. If I had, well, I'd have done things differently," she said honestly.

"Didn't Mom tell you about me?" he asked.

Nick looked at the flawless face, anxious to hear the answer to that question himself.

DeShea read the challenge in the man's dark eyes and decided the truth would be the only thing that would satisfy him. "I'm sure she tried. I just never got the message."

This farce of a reunion was trying Nick's remaining patience. He had a few things to say to Ms. Ballard, and he wasn't going to wait any longer to say them. "Danny, your aunt and I have a lot of things to discuss. Why don't you get cleaned up, give us a few minutes alone, then we'll all sit and talk, okay?"

"I can get cleaned up later." Danny whirled on his uncle. "I just met her. I want to talk about Mom."

The already shortened fuse on Nick's temper burned out. "*Now,* Daniel. I warned you before about back-talking me. Do what I tell you. And get the jug out of the van."

He hadn't meant to shout, but the Ice Princess seemed to have chilled his usually temperate state of mind. He took a deep breath and sent his nephew an apologetic glance. "Go on, son."

With a loud, irritated sigh, Danny replied, "Yes, sir," but not before favoring his uncle with a glare of his own. When he reached the stairs, he turned and looked back at De-Shea. "You'll still be here, won't you? When I'm done?"

DeShea looked into the uncle's intense brown eyes and knew if he had his way she'd be out the door before Danny reached the landing. But she'd not come all this way to merely turn and disappear. Danny was all she had left now, and no one, not even this angry man with the fierce scowl and eyes like smoldering coals, would chase her away.

Squaring her shoulders, she looked directly at her nephew. "I'll be here, Danny. Nothing could make me leave."

Furious, Nick spun on his heels and headed to the kitchen. He needed a drink. Yanking open the refrigerator, he grabbed a can of beer, popped the top and took a long pull. It did little, if anything, to alleviate his irritation.

DeShea followed slowly behind him, stopping inside the archway and watching as he guzzled the beer. For the first time, she wondered just who this man was who was raising her nephew. That he was physically attractive she had no doubts, but that had nothing to do with his ability to raise a child. He'd been, in her estimation, overly harsh in dismissing Danny. And now he was standing in front of the refrigerator downing alcohol like a man lost in a desert. Had Marette approved? Was there no one else to be entrusted with the care of a young boy besides this scruffy, obviously volatile man?

Nick read the disapproval in DeShea's eyes and allowed the rebel in him to taunt her even more. He lifted his nearly empty can. "Want a drink?"

"No, thank you," she replied coolly.

Her response only fueled his already steamy state of mind. Ice Princess to the core. All right. If so, then nothing he could say would melt even one layer of her frigid veneer. "So why the hell didn't you drop in for the burial? Too busy on the Continent?"

DeShea withstood the cutting remark. "I told you, I didn't know about it. If I had, nothing on earth could have kept me away."

"You've had seventeen years to find Marette. Why didn't you look her up before?" He sent her a scathing glance. "She wasn't exactly hiding. Her name's in the book."

Long-buried anger flared and burst forth before DeShea was wholly aware of it. "Marette had *my* address. She knew where I was. Why didn't *she* find *me?*"

The violet gaze that met his was unwavering. A lack of emotion or a sign of truth? Nick's irritation slipped a notch. "Yeah, well, it's too late now, isn't it?"

One hand on his hip, he turned and walked to the table, gesturing abruptly for her to be seated. He sank into the Windsor chair, one leg outstretched, his thumb wiping off the condensation from the aluminum can. "Why come now, after all this time? A sudden surge of sisterly affection or just curiosity? Gee, I wonder whatever happened to good ol' Marette?"

It was a cruel thing to say and he knew he shouldn't have, but at the moment he wasn't too concerned about her feelings. He was concerned with her effect on Danny.

The taunt pierced her heart, but DeShea swallowed the pain. Could she expect any less after her behavior? Lacing her fingers together on the table, she tried to explain in as few words as possible. He would not sit still for lengthy explanations. Of that she was certain.

"I was thirteen when Marette left. Since then I have heard nothing about her or from her. Our mother refused to acknowledge her existence. Last week I found three unopened letters. One was from Pensacola a few months after Marette moved there. She wanted us to know she was okay and that she'd started to work at the Naval Air Station. The second letter was written after she met your brother. The third right after their marriage. Until those letters were given to me, I had no idea where my sister was or even if she was alive."

Nick leaned forward, his expression hard and scowling. "I know for a fact Marette sent your mother a telegram when Daniel was born, and *I* sent the one when she died."

"I'm not doubting your word, Mr. Couvillion," she replied evenly, ignoring the surge of apprehension his fierce look created. "But I never saw any telegrams. My guess would be that our mother...destroyed them."

Leaning back in the chair, he pondered that idea. As much as he hated to admit it, the Ice Princess might be telling the truth. Her explanation matched the tales Marette used to tell about her mother. Except Marette had made several references to the fact that DeShea and their mother had a lot in common. He couldn't remember the specifics, but he remembered the comparison vividly.

DeShea watched the frown on Nick's face deepen, wondering what he was thinking and if this was a good time to ask some very important questions. When the crease between his dark eyes didn't ease, she decided to forge ahead, regardless of his opinion. She had a right to know. "Mr. Couvillion, I'd appreciate it if you could tell me how my sister and her husband died."

He looked over at her, and their eyes locked, each challenging the other but neither one backing down. "Nick," he finally said. "The name is Nick."

DeShea felt as if the first door had been opened. At least he wasn't demanding she call him "Mr. Couvillion."

"My older brother, René, Marette's husband, was a diver. He worked offshore." At the faint frown on DeShea's face, he elaborated. "On the oil rigs in the Gulf. He was killed when one of the rigs collapsed. That was a little more than two years ago. Marette took it hard. They were very close, extremely happy. I'd never seen a marriage that sound and secure."

He shoved the now empty can aside, resting his forearms on the table. "Danny was devastated. He and his dad spent a lot of time together, even though René would be gone for weeks at a time. After he died, I took up the slack as best as

I could. I took over his soccer team and tried to be available whenever he needed someone." He looked away. "But no one can take the place of a father."

The note of sadness in Nick's voice when he spoke of his brother tugged at DeShea's heart, and she had the fleeting impression there was something else behind his statement, someone else for whom he grieved. Nick had kept his gaze averted, but she could easily imagine the dark eyes filled with grief. She realized now that was what she'd seen in his eyes at the field—grief. He had looked at her and seen Marette, and all the pain had been reflected in his eyes. "And my sister?" she asked softly.

Nick released a deep sigh. "Marette died of a toxic reaction to a drug. A minor infection, but her reaction was so swift, so violent, that it was all over before anyone could do anything." He rubbed his forehead in an unconscious attempt to ease the pain. "Maybe if we could have talked to your mother it could have been avoided."

DeShea stared past Nick, searching for some recollection, some memory that would explain Marette's death. She couldn't remember her mother ever saying that either of them was allergic to any medication. But then, Natalie had never handled the mundane aspects of her children's lives. That had been relegated to their endless stream of nurses and nannies. "I don't think Mother knew about any allergies," she muttered softly.

Nick's hands clenched into hard fists as his anger spilled over again. Her sister dead for no reason, and Ice Princess was defending the mother. His words were drenched in sarcasm. "Well, it's all water over the dam now anyway, huh?"

She was puzzled at his obvious anger, but dismissed it as lingering reaction to her sister's senseless death. "Is that when you became Danny's guardian? Did Marette entrust you with his care?"

Abruptly Nick rose and headed back to the refrigerator. *She doesn't waste time, does she? She learns she has a nephew and immediately starts looking for a reason to take*

Daniel away. Damn, the woman. Doesn't the boy have enough to deal with without stirring up a custody mess, especially from a long-lost relative who looks too much like his own mother?

"My guardianship of Danny is legal and sanctioned right down the line," he said loudly, popping the top on a second can of beer. Rarely did he drink two at once—one or two a month was his usual intake—but today was different, in a lot of ways. "The family talked it out, consulted with Dan, and we all decided—me, Danny and the judge—that he should be here in his own home, not carted off to live with relatives he hardly knew or didn't feel as comfortable with. Daniel chose to stay with me, and I chose to take on the responsibility. Marette would have wanted it that way."

This time DeShea understood immediately the motivation behind Nick's harsh tone. He loved his nephew and was afraid she was going to challenge his right to raise him. "Mr. Couvillion, Nick," she said quietly, "I have no doubts that Marette would have wanted the best for her son."

Nick lowered the can and met her violet gaze. Was that a confirmation of Marette's decision or a thinly veiled challenge? Just what was her implication? That *he* was what was "best" for Danny? Or that perhaps she was?

Chapter Two

"Ya'll done talking, or do I have to take another shower?"

DeShea broke the eye contact with Nick and looked over at Danny. His hair was damp and combed neatly to one side. He wore a pair of white shorts and a T-shirt with the flag of Italy emblazoned across it and the words World Cup at the bottom. His brown eyes were large and friendly, and there was a faint smirk on his face that reminded her of Nick. He looked at his uncle, tossing a small soft stuffed soccer ball between his hands as he waited.

"Do you have any homework?" Nick asked sharply. He wasn't ready to deal with all of Daniel's questions yet. He still hadn't dealt with the main problem.

"No, sir," Dan replied. "*Now* can I stay?"

Nick nodded reluctantly and stood, tossing his beer can into the compactor, then resting his hands on the counter.

Leaning one slender hip against the table, Danny looked DeShea directly in the eye. "So do I call you Aunt DeShea, or what?"

"Aunt DeShea is fine," she replied, her heart smiling at the thought. "And may I call you Danny, or do you prefer something else?"

"Danny's cool." He fidgeted with the soft ball, twisting a small tag in one seam. "How old are you?" he finally asked.

"Daniel," his uncle admonished.

DeShea ignored Nick and answered the boy's question honestly. She didn't know any other way to handle the awkward situation. She only knew that too much time had already been lost to silence and unyielding points of view. She didn't want any of that to intrude between her and her nephew. "I'm thirty years old," she answered.

"My mom would have been thirty-five."

Finding herself in the unfamiliar position of wanting to hug the slender boy, she could only nod in response. "I know. January twenty-sixth. When's your birthday, Danny?"

"September twenty-fifth. My dad's was in June. The uh..." He looked back at Nick.

"Thirteenth," he supplied.

"He was a great dad. Mom, too. I miss them a lot."

"I know. I missed your mother very much when she went away. I cried myself to sleep every night for a very long time."

Danny pulled out a chair and sat down, still fiddling with the stuffed ball. "She used to talk about you sometimes. She always wished she could see you again. And she told me about the stuff you used to do as kids. Like the time you got locked in the attic and when you slid down the big banister and Mom broke her arm."

Nick was surprised to see Danny conversing so easily with a stranger. Since Marette's death, he hadn't warmed to many people outside the family. He was grateful that DeShea was giving him her undivided attention, though it was the least she could do.

Turning, he rested his backside against the counter, folding his arms across his chest as his nephew and the aunt talked. For the time being he would give the woman the benefit of the doubt—for the boy's sake, of course. Danny had been through enough in the past years, and Nick's causing a stink about this new relative wouldn't do him any good.

Though he was still defensive, his initial animosity toward DeShea had eased somewhat, and he took advantage of her distraction to make a closer inspection. Her voice was smooth and modulated as she talked to Dan; her answers to his questions were both honest and direct. She was very beautiful in a polished, ethereal way. Her mouth was small and gracefully formed, her cheekbones finely sculptured, her nose slender, straight and perfectly positioned between the wide lavender eyes. She was cool, controlled. Perfection personified—if one liked the type.

But she was a far cry from her older sister. Marette had also been a blonde, but her hair reminded one of ripening wheat, not summer sunshine like DeShea's. Little sister's eyes were the vivid lavender of wisteria, Marette's the deep blue of a Texas bluebonnet. Marette's smile had been ever present and her laughter infectious; DeShea had yet to reveal herself capable of either. Marette had been warm, giving, compassionate and devoted to her family. In comparison, her sister seemed a cold, pale copy.

DeShea was aware of Nick's disapproving scrutiny. He was comparing her to Marette and finding her lacking on all counts. It wasn't a new discovery. She'd done the same thing most of her life. But she didn't need anyone's approval anymore. Only her own. She'd come to Baton Rouge to find her sister and had found a nephew instead. What Nick thought of her or of her mother was immaterial.

She saw Nick glance at his watch, and she took the hint. Her visit had lasted long enough. Perhaps she should find a hotel and make arrangements to see Danny alone tomorrow. It was obvious that she made Uncle Nick very uncomfortable. Turning her wrist over, she ostensibly checked her own timepiece. "Goodness. It's late. I'd better call a cab and find a hotel."

"No. Don't go," Danny said. He turned to his uncle. "She can stay here. We've got plenty of room."

DeShea didn't wait for Nick to respond. "Oh no, Danny. That's very nice of you, but I couldn't impose. I'll get a room and maybe you can come visit me there." She looked at Nick, his jaw working side to side in displeasure.

"No," the boy insisted, going to stand in front of his uncle. "I want her to stay. I want to talk to her and ask about Mom. You *said* I was supposed to talk about her, didn't you?"

"Dan, if Aunt DeShea would be comfortable at a hotel..."

"But she wouldn't," Danny insisted. "Besides, Mom would want her sister to stay. You know she would."

There was nothing Nick could say to that. Wasn't this what he'd wanted, for Danny to come out of his emotional shell? But he doubted DeShea was the right catalyst. In a few days she would grow bored with the boy and life in Baton Rouge and go back to her jet-set existence, leaving him hurt and confused. But did he really have a right to deny Danny a few hours with his aunt? Marette wouldn't have turned her away. She'd always longed for a reunion. Perhaps it was best for now to adopt a cautious wait-and-see attitude. "There's no need for you to leave," he finally said. "If Marette were alive, she'd want you here. You're more than welcome to stay with us."

Her first impulse was to decline. He was only trying to appease Danny. But the echoes of her mantra reverberated in her mind. She *wanted* to stay, to get to know Daniel and to learn about Marette. It would be awkward, but she'd work that out somehow. She'd keep her distance from Nick when he was home and spend as much time with her nephew as possible when his uncle was at work. "Thank you. I appreciate your hospitality."

"Great!" Danny grinned slightly. "You can use the guest room. It's the bedroom upstairs next to mine." He trotted off through the living room as DeShea got to her feet.

"I'll need to send for my luggage. May I use the phone?" she asked.

Nick pointed to the desk near the archway. "Help yourself."

DeShea started toward it at the same time Nick passed by on his way to the living room, and her shoulder bumped into his chest. She tried to step aside but was pinned between him and the edge of the desk. "I'm sorry," she apologized.

Looking down at her, Nick was surprised to find that the top of her head barely reached to his chin. She'd seemed much taller from a distance. Taller, and harder. Up close he had a very different impression. She smelled of flowers, a vaguely familiar yet elusive fragrance. Her eyes were indeed amethyst but flecked with gold. He would have expected a slight chill to emanate from her cool demeanor, but instead he felt a warmth seeping through the heavy jacket on her shoulder that penetrated his shirt. He frowned. He must be imagining things. An Ice Princess couldn't be warm.

DeShea swallowed the lump in her throat as she looked up into the piercing brown eyes. He loomed over her, dark and disapproving, making her feel small and insignificant, yet at the same time she was acutely aware of him as a man. Her shoulder was shoved against his chest, and the way her arm was hanging at her side, she needed only to flex her fingers to come in contact with the crisp hair on his thigh. To her amazement, she had to fight the sudden urge to do just that.

She shifted her gaze to the center of his chest, only to be mesmerized by the rhythmic rise and fall of the broad expanse. She could smell the raw masculine scent of him and felt a twinge of panic. Turning her back, she finally broke the physical contact and reached quickly for the phone.

Only then did she find her voice and a modicum of composure.

"It's not too late for me to find a hotel," she said, looking at him across her shoulder. "I know this is awkward for you."

Nick stepped back and pinned her with a stare. "If Danny wants you here, then you'll stay." Without further comment, he left the room.

After placing the call, DeShea went in search of her room. At the top of the stairs, she found herself in a long, wide hallway, but before she could make a complete survey, something whizzed by her head. She ducked, emitting a sharp gasp.

"Gosh, I'm sorry, Aunt DeShea," Danny said, rushing forward. "Did I hit you?"

"No," she said, taking a deep breath. "I was just startled. What was that?"

Danny shrugged sheepishly. "My soccer ball. It's a soft one, though. It wouldn't have hurt you."

DeShea glanced the length of the empty space and saw a small three-foot goal at one end. "You play soccer here?"

"Yep. It's supposed to be a loft or something, but I use it as an indoor soccer court. Dad and I used to play here. Wanna try it?" He grinned impishly.

"I don't think so," she replied skeptically. "I was never—"

"Danny," Nick snapped from the open door at the far end, "have you done your laundry?"

"No sir, but—"

"Well, what had you planned on wearing to school tomorrow?"

Danny recognized the tone in his uncle's voice and scooped up the errant ball. "I'm going." He looked at DeShea, eyebrows arched in a what's-a-guy-to-do grimace, then started down the stairs. "I'll be right back."

Nick rubbed his forehead, trying to soothe the dull ache behind his eyes. Sinuses acting up again, no doubt. Hardly a good reason to yell at his nephew. It had absolutely nothing to do with seeing the boy in close conversation with his aunt. He walked toward DeShea, stopping several feet away.

DeShea found it odd that a small boy like Danny should have to do his own washing, and she voiced the question before she'd fully considered the implications. "Does he always wash his own clothes?"

The hard line of Nick's jaw grew even firmer. "It's one part of his responsibilities, yes. Along with a lot of other menial tasks. It's part of being a family. Your room is that last door." He pointed. "I think it's in order. If you need anything, just ask Danny. Or me," he added after a slight pause.

DeShea felt as if she should say something, but for the life of her, she didn't know what. She certainly didn't want to argue about the rules and regulations of the household first thing. She finally muttered a quiet thank-you and walked toward her room.

It was large and cheerful, done in muted shades of mauve, cream and green. The bedroom furniture was traditional in medium-toned wood. Tucked away in the corner near the large window was a comfortable swivel rocker and footstool. A small TV completed the area. Laying her purse on the mirrored dresser, she smiled inwardly at the homey atmosphere as she began to unbutton her jacket.

"I'm back," Danny called as he strolled into the room and plopped down on the foot of the bed.

She didn't know how to respond to his easy manner. She wished she could be as openly friendly as her nephew—but she had no guidelines on how to begin. Searching her brain for conversation, she decided the obvious was best. "You play soccer," she stated, assuming he'd carry it from there.

"Yep."

So much for that idea. Now what? Perhaps pressing for details would work.

"I was at your game today for a few minutes. Did you win?"

"Nah." Danny scowled. "We tied. We were ahead at the half by two goals, but—" he shrugged "—the Raiders are tough."

Oh good. Progress. They were up to multiple sentences now. She waited but Dan seemed content to lie across her bed and toss the ball.

"Have you played long?"

"Since I was five. But I went select three years ago."

"Select?"

"Yeah, it's sort of the all-stars. We're a traveling team. We go all over and play other select teams—Houston, New Orleans, Alabama, Mississippi, Tennessee. We've been to Florida a couple times, and we're going to Dallas in a few weeks."

DeShea frowned. "You travel during school?" Surely his uncle wouldn't forgo the boy's education for sports.

"No, ma'am, on weekends and holidays." He rolled onto his back and tossed the ball in the air.

That was a relief. Still, she couldn't help but wonder if a thirteen-year-old shouldn't be home and carefree on weekends instead of journeying from state to state. But Danny said he'd been doing this for three years. That meant that his parents had approved, so she'd withhold any judgments for the time being. "Do you enjoy it? The travel, I mean."

"Sure. It's pretty cool."

"Do you play any other sports?"

"Nope. Just soccer." Danny rolled off the bed and got to his feet. "How do you like the room?"

"It's nice. The colors are very relaxing." She thought of the stark black and white of her apartment. Why had she never considered softer colors? Natalie's influence, no doubt. For her, having the right "look" was paramount in all things.

"Did you see you have your own bathroom?" Danny asked. "Dad made the guy who built the house put a bath in every bedroom. He said he didn't want to share a bathroom ever again."

"Why would he say that?" DeShea wondered aloud.

"He came from a big family, and he was always having to fight to use it." The ball now positioned between his bare feet, Danny began to dribble it around the room.

DeShea considered this bit of information. She'd just assumed that René and Nick were the only children. "How many are in your father's family, Danny?"

"Well, let's see. Dad was the oldest, then Uncle Nick, I think. Then I get confused who came next, but there's Aunt Jessie, and Aunt Cherie, Uncle Hugh and uh...oh yeah, Aunt Dixie. She lives in Houston. Then my granddad had a bunch of brothers and sisters. I never have gotten them all figured out."

"I had no idea the family was so large." She said wistfully, trying to imagine what it would be like to have so many relatives you couldn't count them.

"Oh yeah." He grinned, tossing the ever-present ball into the air and heading with it across the room. "When we get together, it's like a major serious event." He spread his arms wide. "Man, there's Couvillions everywhere."

"Danny!" Nick's voice came from downstairs. "I could use a hand down here."

"Yes sir," he shouted back. "Geez," he said to his aunt. "He's a real grump today."

"Is he usually?" she wondered. He did seem to be perpetually angry.

Danny shrugged and caught the ball. "Only when we lose." He whirled and disappeared out the door again, leaving DeShea with a frown on her face.

Nick tipped the cabdriver and took the two small cases from his hands. "Is that all?"

"That's it, bud," the craggy-faced man assured him.

When Danny reached the foyer, Nick handed him the small overnight bag and picked up the other himself. He'd expected about three times this much luggage. DeShea looked the type to travel with six trunks and an entourage.

Danny held out the small case at arm's length, raising it and lowering it slowly as if judging its weight. "Man, if you need help with this, you must be getting old." He drew out the last word for emphasis.

Nick grimaced good-naturedly and jerked his head toward the stairs. "Get up there, hotshot."

They set the luggage near the foot of the bed, and Nick heard Danny voice the question that he himself had asked a few minutes earlier. "Is this all your stuff?"

DeShea picked up the small case and carried it into the bath. "I didn't know how long I was going to stay, so I just grabbed the necessities." She stopped in the doorway and found her eyes meeting Nick's. Strange how he always seemed to be studying her. Or was she the one seeking a better understanding of him?

Danny was babbling on now about how his mom packed hundreds of suitcases just for a weekend tournament, and Nick looked at DeShea with curiosity. Was Danny's easy acceptance of this woman because she looked so much like his mother? Or was there something else?

DeShea had shed her jacket, and the white silk blouse she wore underneath caressed her upper body. Through the sheer, delicate fabric he could see the intricate lace that cupped her breasts. His eyes traveled upward, meeting hers, and he saw them darken. Feeling as if he'd been reprimanded, he turned and left the room, shouting back over his shoulder, "You want some ice cream, Danny?"

"Yes, sir." He turned to DeShea. "You want some, too?"

She suddenly realized she was very hungry. There had been no chance to stop and eat since she left New York, and the light snack served on the plane had been tasteless. Ice cream, however, didn't seem appetizing at all. "No, thank you. But I'll be down shortly."

When Danny left, she leaned against the doorframe and pursed her lips. She hadn't missed the appreciative leer that had appeared in Nick's eyes as he appraised her. Not only did he have a fondness for alcohol, but apparently he possessed an eye for the ladies as well. Neither quality met with her idea of a proper guardian.

Staunchly, she tried to fan the flames of her indignation to expand it into full-fledged disapproval. It would be much easier to deal with this whole situation if Nick remained the villain. But all she could really generate was an intense pleasure. His eyes had skimmed over her, a mere glance, but even now she could feel the little tingle deep inside that his appreciative gaze had spawned. She couldn't remember the last time a man had looked at her solely as a woman, and she didn't have the slightest idea how to deal with it.

DeShea deliberately lingered in her room, taking more time than necessary to unpack. She needed some time to get her emotions under control. When she finally went downstairs Nick and Danny were sitting in the living room. Nick was on the recliner, a bowl of ice cream in his hand. Danny was sprawled on the floor in front of the TV. He looked up at her. "Ya want something to eat?"

She really was hungry, but it was too late in the evening to fix anything. "Maybe a piece of fruit?" She thought she'd seen some on the counter in the kitchen and looked at Nick for permission.

"Help yourself. The paper towels are near the sink."

After selecting a small cluster of grapes, she returned to the living room and sat on the sofa. The men seemed to be absorbed in the TV program, but she ignored it. Her mind was full of other questions, the main one being why Danny was still up. It was a school night. A boy his age should be in bed. How could he be expected to do well in class if he was overtired? And what about dinner? Ice cream was hardly a proper meal for a growing boy. He needed meat and vegetables, protein and vitamins. Double chocolate fudge wasn't her idea of a nourishing meal.

Out of the corner of her eye, she studied Nick. He had made Danny clean up immediately today, but he still wore the same clothes. His five-o'clock shadow was now a full-fledged stubble, and his hair was mussed. Apparently he wasn't concerned with his own personal hygiene. Though she had to admit, even in his disheveled state, he was very attractive—in a gritty, earthy sort of way.

Quickly she looked back at the fruit in her hand, surprised at the direction her mind had been traveling. Nick was not her concern. Danny was, and in her estimation, he was not being raised properly at all. It didn't seem right. Still, she had to remind herself that she knew next to nothing about family life. Her own could never have been called normal by any stretch of the imagination. Perhaps her perceptions were in error. For the time being, she would keep her comments to herself. But for the next few days, she'd keep her eyes open just to make certain Danny was being treated properly.

"Danny, time to turn in," Nick suddenly announced.

DeShea blinked, wondering if he'd read her mind. She waited as her nephew stood and headed toward the kitchen, carrying his bowl and collecting his uncle's along the way. She heard rattling around in the other room, and then the electric hum of a clothes dryer. Danny was finishing his laundry. At least the boy was conscientious. Marette's influence, no doubt. As Danny strolled back through the room, he planted a light punch on his uncle's shoulder. "Night."

Nick muttered a soft "G'night, kiddo."

"Night, Aunt DeShea," he said, stopping in front of her. "I'm glad you're here. See ya in the morning."

"Good night, Danny." It was hard to speak around the warmth clutching her heart. He was so sweet, so easy to like. Marette must have been very proud of him. She watched him start up the stairs, realizing that she was alone with Nick now. She also knew she was much too tired to deal with him anymore tonight. Getting to her feet, she held up the paper towel and asked, "Where should I put this? I think I'm going to retire as well."

Nick's eyes touched her briefly then looked away. "The compactor is next to the sink."

Walking into the kitchen, she discarded the trash, aware of Nick on her heels. He spoke before she could turn around. "I suppose you'll be calling your mother now to tell her about her heir to Clotilles?"

The cold, hard edge to his voice angered her, but she carefully composed her features before turning to face him. "That would be impossible," she replied evenly. "My mother died two months ago." She waited for the words to take effect, then offered a flat good-night. Turning, she walked briskly through the house and up to her room, shutting the door quietly but firmly behind her.

She went through her nightly routine with little conscious thought and then climbed into bed. It wasn't until she was alone in the confines of the room that she allowed herself to succumb to the emotions that had bombarded her that day. Darkness was her special time to let go and release the feelings she kept carefully controlled during the day. Natalie had hated any displays of emotion, and DeShea had learned her lesson well. Never let others see your true feelings. It was not only bad form but gave them a kind of power over your life.

She had embarked upon this journey so full of hope and excitement. It was going to be a new beginning for both her and Marette. How tragic that it had taken the death of their mother to open the doors to their reunion, only to have fate slam them cruelly shut again.

DeShea closed her eyes, remembering the day she had awakened to the news that her mother had passed away in her sleep. Her first emotion after the initial shock had been one of deep, profound, soul-lifting relief. At last, she was free. Free from the demands upon her time, her thoughts, free from the meticulously arranged life that allowed no room for creativity or relaxation. No longer did she have to fulfill her mother's expectations to run Clotilles, to dress, talk and think like her mother. The sense of freedom had been intoxicating and frightening. Her second overwhelming emotion had been guilt. She should feel a sense of loss, of grief. What she actually felt was…emancipated, and that knowledge took precedence over all other considerations.

Since she was thirteen, her life had been directed, shaped and molded to suit Natalie's master plan; she'd been carefully, meticulously groomed to assume the mantle of her mother's one passion—Clotilles.

Without a father to temper Natalie's obsessive ways and with no sister from whom to seek solace and understanding, DeShea had been no match for Natalie's forceful personality. In the beginning she had tried to stand up to her, to fight for her individuality. Marette had waged an ongoing war, but had found that running away was the only means to winning.

Once her older daughter had left, Natalie became even more determined to shape her other child to her will. By the time DeShea was fifteen, she'd resigned herself to her fate. Marette had abandoned her, left her no choice. If she wanted to survive at all, she would have to bend to Natalie's will in all things.

Besides, she wasn't as strong as Marette. How could she ever have found the courage to do what her sister had done?

In the end, Natalie's way hadn't been as difficult as she'd imagined. She found a certain measure of escape in doing her mother's bidding. In becoming the perfect daughter, her interaction with Natalie was held to a minimum, which meant fewer arguments, fewer harsh words, until eventually Natalie began to refer to DeShea as her "clone" because she was "so much like me." Natalie never understood that by complying, DeShea was actually escaping.

After college, when DeShea assumed her position in Clotilles, life had become a little easier. At least she'd had her own apartment, and within those walls she could do and think as she pleased. She could eat in the living room, watch TV, sleep late on weekends and spend Sundays puttering in the kitchen. At last she was free to indulge in a few of the things Natalie had frowned upon. DeShea began to lead two lives: the well-ordered existence within the boardroom of Clotilles and the private, simple world in her apartment.

Over the years, she grew to know her mother intimately. She could second-guess her every move and every decision. Natalie saw this as her daughter's unparalleled business aplomb. DeShea saw it as pure survival. It kept Natalie at a safe distance, no nagging, no unpleasant confrontations. A sweet smile and a quiet "You're absolutely right, Mother" would make Natalie pat her on the head and go away, leaving her alone for another long stretch of time. Eventually, DeShea could even assert her opinions and Natalie would listen, convinced that she would have had the same idea or come to the same conclusion herself in her own good time. It wasn't a good life, but it was peaceful and the most she could expect.

But how different her life might have been if she'd had Marette's courage. To break free, start out on her own. Marette had found happiness and fulfillment. She'd had a devoted husband and a fine young son to love and cherish.

Why had DeShea herself never found the strength to defy Natalie and find Marette long ago? If she'd only made the attempt, perhaps they could have had a few years together. Even a few months, a day. But the opportunity was lost forever now. She'd waited too long. It was too late. Eight months too late.

DeShea knew she couldn't fight the pain any longer. She rolled onto her side, trying to muffle her sobs in the thick pillow. Tears sprang from her eyes—hot, scalding tears of regret and grief at years of lost opportunities never to come again. She lost track of time and space and reality. There was only the excruciating sadness and the memories of the sister she would never see again.

Nick was in the wide hallway, collecting the half dozen small soccer balls that Danny used to practice with. As he bent down to pick up the one outside DeShea's door he thought he heard a muffled sob come from inside. Leaning closer he waited, straining to hear, but only silence came back to him. His forehead creased in a thoughtful frown as he turned and tossed the three balls into the miniature soccer goal. He must be hearing things. An Ice Princess like DeShea couldn't cry! She was incapable of tears. Dismissing it, he went downstairs.

Stretched out on the sofa Nick tried to watch the sports segment of the news but found he couldn't concentrate. Rubbing his forehead absently, he finally gave up and turned off the set. He really should go to bed. But he wasn't feeling tired. What he *was* feeling... was guilty.

DeShea's announcement that Natalie Ballard was dead had caught him off guard. His cutting comment about her mother seemed unnecessarily harsh now. But he'd been angry and scared at DeShea's sudden appearance in their lives. Nothing good had come out of Marette's family, except for Marette herself. Her mother was a cold, hard, unfeeling woman, and Nick saw red whenever he heard her name. DeShea's icy composure had initially reminded him of all the stories Marette had told of Natalie. But contradicting impressions said DeShea wasn't like her mother. That there might be some warmth, some softness in her more like her sister.

Was it possible that DeShea was telling the truth? Maybe she'd never received those telegrams. Maybe she really hadn't known anything about Marette.

He was sorry DeShea had lost her mother, but that still didn't give her the right to appear on their doorstep and put Danny's emotional state at risk. Not to mention complicating his own life.

Strangely enough, Danny didn't seem the least bit upset at his aunt's arrival. On the contrary, he seemed drawn to her. He'd talked with her easily, as if they were old friends. And it was Danny's insistence that had placed her in the spare room.

For now he'd let things ride. DeShea was, after all, Marette's sister and Danny's aunt. The least he could do was be civil, despite his personal opinion that she was cold and unfeeling. In a few days, she would have paid her respects and moved on, back to New York and out of their lives. But in the meantime he'd keep a close eye on her, and at the first sign of trouble, the Ice Princess was history.

Chapter Three

DeShea woke with a start. It took her a few seconds to place her surroundings, and when she did, she closed her eyes again. A thudding sound from outside her door alerted her that Danny was up and bounding down the stairs. Tossing off the covers, she padded to the bath, catching a glimpse of herself in the mirror. She felt surprisingly well rested this morning, considering she had cried herself to sleep. Unfortunately, she didn't look as good as she felt. Her eyes were puffy and faintly bloodshot, and her complexion was blotchy.

What she needed was a cup of coffee and something to eat. She was starving. A second look at her reflection, however, prompted her to take the time to get properly showered and dressed before going downstairs. If she appeared in the kitchen looking haggard and disheveled, her young nephew would start asking questions. She didn't relish the idea of lying to him, and she wasn't ready to tell him the real reason for her crying spell. In her rather precarious position, neither prospect seemed a good way to start the day.

Twenty minutes later she belted her blue slacks, fastened the top button on her matching blue blouse and gave her reflection one last inspection. She had no idea what would be happening today, no way of knowing if she was over- or underdressed. Slacks seemed an acceptable compromise. With a nervous release of breath, she opened the door and went downstairs. She found Danny and Nick in the kitchen.

"Good morning, Aunt DeShea," the boy called as he grabbed up his books from the breakfast bar at the end of the counter.

"Good morning," she replied.

Nick merely nodded in her direction and turned to Danny. "Money?" he asked.

"Yes, sir," he replied. "Don't forget, two o'clock."

"I won't. Auditorium?"

"Theater."

Puzzled by the verbal shorthand that passed between the two, DeShea stood in the archway, watching as Danny darted around the room gathering pencils and other items. He started out the back door, then stopped and looked at her. "You'll be here when I get home, won't you?"

She answered without thinking. "Yes, of course."

"Great. Hey, Uncle Nick, why don't you ask her to come?" he called over his shoulder. "I'll bet she'd like it. Bye."

The door slammed shut, and DeShea walked toward the counter, a curious expression on her face.

Nick glanced up at her. "Coffee?"

"Yes, thank you," she answered, taking a seat on one of the tall stools at the counter.

Suddenly the door opened and Danny raced through.

"What now?" Nick shouted after him.

"Horn," came the distant reply.

In seconds he raced back through the kitchen, a black case in one hand, and disappeared again. Nick poured her coffee and offered an explanation. "He has a band concert at school today. You're welcome to come." He turned away to set down the pot and added, "It's just the eighth-graders. Nothing professional."

DeShea hid her displeasure with lowered lashes as she helped herself to the sugar. Did he think she wouldn't be interested in a band that wasn't top quality? "I'd love to go," she replied, feeling a rush of pleasure when she saw surprise reflected in the brown eyes.

Nick knew she'd done it to prove a point and assert herself. He had no doubts that once they were at school she would be bored to tears. An Ice Princess wouldn't be impressed with the struggling attempts at music made by a group of teenagers who were still learning to play.

But that was her problem. The sooner she was bored here, the sooner she would leave. His conscience stung, and he reminded himself about his pledge last night to be civil. It was hard to remember when she sat only a few inches away, cool and calm in her expensive blue outfit, her violet eyes assessing what they saw. The only noticeable difference in her today was her clothes. The slacks revealed long, slender legs and a pleasing, rounded derriere that had been hidden in the severe suit she'd worn yesterday. Too bad such an attractive package housed a hollow interior.

"You want some toast?" he asked, busying himself in an attempt to distract his thoughts from DeShea.

"Yes, thank you. I'm starving. I haven't had anything to eat since lunch yesterday." She bit her tongue. What had made her admit that? Now he would think she was asking him to fix her a large breakfast.

Nick's animosity was punctured again. It had never occurred to him that DeShea might not have eaten last night. All he'd offered her was ice cream. He held out a hand apologetically. "I'm sorry. I didn't think to offer you anything last night. Danny and I grabbed a bite on the way home after the game. Can I fix you some eggs or something? There's not much here right now—I haven't had time to get to the grocery."

"No. Toast will be fine, thank you," DeShea assured him.

While he fiddled with the toaster, she noticed how different he looked from yesterday. His face was clean-shaven, his hair neatly combed, and he wore casual slacks and a striped shirt, the sleeves of which had been rolled up, exposing strong forearms covered with dark hair. She could smell the tangy aroma of his after-shave across the distance between them. As he handed her the toast and butter, she grinned, hoping to ease the tension she felt growing.

He looked at her, then rubbed his fingers across his forehead. "Look, DeShea, I think I owe you an explanation for yesterday."

"No," she interrupted, shaking her head. "I should be apologizing to you. I didn't stop to think what effect my arrival might have. I was so anxious to see Marette that I never considered anything else. When I found those letters, all that mattered was getting here as fast as I could. I didn't mean to disrupt your life or Danny's, and if you think I should leave now, before he gets back... I'll understand."

Nick felt an odd tug in his chest. Could it be that there were some feelings inside the glacier after all? "No. You don't need to go," he said, taking a gulp of his coffee and setting it on the counter. "Danny wants you here. He seems to have taken to you, and I think it'll do him good to talk to you about Marette."

DeShea felt a surge of relief. She'd been terrified that Nick would insist that she leave, and she desperately wanted to stay and spend time with Danny. Smiling across the counter, she offered a soft "Thank you."

Nick watched the change in her with amazement. She had smiled—not a big smile, just a small, hesitant one—but it touched her face with a new softness and put a glimmer of light in her eyes. It turned the perfectly formed features into something unbelievably attractive, and he found himself

wondering what a full-fledged smile would do to her delicate lips and smooth silky cheeks.

Walking around the counter, he took up a seat on a stool,
keeping an empty one between them. The sudden change
had made him momentarily forget his reservations about her
motives. She might be attractive, but that still didn't mean
there was a heart inside.

Nick's cautious attitude was understandable, and while
it made DeShea very uncomfortable, she couldn't let it prevent her from finding out the things she needed to know.
Perhaps with Danny at school Nick would be more willing
to answer some of her questions. "Danny is a very nice
young man," she finally said. "Marette and her husband
did a wonderful job raising him."

"Yeah, he's a good kid. But he's been through a lot.
Losing both your parents within three years isn't an easy
thing to adjust to. He's very fragile emotionally."

The warning wasn't lost on DeShea. Nick was telling her
to tread softly, carefully. Was he afraid she'd abandon
Danny? Didn't he know that now she'd found him she
would never lose touch again? No, of course he didn't know.
How could he? She would just have to try and prove it to
him somehow. "Is he like his father?" she asked after a long
pause.

Nick took another sip of his coffee, his eyes softening as
he called up memories of his older brother. "Yeah, quite a
bit. René was friendly, outgoing, a good athlete and devoted to his family. He was fiercely protective of their happiness."

Again a warning hung in the air. He was questioning her
intentions. Convincing him she meant no harm to Danny
might prove to be difficult. "And Marette. What was she
like?"

There was no hesitation in his response. "Marette was one
of a kind. She was pretty and funny, a bit wild at times, but
she had a wholesome quality about her that was very down-
to-earth. It always surprised me when I'd see her working

around the house or digging in the yard or fixing one of Dan's toys. You'd never guess she came from money.

"She was talented, too. She could do just about anything she put her mind to. And she mastered them so easily. It was almost as if she had a demon inside her that pushed her to excel at everything."

"Like marriage and motherhood?" DeShea commented softly.

Nick nodded. "She excelled at both. She was caring, generous and devoted. She made a commitment to René and Danny and never once looked back." He eyed her boldly, not surprised to see her look away, as if she was totally unaffected by his statement. Marette had fit into the family so quickly, so easily, it was as if she'd always been part of them. By no stretch of the imagination could he see this remote, emotionless woman fitting in with the Couvillions.

DeShea thought how different her own life would have been if her mother had shared Marette's views, or if she and Eric had been blessed with a child. But that was in the past. And she doubted if her future held any such prospect. Some things were just not meant to be. "For some, a career is the only way," she said softly.

Her reply didn't surprise him in the least. He'd have been more surprised if she'd agreed with him. He studied her intently, a faint frown creasing his forehead as he tried to draw some sort of correlation between the two sisters and found it a difficult task. "If you didn't look so much like her, I'd never believe..." He stopped when he realized what he'd been about to say.

"You can say it," she said, meeting his gaze. "You wouldn't believe we were related. You're right. Marette and I are... were very different. Total opposites in many ways. But I thank you for your kind words about her. It helps to know she found happiness and people who admired and loved her. We...never had that growing up, and she wanted desperately to belong to someone."

"She belonged to us. All of us," he stated possessively.

Nick's blunt statement filled her with envy, but his description of her sister warmed her heart and reaffirmed her long-cherished beliefs of what her sister had become. Breaking free from Natalie had allowed Marette to fulfill her potential. Perhaps it would give her the same chance. But she had a long way to go and a lot to learn.

When Nick rose and walked back around the counter, DeShea realized the time. "I hope I haven't made you late for work by asking all these questions."

"I'm not working today," he replied smoothly, lifting one eyebrow at her not so subtle hint to get rid of him.

"Oh?" Had she missed a holiday somewhere? Easter was nearly three weeks away yet, but she'd been so preoccupied she could easily have forgotten some vital date.

The frown on her face was easy to interpret. She was trying to figure why he was hanging around the house instead of out earning a living for his nephew. "It's okay," he drawled. "I'm the boss. I can take a day off whenever I want."

"It wasn't meant as a criticism," she explained quickly. "I just—"

He held up a hand. "I promise you. I'm not really a lazy lout. Only on weekends. During the week, I'm a perfectly respectable and hardworking branch manager for Beller Electronics in Baton Rouge."

"I've heard of them."

"No doubt. I believe our New York office provides the alarm systems for Clotilles."

"Yes, that's right. A good company. Have you been with them long?"

Nick's eyes narrowed. The lady was determined to make sure he measured up. "A long time. Since I got out of college. It's not as lucrative as the family business was, but it has other compensations."

"Family business?" Her curiosity was piqued.

"My dad and his brother were grocers. There are five stores in town now. We all worked there growing up, but none of us wanted to continue with it so my uncle bought us out several years ago."

It wasn't easy to walk away from a business that had emotional and familial roots. DeShea understood the situation only too well. But if Nick had done it successfully, maybe she could learn something from his experience. "Why didn't you stay with it?"

The muscles in Nick's jaw tightened. Didn't she really mean "Why did you give up the money?" He knew full well how Marette and the Ice Princess were raised. Their silver spoon had been gilded. Remembering his pledge, he took a deep breath before answering. "Because it demands your attention twenty-four hours a day, robs you of time with your family and friends and leaves no room for anything else. I wanted a job that I could leave behind at the end of the day, that didn't enclose me like a second skin.

"My dad made a good living, but he was never home. The store claimed all his time and mental energy. When he did show up, he was too tired to play ball or take us to a game. Most of the time he was even too tired to talk to Mom. I wanted more than that. Running my own business was too high a price to pay for financial independence." He looked at DeShea, surprised to see the violet eyes clouded to a deep purple.

"It's an insatiable beast," she said softly. "It wraps itself around your throat and squeezes the life from you. It devours your energy, saps your strength and depletes your emotions until you're all used up and exhausted."

Nick stared at her, stunned to find that she understood. He remembered Clotilles, the business her mother had created, and met the violet eyes that now looked clearly into his. "It eats away at your insides until only an empty carcass is left behind," he heard himself say softly.

DeShea nodded, feeling a tenuous bond form between them as his eyes touched hers. Nick understood. No one else she knew had ever seen the hidden traps and unmarked chasms that lie within a family business. Everyone assumed that because Clotilles was world-renowned she enjoyed the unrelenting task. They thought being your own boss was akin to owning a bottomless treasure chest of wealth and fulfillment, a life where you could do as you pleased, never having to worry where the next paycheck was coming from, never having to answer to a higher command. She'd tried to explain to her mother and to others that Clotilles was a relentless master—never satisfied, always demanding more and more time, slowly claiming your soul. But until this moment, no one had understood her point of view.

Their mutual understanding flowed between them. DeShea felt Nick's quiet kinship lift the tendrils of guilt she had about wanting to rid herself of a business her mother had worked so hard to establish. Her decision to sell Clotilles had been reached shortly after Natalie's death. DeShea had only to say the word and the matter would be out of her hands. Until this moment she'd been reluctant to take the final step. But in Nick's understanding—his personal testimony—she found the courage to sever those ties. She would call Howard in New York today, now, and start the ball rolling.

"I need to make a few phone calls," she said, breaking the silence between them. "Would you mind if I used the phone in my room to call New York? I'll put it on my credit card."

The delicate, tentative bond snapped. Nick set his jaw and turned his back, slamming his cup into the sink with a loud bang. "Suit yourself. If you're going to the concert, we need to leave at one-thirty."

DeShea felt as if he'd just thrown a glass of cold water in her face. Only seconds ago he'd seemed so sympathetic, so warm. Then without warning he turned steely. What had she done or said? Sliding off the stool, she started slowly toward the living room, glancing back to see his shoulders hunched angrily as he stared out the window.

"I'll be ready," she said, hoping he'd look at her and she could find some explanation in his eyes.

He only nodded and uttered a curt, "Fine."

Once DeShea had left the room, Nick slammed the palms of his hands against the counter. The woman really was made of ice. For a moment he'd felt a closeness, an understanding between them. He'd even thought he saw a trace of warmth creep into her eyes—a hint of softness that he wanted to see more of. They'd been talking easily, and he'd felt his opinion of her beginning to shift ever so slightly. But he'd been wrong. She spoke all the right words, but she didn't mean them. She offered a false understanding, then hurried to the nearest phone to make her "power" calls and check on the million-dollar business Mama had built.

It was the same sort of ploy she was using on Danny, he realized. She offered fake affection, pretending to listen to him with wide violet eyes, patting him on the head with the proper amount of emotion until he grew attached to her, and dependent upon that attention. But what would happen to Danny when DeShea disappeared back into her own world? It would be like losing his mother all over again. Danny wouldn't be able to endure another such trauma.

It had been a mistake to let her come into their lives. He should have sent her packing the moment he'd seen her at the door. DeShea was right, she and Marette were nothing alike.

What the hell did he care anyway? Why was he so determined to find a little of Marette in the Ice Princess? He would have more luck getting a smile out of the Rock of Gibraltar. Smile. He remembered the little smile she'd given him and how it had altered her image. Was there another woman within the glacial shell, or was he only imagining it, reluctant to believe that Marette's sister was so cold?

There had been that one moment when she seemed to understand how he felt about his father's business and why he had chosen a different career path. But before he could fully grasp the implications, she had chilled him out like a mountain storm. Damn. Why was he so confused by the woman? One minute he wanted her gone, the next he wanted to dig inside and find out if there was a real person behind the frosty shell.

Unfortunately, there really wasn't much he could do now. He'd committed himself to letting her stay. Danny wanted her here. But she'd better not ignore the boy or upset him in any way, or she was in for a fight.

DeShea hung up the phone, her nails playing an absent tattoo on the cradled receiver. Howard Roth, vice president of Clotilles, was not happy that the final moment had come. He realized, though, there were very few options open to them. Clotilles was doomed. Beyond redemption.

In its heyday, the elegant beauty-and-health spa had been exclusive and unique. It had catered to a select clientele—the very rich and the obscenely rich. Women with time on their hands and money to throw away. Mature women who wanted to "diet" and "exercise" without actually exerting any effort. For nearly thirty years, Clotilles had been an unparalleled success. From the first "salon" in New York, it had grown to include six locations from L.A. to London.

But during the past decade, business had taken a sharp downward turn. Women were no longer satisfied with going through the motions of diet and exercise. The new fitness craze and health-awareness attitudes demanded results. The rich wanted to lower heart rates, firm muscles and shed pounds, not merely gather with friends in swank spas and share wine and cheese beside a pool of "healthful water."

DeShea had tried to warn her mother that Clotilles needed to change with the times. But Natalie had refused to read the handwriting on the wall. Ultimately they'd been forced to close down the less profitable salons, until only the London and New York locations remained open. The company had been running on borrowed money and the fading strength of Natalie's name and reputation. When she died, DeShea was forced to make some hard decisions about the future of Clotilles. The decision to sell everything was an attempt to alleviate the huge deficits that had accrued in the past six years.

She'd also arranged for the sale of the family home in Connecticut. The sprawling stone structure held no particular memories for her, and the money would go a long way toward paying the debts. The Victorian house in Galena, however, she'd decided to keep. It was a quaint house in a quiet town, her maternal grandmother's home. Once she left Baton Rouge, she would settle there until she could decide what to do with the rest of her life. With any luck, she would come away from Clotilles with a small nest egg as well, but even if she didn't have a dime left she'd have her freedom. She was young, healthy and educated, with a wealth of experience. If Marette could make a new life with less than that, she could, too. Right now, though, she was going to concentrate on Danny and enjoy her visit while she could.

The rest of the day passed quickly. Whatever had been bothering Nick that morning had dissipated by afternoon. When she returned to the kitchen, he wasn't pleasant, but was at least civil. They talked about René and Danny and Marette, ate a light lunch and then left for Danny's school. DeShea felt herself relaxing, and hopeful of establishing a tolerable relationship with Nick. For Danny's sake.

The concert was the most inspiring thing DeShea had ever seen. She marveled at the ability of the young musicians and felt her heart swell with pride at Danny's accomplishment. Nick was every inch the proud father, and she found herself wondering what he would be like with a son of his own.

On the way home, they stopped at a chicken place for supper, and within moments a bemused DeShea was seated at a small cramped table looking at a box full of chicken and a soft drink in a paper cup with a plastic lid.

Nick and Danny attacked the food with relish. Following their example and not wanting to reveal her lack of experience in these matters, she gingerly selected a piece and took a healthy bite. Her eyes widened in surprise. "This is very

good," she blurted out, instantly embarrassed by her remark.

Danny and Nick exchanged glances, then Danny asked,
"Haven't you ever had Ragin' Cajun chicken before?"

She shook her head.

"How about Boudreaux's?"

Again she moved her head from side to side.

Danny gaped. "Man! Don't they have fast food in New
York?"

"Yes, of course. I've just never—" she shrugged awk-
wardly "—eaten it."

"Then what do you eat?" Danny asked, his eyes wide in
amazement.

"Uh, well," she said, wiping her hands on the flimsy paper napkin. "I'm usually conducting business over lunch,
so we go to a nice restaurant, and then when I'm at home I
fix a small meal for myself."

"Welcome to the real world, DeShea," Nick drawled
sarcastically.

She couldn't tell from the tone of his voice if he meant to
be humorous or condescending. But when she looked into
his brown eyes, she saw a twinkle and had to assume he'd
only been teasing her. It was something she'd never dealt
with before, and it gave her a warm sensation in her stomach. Almost as if she was beginning to be accepted.

Danny led the conversation for most of the meal, keeping DeShea entertained with stories about school, friends
and teachers. She understood only bits and pieces, but she
was enthralled by it all. When they returned home, Danny
went immediately to his room to change and Nick ducked
into the study, so DeShea took the opportunity to freshen
up. When she emerged, she found the pair back in the living room, comfortably draped over the furniture.

An odd feeling crept over her as she looked upon the
scene. Was this what Marette had enjoyed every night—her
husband resting in his favorite chair, their son comfortably
sprawled on the floor, a companionable silence drawing

them together? She found she liked this quiet domesticity. It was mellow, soothing to the nerves, and for a fleeting moment she allowed herself to pretend that this was her house, that Daniel was her son and Nick was the only man in the world for her.

That last thought brought her back to reality with a cold, hard jolt. What was she doing? Nick didn't even like her. She wasn't entirely sure how she felt about him, either. Shaking off the thought, she joined the two Couvillions, catching the tail end of Nick's words as she sat down.

"...could do it tonight. There's plenty of daylight left."

"Okay," Danny relented with a sour tone in his voice. He glanced at his uncle as he rose. "I just wish it wasn't open season on all us little guys."

"It's a hard-knock life, kiddo," Nick responded with a grin.

DeShea wasn't sure if they were serious or not, but decided to at least let her opinion be known. "I think you're very big for your age," she said.

Danny and Nick exchanged amused glances, and both began to chuckle.

"Me?" Danny finally asked, pointing to himself. "Big? Aunt DeShea, I'm the smallest guy in my whole class. Didn't you notice that today?"

"No, I guess I didn't," she admitted. She didn't add that she'd been so fascinated with his performance that she'd not taken her eyes off him from the moment the concert had started.

"Believe me, I am. That's why Dad wanted me to play soccer," Danny explained. "You don't have to be big to play it like you do football."

"You'll grow soon enough," she commented, hoping to correct her earlier faux pas. "You'll probably be as tall as your uncle."

"I don't know," he said doubtfully. "Dad wasn't very tall, either." He turned to Nick. "What was he?"

"Five-nine," he answered with a smile.

"See? Not much hope. Besides, who said The Nickster was so tall?" he teased, a broad grin slashing his attractive features. "He missed six feet by a whole half an inch." Holding up his thumb and forefinger, he illustrated the exact amount.

"You should be so tall, kiddo," Nick joked back.

The friendly banter continued, but DeShea's attention was riveted on the look in Nick's eyes as he teased Danny. There was such affection, such profound love in the brown eyes as he looked at his nephew, it created a physical ache in her chest just watching it. Eventually she was forced to turn away, feeling as if she'd intruded on something private and intimate between them. Danny's voice filtered through her mind, and she focused on the sound.

"...who's tall is Uncle Hugh. He's about six-one or -two. Maybe I'll end up like him."

"In your dreams, pal," Nick drawled.

Daring another glance at Nick, DeShea was again forced to look away. Never had she seen such pure, unconditional love reflected in one pair of eyes. It hurt, squeezed at her heart. She had to get away. Slowly she got to her feet, feeling as if she were moving underwater, struggling to breathe. She muttered something about not feeling well, then retreated quickly to her room.

"What's wrong with Aunt DeShea?" Danny asked as his aunt rushed from the room.

"You heard her. She doesn't feel well," Nick said in a curt tone. "You better get the grass cut before it gets dark."

Safe and secure behind the closed door of her small room DeShea cringed inwardly with embarrassment. She walked slowly toward the swivel rocker in the corner and curled up, clutching a small decorative pillow to her chest as she stared at the ceiling.

What must they think of her, running out that way? No one had ever looked at her with the expression she'd seen on Nick's face. Her mother had barely looked at her at all, and never with affection, let alone love. Even her husband during their brief marriage had never gazed at her with the deep love Nick had shown for Danny. The best she'd ever gotten from Eric was a warm affectionate glance. But then their marriage had been one of Natalie's great plans. DeShea hadn't fought it because she had had a crush on Eric. Eric had complied because he recognized a golden opportunity when it was handed to him.

Strangely enough, her marriage had proved to be a good thing for both of them. Confident in her plan, Natalie sent them off to run the London salon, and away from her influence DeShea had started to blossom. Her confidence developed, as well as her self-esteem. She didn't really enjoy Clotilles, but she did discover she was good at the work, and Eric was an innovative partner. With his new ideas and her business sense, the London spa soon became the most successful of all.

Her feelings for Eric had grown and his affection for her deepened, and while the marriage was never a union of passion, they were compatible and content with their lives. Their unique arrangement had worked well for several years until Eric found a woman he truly loved and asked to be released. DeShea had not stood in his way. The woman had been a friend of both of them and DeShea had given them her blessing. Eric had looked at Angela in nearly the same adoring way Nick had looked at Danny.

How she had envied them. What must it feel like to have someone touch you with eyes of love? Would she ever feel the burning, all-consuming passion that she read about, fantasized about? Or was love reserved for everyone but her? What was missing within her that kept it so firmly out of her life? She knew the answer. It was her fault Eric had left. Her inability to open up and allow him access to her heart had eventually sent him into the arms of someone else.

But that was in the past. This was a new life, a new direction. She had to concentrate on her strengths not her weaknesses, take pride in her many accomplishments and not the failures. Everyone had a cross to bear in life. Hers was to be forever on the outside looking in. After all, no one could have it all.

Later, in the master bedroom on the first floor, Nick undressed in a fit of irritation. What had come over the Ice Princess tonight? All afternoon she'd been pleasant and easy to talk to. Even his gentle teasing about fast food had been taken in stride. He'd thought he was making progress, starting to melt the ice floe, then tonight, for no reason he could see, she jumped to her feet and left the room. Why? And how was he supposed to answer Danny's question when he wondered what was wrong? *Sorry, pal, but she's probably bored with you?*

He went over the evening's conversation once again, searching for something he might have said or done to upset her, but he could find no explanation. Damned if he could figure her out. He balled up his shirt and tossed it into the corner, wondering why the hell he even cared.

Climbing into bed he turned out the light, but images of DeShea joined him in the dark rooms of his mind. He saw her stiff-backed and composed, telling him that her mother had died two months ago. It was the same posture she'd assumed when she left the living room tonight. He opened his eyes, staring into the darkness, his hands clasped behind his head. First her mother, then Marette. He knew what it was like to lose family. Was that why she left the room? Because she was hurting? Maybe he should have tried to talk to her, find out what was really wrong. Or maybe he should mind his own business.

Rolling over, he punched the pillow and closed his eyes. If she was still behaving like a walking icicle in the morning, he'd see if she wanted to talk. It was the least he could do for Marette's sister.

But DeShea didn't put in an appearance the next morning as Nick got ready for work. Danny had already gone to school. The back door crashed loudly behind Nick as he left

the house. She could at least have gotten up to say goodbye. Apparently an Ice Princess needed a lot of beauty sleep.
Well, she could sleep all the damn day as far as he cared.

Chapter Four

It was after eleven o'clock when DeShea finally awoke. She stared in disbelief at the numbers on the clock radio, then checked them against her wristwatch. The numbers matched.

Quickly she rose, showered and dressed, feeling like a naughty child. The last time she'd slept this late she'd been ill with a virus. But she wasn't sick now. At least, not physically. Heartsick, perhaps, but that was not a medical ailment.

Unable to face Nick and Danny again last night, she'd stayed in her room. The memory of Nick's loving look had haunted her until she dug out a notebook and pencil and tried to capture what she'd seen in writing. It had been an arduous task and emotionally painful, but when her crude poem was completed, she was gratified with the result, almost as if by capturing her feeling on paper she had undergone a type of catharsis.

Writing had been her one secret vice since she was ten years old. It was her only creative outlet, her sole means of expressing the emotions her mother found distasteful. For a long time only Marette knew her secret.

It was after Marette left that DeShea had started to write seriously, filling page after page until she had a box full of notebooks. Then in her last year of high school, her mother found a tablet she'd left unguarded and forbade her to waste any more time on such nonsense. The ensuing ridicule was sufficient to halt further attempts.

It wasn't until she married Eric that she started writing again. He had encouraged her to put her thoughts and feelings down on paper as a kind of therapy, a way of sorting out all her confused and repressed emotions. She had started a personal journal and as a result felt her confidence and self-esteem begin to grow. It had become a very important part of her daily life. Sometimes she would hastily scribble her thoughts or impressions in her book. Sometimes a poem was the only way to capture and express her deepest feelings, like last night, when she'd seen that look of love in Nick's eyes.

During the past couple of years she'd taken to writing short stories. She found it gave her a type of satisfaction she'd never known before.

Now DeShea took the small notebook from where it rested beside the bed and slipped it into the drawer of the nightstand, then ventured downstairs. The house was strangely empty and silent. The only sounds were the soft buzz of the ice maker in the kitchen and the faint rustle of the ceiling fan as it stirred the air.

Usually she found total silence unsettling. Alone in her apartment, she generally had a radio or stereo playing softly in the background just for company. But the silence in Marette's house this morning wasn't disquieting at all. Instead she found it peaceful and cozy.

In the kitchen, she found the coffeemaker cold and nearly empty and opted for reheating the last of it in the microwave. Mug cradled between her hands, she wandered back through the house, taking the time to inspect each item and commit it to memory. She would never know the adult woman her sister had become, but perhaps she could gain some insight through the things she'd left behind.

Staring at the bookcase, she read each title and speculated on whether the book had belonged to René or Marette. She touched the bric-a-brac, analyzed the decor. Tears welled up in her eyes at the collection of photos she found in an album—Danny as a baby, Marette and her son in the backyard, a snapshot of René and Nick. The resemblance between the brothers was startling.

She drifted into the formal dining room, imagining the holiday dinners served here and wondering if Marette had been a good cook. She glanced into the small study on the other side of the foyer, which she'd learned was Nick's at-home office. The only other room downstairs was the master bedroom, and she took only a quick glance into it. Nick's room. The temptation to inspect it was immense, but she forced it aside, refusing to snoop through his room. She did, however, take a quick peek into Danny's room upstairs and smiled at the cluttered floor and walls plastered with soccer posters.

When she stood in the living room again, her eyes were drawn to the large windows that looked out over the patio and the generous yard. Her focus came to rest on the glossy black baby grand piano that stood in the corner. The smile on her face faded as she ran a hand across its smooth, shiny surface. Marette must have gotten her wish. As long as DeShea could remember, her sister had wanted to play the piano. She'd loved music. But, like writing, Natalie didn't consider musical ability necessary for a future in business.

While it gave DeShea immense comfort and satisfaction to know that Marette had finally achieved her heart's desire, her pleasure was marred by the tenuous thread of resentment that she could never quite break. Marette had broken her promise, and left DeShea behind. There'd been no warning given, no goodbye offered. Nothing to tell of her plan to run away. No call, no note to express regret or sorrow, or even a promise to come back. Just a clean, bloodless amputation of a mother and of a little sister who had depended on her.

She looked around the room again. Marette's life had begun when she removed herself from Natalie's influence. Would she be as fortunate? Now that she was free from Natalie, would she find her heart's desire as her sister had?

Nick's image immediately filled her mind, and she felt a surge of loneliness. She knew now what had bothered her most about the loving look Nick had given Danny. Envy was only part of it. The other factor was exclusion. She'd felt shut out, barred from the inner circle and the bond between them.

And she wanted desperately to be inside it. She wanted what her sister had—a home, a family, a place to come to where she felt safe and loved. Nothing like the sterile mansion they'd been raised in or even the oh-so-contemporary apartment she had now. Marette's home was slightly dusty, moderately cluttered. The furniture was pleasantly worn, the carpet and floors faintly soiled, but it was real, normal, comfortable and homey. The silence enfolded her again. Was it the lingering essence of Marette and René that gave this place such an aura of contentment? Or was it the people who lived in it now, Nick and Danny, who made it feel like a safe haven from the outside world?

So deep was she in her inner wanderings that she failed to hear the man enter the house until he stood in the kitchen archway and said, "Hello."

Stifling a startled cry, she whirled around.

"Oh gee, I'm sorry," the stranger apologized. "I didn't mean to scare you. Honest. Nick was supposed to let you know I was coming."

DeShea stood stiffly by the piano as the stranger stepped farther into the room. The mention of Nick's name removed the panic, but she remained alert and cautious nonetheless.

"I'm Hugh Couvillion. Nick's brother." He stopped and waited for the introduction to sink in.

She felt her tension ease and raised a hand to her throat as her heartbeat slowed to a normal level. "Hello, I'm DeShea Ballard."

Hugh came toward her, a broad grin on his face. "Yeah, I know." He shook her hand, keeping it clasped tightly between his palms long after the contact should have ended. "I just came by to borrow his crawfish pot. I talked to him this morning and he said he'd call and tell you I'd be over. I really am sorry I barged in." He grinned again in apology.

DeShea found it hard not to return his friendly smile. He had all the guileless charm of her nephew. As Danny had said, Hugh was very tall, long and lean. He had a mane of curly brown hair that set off his twinkling blue eyes. He walked with a loping, boyish gait, though he was probably the same age as she was. "That's all right."

"So, you're the long-lost sister," he said, shifting his weight with a nonchalance that pointed up his attractiveness. "Welcome to the family. Hope you'll be here a while so we can get to know each other."

"I guess that'll depend on several things," she commented.

Hugh nodded in an understanding way. "Brother Nick getting to you, huh?"

Color stained DeShea's cheeks before she could prevent it. "Getting to me?"

"Yeah, he can be a real pain at times. 'Specially when he's caught by surprise. And you—" he pointed at her "—threw him a major-league curve."

"I know," she admitted with a sigh. "It wasn't intentional, though. I've been out of touch for a long time, and my arrival stirred up some very painful emotions."

Hugh's voice softened. "I'm sorry your visit came too late."

DeShea glanced over at the piano, wondering if Hugh's sympathy would have been so heartfelt if he'd read her thoughts about Marette a few minutes ago. "I don't blame Nick for being upset. I've disrupted things around here considerably."

"Ah, he'll get over it," he said, waving aside her concerns. "He inherited more than his share of Mom's Italian blood. Don't pay any attention to him. Concentrate on me instead. I have Dad's romantic, passionate, French genes in me." He leaned toward her, the dimples in his cheeks in full force.

DeShea raised her eyebrows in faint surprise. "Aren't you rushing things a bit?"

"Nope. Wastes time. I like to cut right to the chase, keep things up front." He grinned at her, shoving his fingers into the back pockets of his tan jeans.

His playfulness brought a chuckle to her throat. Hugh was absolutely adorable. She wasn't sure that was the right word for a grown man, but it certainly applied. His smile was easy and quick and revealed white teeth and deep dimples at the corners of his mouth. The most startling thing about him was that he didn't resemble Nick even vaguely. Where Nick had a dark, brooding, European handsomeness, Hugh was the wholesome, all-American boy-next-door type. The contrast was fascinating.

"You're nothing like your brother," she commented.

"Lucky for me." He laughed heartily. "What a boring life."

"Don't you like him?"

"Sure. But he takes life too seriously. He gets too hung up on responsibility and forgets to just be a man. Sometimes I wonder if he has any red blood in him at all."

"What do you mean?" Hugh's opinion of his brother didn't match hers at all.

Hugh gave her a long, appreciative inspection with his blue eyes. "If he did, he'd never leave a luscious thing like you out of his sight for a minute. And he *definitely* wouldn't

leave you lying loose for the likes of me to find. But Nick
didn't tell me how beautiful you were. Guess he was trying
to keep you to himself, huh? The rascal."

DeShea was embarrassed and confused by Hugh's effu-
sive compliment and had no idea how to respond.

Hugh noticed her discomfort and frowned. "Don't tell
me you've never been told that before?"

She almost lied to him but decided against it. "Not very
often," she admitted with a grimace.

"I can't believe it," he wailed. "You're gorgeous. You
been living in a convent or something? Some Himalayan
retreat with no men allowed?"

DeShea blushed and searched for something to say. She'd
never been a flirt, or a master of small talk. For her, conversation was either about business or it didn't exist. Except with Eric, of course. He was the only person with
whom she'd felt comfortable enough to be totally herself.
"Sort of." She shrugged. "I've been running Clotilles."

Hugh let out a low whistle. "Oh, yeah. Sorry. Excuse me
while I pull this size-eleven foot out of my mouth."

An awkward silence descended between them until she
realized that with Nick and Danny gone, she was the sur-
rogate hostess. That gave her a direction, something she
could handle. "I'd offer you something to drink, but I'm
not sure where everything is."

"No problem. I do. I've got the rest of the day off, so you
can tell me all about yourself." He smiled and motioned her
to the kitchen. Not only did he find a drink, but he threw
together sandwiches as well.

They'd been chatting for the better part of an hour when
he set down his glass and stared at her. "So are you going to
have dinner with me this week, DeeDee?"

DeShea's eyes widened in surprise. No one had ever given
her a nickname before, not even Eric. The simple gesture
made her feel oddly warm and soft inside. "Dinner?"

"Yeah. Someplace romantic, soft lights, expensive wine,
classical music." His blue eyes smiled intimately into hers.

"Oh, I don't know." She hesitated. "I want to spend as much time with Danny as possible. I'm not sure how long I'll be here, and Nick might . . ." She faltered.

"Nick might what?" he prodded.

Good question. What had she intended to say? Nick might not like it? Nick might want to talk? Nick wouldn't care because Nick didn't even like her. She was merely a temporary inconvenience.

Hugh studied the changing expressions on DeShea's face and realized he'd lost the game before it had even begun. DeShea's interest was already focused on his older brother. With a little shrug, he merely shifted mental gears and started again. "I think we should have dinner on Thursday. You'll be ready by then," he stated matter-of-factly.

"Oh?" She grinned at his blatant egotism.

"Absolutely. After two more days with Nick and Danny, you'll be sick of soccer talk and begging to spend an evening with an urbane, handsome man of the world who can converse on a vast assortment of topics, none of which relates to sports in any way."

"Well . . ." She hesitated.

"No strings attached, DeeDee. I just thought maybe you could use a friend. Someone to talk to."

There was no humor in his voice now, no boyish flirtation. Only a sincere offer of friendship, and DeShea was overwhelmingly grateful. "Thank you. I could use one right now. And I'd love to have dinner with you."

Hugh stayed through the rest of the afternoon, and DeShea couldn't remember a more enjoyable time. She learned he was only twenty-eight and that he worked as an accountant for a local firm, though she had trouble imagining him as a pencil pusher. She also found that he was funny, easy to talk to, and she felt herself letting loose, joking, laughing—things she'd almost forgotten how to do since Eric left.

Nick saw his brother's car at the curb the moment he turned the corner and remembered he had been supposed to call DeShea and tell her Hugh would be dropping by. But he'd been swamped with work, and it had completely slipped his mind. That had been around noon. It was now three-thirty. Why was Hugh still here?

They were standing in front of the large rear window when he stepped through the front foyer. A shaft of afternoon sunlight was streaming in, bathing DeShea in a soft golden glow. She was smiling, and the sight stopped Nick's heart as he looked at her. It was as if something magical had touched her. Her hair was the color of spun gold; her eyes were clear and lit from within, turning the violet into lavender fire. Her smile was dazzling, rivaling the sun in its warmth. He was aware that he was staring like an imbecile, but he couldn't find his voice or the ability to look away. She was beautiful, alive and exciting. Where was the Ice Princess? And where had this living ray of sunshine come from?

Even as he formed the question, her smile dimmed, and he saw that her hand was held firmly in Hugh's fingers. A cold chill swirled inside as he realized the dazzling smile had not been for him but for his brother. Setting his jaw, he started toward his room. "What are you still doing here?" he growled as he walked past them.

Hugh's eyebrows rose. "Hello to you too, big guy. I was just on my way out."

Nick stopped and took a breath. No need to bark at his brother. Most women found his charming sibling irresistible. Why not DeShea? "Sorry. We've got soccer practice today and I'm running late."

Hugh watched his older brother disappear down the hall and frowned. "Wonder what's got a burr up his—" he glanced at DeShea and amended his statement "—why he's so ticked?"

DeShea felt as if the wind had been knocked out of her. The sight of Nick had sent a strange weakness into her legs. He'd come directly from work, and it was the first time she'd seen him in business attire. The brown suit did little if anything to take away from his athletic build. On the contrary, the conservative lines only made his bold masculinity even more apparent. The jacket called attention to his broad shoulders and narrow hips. The starched white shirt with its perfectly knotted beige-and-navy tie was a pleasing contrast to his bronze skin and brought out the deep-set sable eyes. The trousers hung perfectly along the long, muscled legs. Nick did things to the suit that the tailor had never intended, and it made him dangerously handsome.

DeShea felt her smile fade as she looked at him. She was captivated, breathless. He was without question the sexiest man she'd ever seen. At the same moment she made that discovery, she realized she'd been staring and saw the muscle in his jaw tighten. Had she offended him? He frowned, marring the strong, handsome features, then snapped a curt comment to his brother and turned down the hall to his room. She immediately understood the cause, even before Hugh voiced the question. "It's me. He doesn't like me much, I'm afraid." She realized as she spoke the words that she wanted him to like her. Wanted to be friends, like Hugh. For Danny's sake, of course.

"Why doesn't he like you?" Hugh asked in surprise.

DeShea shook her head. "I'm not sure exactly. I suppose because I barged in here and upset Danny by dredging up memories of his mother."

"Hey, Uncle Hugh," Danny called as he breezed into the room. "Aunt DeShea."

His relatives returned the greeting, chatted a few moments, then when Danny went to change, Hugh decided it was time to leave. "Don't worry about Nick," he said. "Like you said, your coming knocked him off track. He'll come around once he has a chance to think things over and see that you're not some evil, wicked aunt set on gobbling up his favorite nephew."

Nick walked into the kitchen then, dressed in shorts and a shirt similar to the one he'd worn on Sunday, and began puttering around.

Hugh winked at DeShea then waved at his brother. "See ya later, Nicko."

Nick grunted, and Hugh leaned over and whispered rather loudly in DeShea's ear, "If he doesn't lighten up, you can come and stay with me. I've got plenty of room. King-size bed, too."

She blushed and said goodbye, watching him disappear out the back door. When she returned her attention to Nick and Danny, they appeared to be in an organized state of chaos. Nick was fixing a sandwich; Danny was darting around the kitchen putting ice into two water jugs. DeShea tried to stay out of their way as they came and went from the house to the car, but it was difficult. Danny, sandwich in one hand and ball in the other, smiled at her during one trip.

"You wanna come to practice?"

Nick elbowed through, answering for her. "She'd be bored out of her mind. I'm sure she'd rather stay here."

His presumption sparked a sudden defiance in DeShea. Did he have to be so sly about not wanting her around? Why didn't he just come right out and say it?

"No, she wouldn't," Danny argued. "She'd like it. There's always other moms to talk to."

Danny's plea helped her make up her mind. Nick might not want her here, but Danny seemed to, and he was the reason she was staying. "I'd love to go, Danny," she said firmly.

Nick set his jaw. "Look, we're not talking about some nice city park with paved sidewalks. The fields are going to be mud holes after all the rain last week."

"I don't mind," DeShea assured him. "I'd like to see Danny practice."

Nick looked at the pale pink slacks and blouse she wore, his frown deepening. "There aren't any bleachers. You'll have to stand for two hours, and I doubt if your expensive clothes or your shoes will stay clean longer than ten seconds."

DeShea stood her ground, looking Nick squarely in the eye. "Then I'll have them cleaned."

Running a hand sharply through his thick hair, Nick fumed silently. The woman was stubborn on top of everything else. Fine. If she didn't mind standing on a muddy soccer field up to her knees in grime, then he didn't, either. "Then let's go," he said brusquely. "We're late already."

"I'll just get my purse." Quickly she returned to her room, then hurried back to the kitchen just as Nick came through the back door again. Their eyes met and he muttered, "Forgot the water jug."

"Oh, I'll get it," she offered, grabbing the container off the counter at her side. She turned toward the door and collided with the oncoming Nick.

Reflexively he grabbed her shoulders to steady her, pinning her against his chest. With one hand holding the water jug and the other clutching her purse, she had no choice but to lean against him for support.

His nearness sent fingers of awareness through her nerve endings, waking them to his potent sexuality. She could feel the warmth of his body even though she barely touched him. His hands were firm but gentle on her arms. Up close the sable eyes were more beautiful and fascinating than she'd first thought. His lashes were so long they cast shadows on his high cheekbones. His nose was straight, classic, evidence of his Italian heritage. Her gaze drifted to the sensuous lower lip and stopped there as her mind began to tease her with thoughts of how it would taste against her own. The scent of him filled her nostrils, and she committed it to memory.

Realization like quicksilver dawned, and she knew why she wanted Nick to like her. It wasn't for Danny's sake but for her own. She wanted him to like her as a woman, to find her attractive and desirable. But heaven help her, how did she begin? Where did she start? Outside of her marriage, she'd had painfully little practice in relationships with the opposite sex. While there had been many men to seek her company, few seemed to develop past that initial stage, which brought the conclusion that the fault lay within her. Probably because she usually felt so nervous and uncertain around them. Eventually she'd put dating out of her mind altogether and concentrated solely on her work. Now she suddenly wished she were more experienced, and more self-assured with men.

With DeShea so close, Nick found it hard to maintain the image of her as the Ice Princess. It was a conflict he'd yet to sort out, but he knew it was one he must tackle quickly. When she was at a safe distance, he could easily see cool detachment in her eyes and feel the wintry chill of her aloof personality. But when she stood close, as now, he felt only warmth emanating from her small frame, and he sensed something fragile and wistful behind the violet eyes. And once he looked into those unusual wisteria-colored eyes, he was reminded that she was a very attractive woman.

The arms in his grasp were warm, soft, and he could feel the blood pulsating through her veins. The tips of her breasts brushed against his chest, and he fought the response in his loins. He looked into her eyes and felt himself being drawn in, pulled toward the center of her.

Her lips were moist, parted, and he wondered what she would do if he kissed her. Would she freeze him out or turn into sweet sunshine under his hands? The sunshine he'd seen when she was in front of the window... with Hugh.

The memory sobered him, and abruptly he set her away. "Let's go."

Thanks to Danny's continued chatter and the screaming guitars coming from the van radio, DeShea didn't have to talk to Nick on the ride to the field. Instead she kept her eyes averted, tried to figure out what it was about her that seemed to irritate Nick so. For a brief second, when she was close against him in the kitchen, she'd thought he was going to kiss her. Then suddenly he'd thrust her away as if repulsed.

That he should feel that way about her hurt more than she would have thought possible. To be honest, she'd liked the feel of his hands on her arms, liked being held so close. But what she felt wasn't the issue. Nick was the boss here. She'd be wise to remember that and keep her mind on her real reason for staying in Baton Rouge. Danny. Anything else was irrelevant.

Nick stopped the van in a parking lot beside an open area that Danny explained used to be an airport. The city had converted it into eight soccer fields and several baseball diamonds. The old hangar housed indoor tennis courts with outdoor courts alongside.

After picking her way along the edges of the muddy parking lot, DeShea perched against a low iron railing and watched as Nick took the boys through their paces. It wasn't hard to see that they all worshiped the coach. He was firm but not harsh in his demands. He pushed them to their limits but never beyond. He tolerated no horseplay but encouraged humor and the fun of the game. Her admiration for him grew tremendously.

When practice was over, DeShea watched as Nick spoke with several of the parents who had come to pick up their sons. He joked and laughed, a broad, genuine smile that revealed strong white teeth and gave his stern features a boyish quality. Her pulse skipped a beat, and she found herself hoping he didn't flash it around too carelessly or her emotions would be in a constant state of upheaval.

The smile lingered around his eyes as he walked toward her but faded into a puzzled frown when he saw her staring at him. "Is something wrong?"

"No." She grinned. "I was merely thinking about practice. The boys have a great deal of affection and respect for you."

For some reason her unexpected compliment made him feel awkward and he turned away, handing his binder to Dan as he jogged past. "They're good kids," he answered.

"You have a real understanding for them. Not everyone could handle sixteen spirited teenage boys. That takes a special ability."

"Not really," he replied with a shrug. "You just have to like them." He looked down at her feet and frowned. "Your shoes are ruined."

She smiled up at him. "They're only shoes."

The ride home took a detour through another fast-food restaurant. DeShea's admiration for Nick had grown considerably today, except in the area of nutrition. She was beginning to wonder if he ever fed Danny real food.

Chapter Five

Hugh Couvillion leaned over the large desk in his brother's office and got right to the point of his visit. "So you want to tell me what the hell's eating at you?"

Brown eyes narrowed, as the older Couvillion glared at the younger. "What are you talking about?"

"You. Mr. Nice Guy. Or at least you used to be. But from what I saw last night, you've had a change of heart."

Nick leaned back in the leather chair, rubbing his fingers against his forehead. "I'm sorry I snapped at you, okay? It's inventory week."

The explanation didn't satisfy Hugh. "I don't care about me. I was thinking about DeShea."

"What about her?" Nick asked sourly.

"Exactly. What about her? From what I saw, she's a terrific lady. She's beautiful, smart, easy to talk to, not to mention family. But I got the distinct impression you detest her."

Nick released an exasperated sigh. "That's ridiculous. I hardly know the woman."

"That's my point, pal. Have you bothered to try?"

"She's only been here three days."

Hugh raised his eyebrows in response. "It only took me one afternoon to know I like her, and Danny certainly seemed comfortable around her."

"Yeah, I know," Nick muttered softly.

"Why do you say that?"

"Because I don't know what effect her visit will have on him. I'm not sure it's wise to have Marette's sister barging into his life when he's still coming to terms with her death. You know he's got a lot of bottled-up emotions inside him. What happens to Danny when she gets bored with life in Baton Rouge and flies off?"

"What makes you think she'll get bored?"

Nick thought about her sudden departure from the living room the other night. Almost simultaneously he saw her patiently standing on a muddy soccer field for two hours during practice. She'd looked so out of place. "She's not cut out for ordinary day-to-day living. She'll grow tired of it in a hurry."

"And that bothers you?"

"Of course. Danny gets used to having her around, feeling secure, starts depending on her, and them bam—she's gone. Just like Marette and his dad. How much loss do you think he can take?"

"I think you're making a mountain out of a molehill. I don't think DeShea will leave. I think she just might like to stay here. Permanently."

"You're dreaming, little brother," Nick scoffed. "She's a self-centered, unemotional woman who waits until her sister's death to find the time to locate her."

"Are we talking about the same woman here?" Hugh asked, a look of stunned surprise on his face. "'Bout five foot three, blond hair, violet eyes, great smile?"

The memory of DeShea's dazzling smile darted through Nick's mind, but he ignored it. "A woman who didn't even flinch when I told her that the sister she'd come to see was dead."

"Well, what did you expect? Hysterics?"

"If she didn't know about Marette, then I would have expected some sort of emotion. A reaction of any kind would have been nice."

"She was in shock," Hugh defended, getting to his feet. "How did you react when you found out René was gone? Did you scream and wail? As I recall, you stood in Mom's kitchen like a damned zombie."

"I hadn't ignored my brother for seventeen years, either. Where was she when Marette was married, when Danny came? You know how badly Marette wanted a reunion."

"We all know, you more than the rest of us, the family situation with Marette. But why are you blaming DeShea? She was only a kid when Marette ran away from home."

"Because she's a chip off the old block. Even Marette said her mother and her sister had a lot in common."

Nick's persistently harsh attitude began to get under Hugh's easygoing skin. "Now you hold it right there. I remember that conversation," he said firmly. "What she said was that DeShea and Natalie were both intense, passionate people. That once they found their purpose in life they would give it all they had."

"The point is, just *what* is her purpose here?" Nick countered. "Danny is my responsibility. He's been through a horrible couple of years. He's fragile. He doesn't need to lose anyone else close to him." Rubbing his lower lip, he pierced his brother with a stern glare. "I just want her out of here as soon as possible before she does any harm to Danny."

"She's not going to harm him," Hugh replied confidently. "She seemed really fascinated by everything here, and especially with Danny. In fact, I think she'll be very good for the kid. I think you might be surprised at just what she might contribute to his life.'' He paused and grinned slyly. "And to ours.''

"I'm not going to argue with you," Nick said. "But you can get off my case, little brother. I've already decided, for Danny's sake, to give the lady the benefit of the doubt. I won't toss her out of the house unless—'' he pointed his finger directly at his brother to emphasize his point ''—unless I see that she's treating his delicate emotional state lightly. Then she'll be out on the sidewalk faster than you can blink.''

Hugh shrugged and nodded slightly. "I can live with that. But before you chase the lovely DeeDee away with your nasty attitude, I'm at least going to have one romantic dinner to show for it.''

Nick raised his head sharply. "DeeDee?''

"Yeah.'' Hugh grinned, perching one lean hip on the desk. "She looks like a DeeDee, don't ya think? DeShea is too stuffy. We're going to dinner tomorrow night.''

Reaching for the papers in front of him, Nick sat back down in his chair, hoping Hugh would take the hint and leave. Did DeShea like the nickname Hugh had given her? He couldn't picture her as a DeeDee. In fact, he thought her unusual name suited her perfectly. "What did you do, offer her a meal at Chalet Brandt to get her to go out with you?''

"Nope,'' Hugh replied, ignoring the disparaging remark. "Actually, I was quite clever. I used one of my surefire lines to snag her and reel her in.'' He glanced searchingly over the desktop. "Ya got a piece of paper handy? You might want to write this down. It's never failed.'' Nick scowled at him, but Hugh wasn't affected in the slightest. "First you smile. Uh, you do remember how to do that, don't you? Then you say, 'DeeDee, would you have dinner with me on Thursday night?''"

Nick had heard enough of his brother's nonsense. "Hugh, I've got work to do here.''

Hugh frowned and shook his head. "You know, I don't get you. You're usually so patient and understanding with everyone. Always the sympathetic shoulder in the family. Especially with Danny. In case you've forgotten, DeShea is an orphan, too. She was a victim, just like Marette was. Where's your understanding and patience where she's concerned? You've been acting like a real jerk, and I suggest you rethink your attitude toward Marette's only sister."

Nick's conscience smarted at the direct hit. He'd forgotten about Natalie, still had difficulty linking DeShea to Marette instead of their mother. Hugh's observations forced him to take a good look at the way he'd behaved in the past few days. What he discovered wasn't pleasant. "You're right, I have been acting like a jerk," he admitted.

He'd realized it himself yesterday, then promptly taken the offensive against DeShea at the first opportunity. Rising, he strode to the office window, hands shoved deeply into his trouser pockets, Hugh's first question still echoing in his mind. "I don't know what's eating at me. I guess my concern for Danny makes me overly cautious sometimes. He's never fully released his emotions regarding his mother's death. I want those feelings to be uncovered naturally, in the proper time—not ripped from him by another trauma."

"Has DeShea actually made moves to harm him?" his brother asked.

Nick shook his head. "There's just something about her. She's so aloof and distant."

"Hey, big guy, don't forget she lost her mother barely eight weeks ago, and then she gets down here to Louisiana and finds out her sister is gone as well. That's bound to make a person a little distant. She's grieving."

A wave of sympathy swelled inside Nick, laced liberally with shame. Gnawing at the inside of his lower lip, he faced some truths about his behavior. He'd been more than a jerk. He'd been unfeeling and callous—the very things he'd accused her of. Worse, he could find no logical reason for his uncharacteristic resentment. Perhaps the strain of the past eight months had warped his own emotions. His concern for Danny had taken precedence over everything else and made him blind to another's pain. He remembered that one moment of understanding they'd shared—the sense of empathy. Had it actually happened, or had he imagined it?

"Tell me the truth," Hugh urged, going to stand by his brother's side. "Has she really given you a hard time? Or Danny, for that matter?"

"No," Nick replied quietly. "She's been very cooperative, though I don't think she approves of some of my ideas on child rearing."

"What about with Dan? Any real problems?"

Nick shook his head again. "No, she seems genuinely interested in Dan and what he's doing. And so far, when he asks questions she's responded with frankness and honesty."

"So what's the deal?" Hugh said with a smile, clapping his brother on the back. "Chill out. Don't look for potholes before the road is even paved, dude."

Nick smiled and turned back to his desk. "Good advice. I'll try and keep it in mind."

"That's better. I'll see you later."

Nick tried to sort through his muddled emotions after Hugh left. If only DeShea was more like Marette, this whole situation would be easier. You always knew where you stood with Marette. She didn't hesitate for a minute to speak her mind or put you in your place. Little sister was just the opposite. She kept everything carefully guarded behind that Ice Princess mask of hers, as if everyone could read her mind. Well, he was no mind reader. How was he expected to feel sympathy for a woman who refused to communicate?

But then he remembered the sight of her, haloed in the sunlight, and was forced to admit another fact. DeShea was a very beautiful woman, and he was attracted to her. He resented that knowledge, too. But he soothed it with the rationalization that he was drawn to her the way any man would be drawn to an object of beauty. He was merely feeling an appreciation for a lovely work of art. Nothing more.

Yet something about DeShea nagged at the back of his mind. Warned him to beware, be cautious and tread slowly. There was something unseen about her, something below the surface that she was protecting.

There was that unexplained look in her eyes, the one he could only describe as cold. And then there were her sudden withdrawals into silence and her unexplained retreats to her room. Those actions didn't match with the woman he'd seen in the sunlight or the one that had pressed against him in the kitchen. The woman was one huge question mark. But he couldn't find the answers hampered by anger and suspicion. For the sake of everyone concerned, he'd better let go of the anger and try to look at the situation more objectively. No matter how difficult that might be.

DeShea looked anxiously at the clock, waiting for Danny to come through the door. She couldn't remember exactly when he was due home from school, but she thought it should be soon. Before she could glance at the wall clock again, she heard the back door open. Her nephew sauntered in, dropping his backpack on the kitchen table.

"Hello," she said with a smile, thinking again what a charming young boy her nephew was. "Did you have a good day at school?"

"It was a day," he replied with a shrug, heading for the refrigerator.

"Do you have homework tonight?"

"Just a few algebra problems. But they won't take long."

"Then I'd like to ask you for a favor. I was thinking about the mothers I saw at practice yesterday, and I realized I don't have a suitable wardrobe to wear to soccer games and around the house. So I thought maybe we could go to the mall and I could pick up a few things."

"Great. When do you want to go?" he asked, taking a huge bite out of his apple.

"How about now?"

"Sure. You gonna use Uncle Nick's car?"

DeShea had already thought of that. "No. I'd rather not. How about if I call a cab?"

A huge grin appeared on Danny's face. "Radical."

His aunt frowned. "Is that good?"

"Yes, ma'am. That's more than good."

When the cab arrived, DeShea let Danny give the driver their destination. They spent the next couple of hours selecting jeans, shirts and sport slacks. She bought a pair of tennis shoes and some black flats as well as a few skirts and sporty dresses. When it came time to select lingerie, however, Danny cheerfully took off to more interesting departments.

When they met again, they wandered through the other stores. DeShea discovered what a wonderful companion Danny was, and she began to feel that they were really becoming friends.

Her nephew was easy to talk to, intelligent and possessed a delightful sense of humor. He kept her constantly amused, either with stories about his friends and school or anecdotes about Marette and his dad. He even gave DeShea a crash course in soccer, from the basics of the game down to the difference between long cleats and turf shoes.

DeShea began to see that Danny was the young man Nick kept telling her he was, not a little boy. And while the realization was a happy one, it also saddened her to think of all the things she'd missed and all the time lost forever.

By the time they returned home it was almost dark, and Nick was waiting in the kitchen as they hauled the shopping bags through the door.

DeShea hurriedly offered a defense when she saw the scowl on his face. "We went shopping. Did you see the note?"

"Yeah," he answered curtly.

"I think Aunt DeShea bought everything in Cortana Mall," Danny teased.

Nick didn't say anything, merely shoved a box of pizza along the counter. "Your supper is still warm if you eat it now."

Turning to Danny, DeShea pointed at the packages he was carrying. "Just put those down and go eat. I'll get them later." With a glance at Nick, she hurried to her room, depositing her purchases on the bed. Nick was obviously perturbed by their absence, though why he should be so upset by a few hours at the mall was beyond her. She hoped she could smooth the situation. Danny shouldn't have to suffer for her actions.

When she returned to the kitchen, however, the pizza box was still unopened on the counter and Nick and Danny were nowhere to be seen. She picked up the rest of her purchases, and was halfway across the living room when she heard Nick's voice coming from the small office off the foyer. She started toward it, intending to apologize, but stopped at the threshold.

Nick was holding Danny tight against his chest while the young boy sobbed against him. One strong hand smoothed his nephew's glossy brown hair tenderly, then Nick bent and rested his cheek on Danny's head.

The sight of Danny so distraught, hurting, was like a physical blow to DeShea's heart. She wanted to go to him, comfort and hold him the way Nick was, but it was clear she wasn't needed. Nick was handling the situation, and he was the one Danny needed now. But what had upset him? All through their shopping trip he'd been cheerful, lighthearted.

Uncertain exactly what to do, she turned back toward the kitchen to wait. As the minutes ticked slowly away, her worry and concern grew. Almost an hour later Danny emerged from the office and went directly upstairs.

DeShea joined Nick in the living room, a worried frown on her face. "What's wrong?" she asked. "What happened? Did I say something to upset him? Is he sick?" Her heart was a tight fist in her chest.

Nick shook his head and ran a hand through his hair. "He just misses his mother."

DeShea closed her eyes. She kept forgetting that she looked like Marette. Of course it would be difficult for Danny not to think of his mother when there was the living image at his elbow all day. "I'm sorry," she said in an unsteady voice. "I didn't mean for this to happen."

"I know."

Nick's comment surprised her. It threatened to bring on the tears she was struggling to keep back. "I'd never do anything to hurt him. He's all I have now."

Nick watched the moisture form in the corners of her violet eyes and felt an urge to draw her into his arms, as he had Danny moments ago. There was nothing cold and empty about her now. She looked small and sad and strangely appealing. For the first time he was able to connect her emotional state to Danny's. They were both alone, without parents. Except Danny had him and scores of aunts and uncles and cousins. Whom did DeShea have?

"Should I go and talk to him?"

Nick shook his head and gestured to the sofa. "Sit down. I think I'd better explain something to you."

DeShea searched his face anxiously. He looked so serious, so unapproachable. She fully expected him to ask her to leave, and her heart contracted further. "What is it? What did I do? If I'm responsible for upsetting him..." Her voice faltered.

"You are—" he started to say.

"Oh, God." DeShea bit her lip. Her shoulders slumped.

Nick cursed himself. He wasn't handling this right at all. "No, DeShea. That's not what I meant." He took a breath and began again. "When Marette died, Danny was understandably distraught. He'd barely adjusted to René's death only to lose his mother. I put him back in counseling, and with the help of the family and time, he was getting along reasonably well."

"Counseling?" It had never occurred to her that a child might need professional help.

"Yes. Marette thought it would help him deal with his grief over René. I was skeptical at first, but it seemed to really help him." Nick rubbed his eyes and continued. "The difference this time is that Danny had never cried for Marette. He'd talked about it, even gotten angry about it, but he's never let the tears come, never given up that final measure of loss. Today he did."

The significance of Nick's words began to take hold in DeShea's mind, and she felt a wave of nausea. She'd been so consumed with her own need to find a family, to spend time with Danny, she'd never fully examined the consequences of her actions upon her nephew.

Rising, she walked to the window, keeping her back to Nick. How could she face him? Despite her good intentions not to harm her nephew, she'd practically forced Danny to face his grief for Marette. Surely it would have been better for him to tap that level of emotion in his own way. "I'm sorry," she said, barely able to keep the tremor from her voice. "Believe me, I never meant for this to happen."

"I believe you," Nick said, and was surprised to find that he truly did.

"I'll leave immediately if my being here only reminds him of his mother. I don't want to add to his unhappiness."

"On the contrary, you've been a tremendous help," Nick said earnestly. "You were the catalyst that finally penetrated his wall of grief. I'm very grateful to you for that, and Danny likes having you here."

DeShea looked at the brown eyes and saw compassion in them—for her. "Are you sure?"

He nodded. "Marette and Danny used to shop together often. Being with you today finally allowed him to come to terms with her death."

"What if I only made it worse?" she asked, still not convinced.

"Doubtful. He is fond of you. He was drawn to you from the beginning."

"Because I look like Marette," DeShea said flatly.

"Maybe. But he knows you're not his mother. I believe he truly likes you for yourself."

The sincerity in his voice eased her concern somewhat. "Will he be all right?"

"I think so. There's still some rough times ahead. Grieving is a long process. But we've made headway today. That's a very good sign."

The magnitude of her mistake was beginning to register. "What should I say to him?" she asked. "Do I apologize? Do I ignore the whole thing?"

"Let him lead you. He'll let you know. Just follow your instincts."

DeShea looked up at him, her mind filled with trepidation. "I'm not sure I have any."

Nick saw the emotion-filled eyes and wondered how he could have thought her cold and empty. "I'm sure," he stated softly. "I've seen you with him. You have good instincts. You just need to learn to trust them." His compliment caught them both off guard, creating an awkward silence.

Nick finally ended it the only way he could think of. "Are you hungry? I could warm the pizza."

"No, thank you," she said with a faint smile. "I think I'll go to my room for a while." Picking up the long-forgotten shopping bags, she looked back at him and said quietly, "Thank you for explaining it to me. I'm sorry if I've made things difficult for you and Danny."

"It's my fault," Nick said quickly. "I should have told you from the start. I tend to be a little overprotective of my nephew. Especially with people I don't know."

"I understand. I'd probably do the same. Danny's very lucky to have someone like you to care for him." DeShea saw the dark eyes soften. She wanted to say more, to tell him how she admired him, how she envied Danny the love his uncle bestowed so freely. But the words wouldn't come. Lowering her eyes, she gestured to her packages. "I'll just put these away."

DeShea woke feeling wonderful. Last night, Nick had seemed friendlier, less distant than he had since her arrival. And just before she went upstairs, Danny had reappeared, apparently none the worse for wear, and eaten six pieces of warmed-up pizza. All in all, the incident seemed to have drawn them all a bit closer and relaxed the tension between them.

Seated at the kitchen counter, she wondered what she could do to repay the Couvillions' hospitality. She'd been here almost a week and had done nothing but follow them around. Maybe she could do some laundry or straighten up the house. Before she could even ferret out a dust rag, however, a cleaning woman arrived. She was friendly, but assured DeShea firmly that she needed no help with the household chores.

It was while she was pouring her third cup of coffee that DeShea spotted the grocery list on the corkboard above the desk. After checking with the cleaning lady, she made a thorough inspection of the cupboards, adding several more items to the lengthy list. The next problem was transportation. The keys to Nick's vintage Stingray dangled from the corkboard, but she doubted if he would appreciate her taking it without his permission.

After much consideration, she decided to rent a car and have it delivered. If she was going to stay here a while longer, she would need a vehicle. She couldn't ask Nick to drive her wherever she wanted to go. Besides, if she had a car, maybe she could help out by driving Danny to school or Scouts.

After obtaining directions from the cleaning lady, De-Shea steered the rented car down the street and out onto the main thoroughfare. When she spotted the sign announcing Couvillion's, she pulled into the lot, nervous excitement racing through her.

* * *

The food was barely stored in the cupboards when Nick came home. The sight of the beaming DeShea greeted him when he stepped inside the door. She was seated on a stool and spun around to face him, eyes sparkling and a dazzling smile on her face. A rush of appreciation coursed through him. She was ridiculously attractive when she wanted to be. But what had her so excited?

"Hello," she said. "Did you have a good day?"

"Yeah," he said, setting his briefcase on the floor. "We have company? I saw a strange car in the drive."

"No. It's mine. I rented it today," she said proudly. "I didn't want to impose on you."

"You could have used mine. I don't mind."

"Well, I wasn't sure, and I hated to take it without asking."

Her consideration pleased and surprised him. She could have just taken it. He'd expected such behavior from someone with her background. The Ice Princess was full of surprises. "You're welcome to use it while you're here," he offered, vaguely wondering why his nickname for her no longer seemed appropriate.

"Thank you. If you're sure. It would save some money. I'll pay for the gas, of course."

Nick tugged at his tie and walked to the refrigerator for a soda. "You look awfully happy."

"Do I?" She grinned. "Maybe it's because I started repaying your hospitality today."

"Oh?"

"Yes. I saw the grocery list on the board, and I went to the store for you. I'm not sure I got all the right brands, but at least your cupboards aren't bare anymore."

Nick stared at her a moment, finding it difficult to digest her words. "You did that?" He wouldn't have expected her to know her way around a food store.

"I hope you don't mind."

She seemed so proud of herself Nick couldn't help but smile. Again her thoughtfulness and consideration touched him. It couldn't have been easy getting a car, finding her way to the store and selecting food for people she hardly knew. Personally, he detested grocery shopping and put it off as long as possible.

"No," he assured her. "Not at all. Thank you. I've been meaning to go, but it's been hectic at work and I just didn't have time."

"Guess that explains all the eating out."

He grinned. "Yeah. We don't usually eat junk every night."

"Good." She chuckled lightly. "I was beginning to wonder."

As they smiled at each other, Nick marveled at the change in her. She seemed so real today, alive, vital. He couldn't explain the difference, but he liked it.

"Would you like to come to practice tonight?" he asked, surprising himself. He hadn't consciously intended to ask her.

"Oh, I'd love to, but I'm having dinner with Hugh this evening," she said matter-of-factly.

Instantly his good mood soured. "Right." He turned and walked out of the kitchen just as Danny came in the back door.

He didn't see DeShea again until after practice. Hugh was waiting for her in the living room when he came in, and the jolt of envy he felt at the sight of his brother startled him. It was no concern of his if she had dinner with Hugh. His brother was a fun guy, the type women fawned over. DeShea was a lovely woman. It was only natural they get together. So why did the idea bother him so?

Probably because he'd set all his own relationships aside for the time being. He had Danny to think of now. His personal life had been tabled until his nephew was on solid ground again. Hugh and DeShea, on the other hand, were both free and unencumbered.

Hugh greeted him with a smile. "Hey, big guy, how did practice go?"

"Fine," Nick answered curtly.

Danny trotted between them on his way upstairs. "Hey, Uncle Hugh. Wha-sup?"

Giving the boy a friendly punch on the arm, Hugh winked. "Got a hot date."

"O-oh," Danny drawled, "with Aunt DeShea?"

"Yep." Hugh grinned, eyebrows bobbing meaningfully.

"Did I hear my name being bandied about?" DeShea asked as she came through the foyer.

She looked lovely. Her long blond hair was pulled up on her head but in a softer, more feminine, style than usual. Her slim figure was sheathed in a soft jade green silk dress that embraced her dainty figure to perfection and highlighted her fragile beauty.

Hugh whistled softly, Danny muttered "wow," and Nick found his vocal cords tied in knots.

"Thank you." She grinned, moving into the room. Hugh was immediately at her side, spinning her around and leading her toward the front door.

"What's your hurry?" Nick heard a voice ask, shocked to realize he'd spoken.

"Are you kidding?" Hugh grinned. "I want to get her out of here before you get any ideas. Bye."

As the door shut behind them, Danny came to Nick's side. "Wow. Didn't Aunt DeShea look great?"

Nick had to make several attempts to find his voice. "Yes," he finally muttered somewhat sourly. "She looked great."

Chapter Six

"Good night, Hugh, and thank you for everything." DeShea smiled as she stood at the back door.

"Any time, DeeDee. But I still say it's too early to call it a night. I hope you know you're putting a black mark on my reputation."

DeShea laughed. "Oh, I think your image will remain intact. I promise not to tell a soul about your uncharacteristic behavior."

After talking a few more minutes, she shut the door and walked leisurely through the house toward her room. The restaurant had been elegant, the food sumptuous and the conversation enjoyable. Hugh had been easy to talk to and she'd found herself discussing things with him she'd never intended. She told him about her difficulties with Clotilles, swearing him to silence until the delicate negotiations were completed.

She had shared her lingering concern for Danny and his emotional breakdown the day before and her part in it. But Hugh quickly and firmly reassured her.

"Don't worry about Nick. He just tends to take his role as patriarch too seriously."

"Patriarch?"

Hugh nodded. "After Dad died, René and Nick sorta became our fathers."

"I didn't know your father was gone."

"Nick was only thirteen at the time, and I was just a toddler. René did what he could, but he went into the Navy after high school so Nick became head of the family. He was the one who listened to our problems, settled our disputes. He still makes himself available to all of us at the drop of a hat. That doesn't leave much time for himself, especially now. When René died, Nick tried to step in and help Marette, and after she died, he got Danny full-time."

"It takes a special kind of man to do that," DeShea observed quietly, more to herself than to Hugh. She understood now Nick's fierce protectiveness toward Danny. He knew the pain of losing a parent at such a young age.

"I agree, but sometimes I think Nick gets so caught up in looking out for us that he never finds time to lead a life of his own. He needs a woman, someone to share his future. Nick isn't the kind of man who was meant to be alone."

He had Danny. But even with her limited knowledge of Nick, she could see it wasn't enough for a man like him. Nick was a family man. He needed a wife. Someone warm, sympathetic, who would love Danny like her own and make a home for them both. But Nick's love life was really no concern of hers. She had to concentrate on Danny. Not on the uncle who didn't want her here.

Nick heard Hugh's car pull into the drive and glanced quickly at the clock radio. It was almost midnight. Apparently DeShea and his brother had enjoyed the evening, though he had trouble envisioning the quiet, elegant DeShea with the gregarious Hugh. The sound of their mingled voices drifted through the walls. He couldn't make out what was said, only the sound of DeShea's laughter. Then suddenly the house was silent and his bed was very empty.

Nick stared blindly into the darkness, unable to sleep. The sound of DeShea's laughter kept reverberating in his mind with a fierce aching need that coiled deep inside his gut. Loneliness. Something he hadn't felt for a long time. So what brought it out now?

He'd been perfectly content with his life. For the past several years he'd been happy to devote all his energy toward giving his nephew the love and support the boy needed to get through the terrible loss of first his father and then his mother. But now that Danny had faced his grief over Marette, he would continue to grow stronger. The fierce wall of protectiveness could be eased.

Nick didn't regret setting his own life on the back burner for Danny's sake. The boy brought joy and happiness, meaning and purpose into his life. But now the crisis was coming to a close, Nick had to admit his relationship with Danny didn't give him everything. It couldn't fill the need for companionship, for the physical blending of two people who had made a commitment to spend their lives together, for a special someone, a woman, who would stand by him, replenish him and help him find the strength to greet each day. He loved Danny, but he wanted a wife and children of his own, living proof of that mutual love and devotion.

But where did he find her? He hadn't found a woman he'd cared for deeply enough to make that commitment. He wanted to be sure, positive she was the right one for him. He believed very strongly in marriage, and when he settled down, it would be forever.

Unfortunately, he was coming to the conclusion that the right woman for him didn't exist. Perhaps the fault wasn't in the women he dated but in himself. Admittedly he was slightly chauvinistic about the type of relationship he wanted. But was that totally bad? He wanted a woman who would put family first. The way Marette had with his brother and Danny.

The memory of DeShea's laughter echoed inside his head. Why tonight? Why the sudden feeling of isolation? Finding no answer that satisfied him, he rolled over and grabbed the remote control, punching the power button and letting the drone of the TV set chase the loneliness away.

The next morning DeShea awoke early, feeling better than she had in years. The atmosphere in the house had eased considerably since Danny's emotional catharsis, and Hugh's affirmation of Nick's attitude further enhanced her good mood. Maybe now that the air was clear and she no longer posed a threat to Danny in Nick's eyes, they could all become good friends. For the first time she entertained the thought of becoming a permanent part of Danny's life. Perhaps Nick would allow her to visit often and let Danny come to Galena.

Dressing in one of her new sport dresses, DeShea braided her hair, added a fancy clip, then went downstairs. Danny was alone in the kitchen eating breakfast when she walked in. "Good morning," she said cheerfully.

The boy looked up at her and smiled, sending a rush of warmth to her heart. Was this what was called maternal love? How wonderful it would be to feel this way all the time, to be greeted with that precious face and endearing smile each day of her life. The memory of another smile flashed into her mind as she fixed her coffee. "Where's your uncle?"

"He left early. But he said he'd be home early today. It's Friday."

DeShea joined him at the counter. "Something special going on today?"

"Nope," he said between bites of cereal. "Everyone takes off early on Friday."

"Oh, really?" DeShea laughed. "Maybe I'd better stay here and find work."

"Would you?" he asked eagerly, his brown eyes hopeful.

"What?"

"Stay here. Live here."

"Oh, I don't know." She'd spoken without thinking, never considering how Danny would react. "I hadn't thought about it."

"You could live with us," Danny continued enthusiastically. "We could be a family again."

Taking a long sip of her coffee, DeShea searched for the right words. She didn't have the heart to crush his dream. But she couldn't tell him bluntly that she wouldn't be welcome here on a permanent basis. Her relationship with Nick had improved tremendously, but not to the point of sharing a house! "Danny," she finally said, her tone cautious, "I don't think it would work quite that way."

A sigh of resignation came from the young boy. "Yeah, I know. It was a dumb idea."

"Not at all," she replied quickly, placing a hand on his arm. "I'm flattered you want me to live here. But I don't think it would be practical. For your uncle or me."

"You could get an apartment here in Baton Rouge," Danny persisted. "Couldn't you open a salon or whatever down here?"

"Well, actually, I won't have any salons at all shortly. I'm getting rid of them. After that, I'm not sure what I'll be doing. I have an old Victorian house in Galena, New York, that I'll be moving into." Danny's eyes reflected his disappointment. "But I tell you what, I'll take your suggestion under consideration. All right?"

Danny grinned impishly. "Does that mean I can try and talk you into staying?"

"Sure." DeShea grinned. "You never know. It might work. Now you'd better hurry or you'll be late for school."

The morning passed quickly, and after a light lunch, DeShea decided to take advantage of the warm sunshine. Slipping into her new bathing suit, she stretched out on the chaise on the patio. The sun felt deliciously warm, intoxicating, and she could feel it lulling her into a dreamlike state. She let her thoughts wander and found them, as was becoming her habit, turning to Nick. But these weren't the usual images, the ones she thought of consciously. Usually she thought of the raw, masculine look of him tired and sweaty after a strenuous practice or the clean, polished, oh-so-sexy businessman in suit and tie.

Instead she found herself replaying the little domestic things, things she didn't normally think of in regard to a man. The way he looked cleaning up the kitchen, making breakfast with careless expertise or folding the clothes with Danny, and the affectionate banter that passed between them. Such ordinary things and in themselves not very masculine, but the mere fact that Nick was comfortable doing such mundane chores only seemed to heighten his masculinity. She wasn't sure she fully understood the concept. But somehow, the contrast between his conspicuous virility and the dull colorless tasks was powerfully seductive.

DeShea found herself daydreaming about staying in this house, taking care of Nick and Danny, managing all the little details that she was beginning to learn were part of family life. Images flooded her mind until she was forced to collect her notebook and spend the next several hours writing about her impressions and feelings toward Danny and Nick.

As she wrote, it became clear that her feelings toward Nick had changed. She was very strongly attracted to him. It was more than just fascination or casual interest. He was beginning to occupy her thoughts on a regular basis, and she wasn't sure how to stop it. Or even if she wanted to.

The tinkling of the phone bell prevented her from examining the question more thoroughly. She hurried into the house. "Hello?"

"Is Mr. Couvillion there?" a crisp voice inquired.

"No, he's not. I'm his sister-in-law. May I help you?"

"This is Mrs. Lenore Fontenot, Danny's English teacher."

DeShea listened intently, her face settling into a thoughtful frown, as Mrs. Fontenot explained the reason behind her call. She had replaced the phone and was still absorbing the teacher's words when Nick walked in. She'd forgotten he was due home early. She'd also forgotten she was still in her swimsuit, and her cheeks burned hotly as his intense brown eyes skimmed over her barely covered body. Every nerve ending in her body came to life, calling to her in unfamiliar ways and reminding her that she was above all a woman. Swallowing past the lump in her throat, she forced herself to move.

"I was lying in the sun when the phone rang," she explained quickly.

"Who was it?" he asked softly, his eyes traveling up her form once again before focusing on her eyes.

"Danny's teacher."

Nick finally broke eye contact, and she took advantage of the moment to retreat into the living room. "I'll just get my robe," she mumbled, turning and hurrying through the French door, and grabbing up her robe. Her heart was pounding wildly as she slipped her arms in the sleeves and tied the belt.

The moment DeShea was out of the room, Nick yanked the constricting tie from around his neck, gulping in a couple of deep breaths. The sight of DeShea standing in the kitchen in the sleek swimsuit had triggered an intense physical response he'd been unprepared to control. The blue suit was modest by most standards—narrow straps, a scooped neckline that barely revealed the upper swell of her small breasts, and a saucy ruffle that angled up from her left thigh over her hip and called attention to her shapely legs. But although he reminded himself that this was Danny's aunt, Marette's sister, and a guest in his home, the male in him couldn't stop his eyes from drinking in the luscious, tantalizing sight in front of him. The delicate throat, the soft swell of breasts, the angle of the rib cage as it dipped into the narrow waist then flared to full, rounded hips, the blush that stained her cheeks as he admired her. When she hastened from the room, he'd breathed a sigh of relief. He also found himself wishing DeShea had maintained her Ice Princess image. This new one—the vulnerable, innocent woman— was going to be more difficult to ignore.

When DeShea returned to the kitchen, she was completely covered in the folds of a terry-cloth robe. She moved directly to the counter and picked up the notepad, avoiding Nick's eyes. "She said Danny missed a test two weeks ago and a makeup that was scheduled for after school last Friday. Apparently he left school early the day of the test?"

Nick took the pad and read it over. "That was the day we left for Houston. I checked him out early."

"You were going to visit relatives?" she asked, remembering Danny's comment about having an aunt there.

"No. We had a soccer tournament," he replied, staring at the note.

DeShea's eyes widened in disbelief. Danny had assured her that he only played games on weekends and holidays, yet Nick was openly admitting to pulling him out of school— totally disregarding an important test just for an out-of-town soccer tournament.

Her clear disapproval made Nick instantly defensive. She was judging on something she knew nothing about. "It's nothing to get upset about. Danny is a good student. It doesn't hurt to miss a class now and again."

Still trying to comprehend his actions, DeShea decided that perhaps he'd not heard her correctly. "Mrs. Fontenot said he missed an important test."

Nick rubbed his temple thoughtfully. "He told me he didn't have any that day."

DeShea lowered her eyes and toyed with the fringe on the place mat to cover her annoyance.

Nick took a deep breath and tried to explain further. "We have an agreement. When he has a test scheduled, I don't take him out of school." He tossed the pad down on the counter. "It's not like him to lie to me."

"Maybe he was too anxious to get to the tournament," she suggested firmly. Nick's overemphasis on sports had distressed her. "Perhaps if Danny had a little more structure to his life?"

"Structure?" Nick snapped, offended at her implication that he wasn't doing what was best for Danny. "You mean like the rigid unbending life you lead? Is that really what you want for him?"

DeShea realized how her comment had sounded and tried to explain. "It's just that I feel that overindulgence can be as destructive as excessive discipline."

"When did you become an expert on raising kids?"

"I'm not. It's just plain common sense."

Nick felt his temper getting out of hand and made a half-hearted attempt to calm it, but the look of disapproval still poured from DeShea's violet eyes.

"I think I know a little more about this than you do. Danny isn't the first child I've raised. Hugh and my sisters were all under seven years old when Dad died."

DeShea blinked, realizing with a jolt of sadness that Nick had devoted his life to raising other people's children and yet had none of his own.

Before she could respond, Danny burst through the door, dropping his books onto the table with a loud bang. "Hi, guys. What's up?"

Fueled with disappointment over Danny's lie and anger over DeShea's disapproval, Nick whirled and stabbed a finger at him. "Why the hell didn't you tell me about that test?" he barked.

Danny blinked and stepped back. "What test?" he asked meekly.

"Dammit, Danny, don't make it worse by denying it," Nick shouted. "You had an English test the Friday we left for Houston."

"Yes, sir."

"Why didn't you tell me?" Nick demanded, his voice growing louder.

Danny stared at the floor and shrugged.

"That's not an answer."

"It wasn't a very big test," he said lamely.

Nick cursed. "What about the makeup?"

"I forgot."

"Forgot!" Nick roared. "Just what's gotten into you? You've never done this before. You know we have a rule about tests. Why would you lie to me?"

Again the boy shrugged. "I hate this teacher. She's a geek."

"Danny! You will *not* talk about your teacher that way. I don't give a damn whether you like her or not. You're there to learn."

DeShea sat on the stool, hands clasped tightly in her lap, as Nick began a lecture on the importance of schoolwork and trust and responsibility. The intense empathy she felt for her nephew was difficult to handle. Nick's loud outburst was bringing up memories of Natalie and her screaming, hysterical outbursts. DeShea didn't want Danny to endure anything like that. Ever. Nick's unexpected temper also disappointed her more than she wanted to admit. Up until now, Nick had seemed eternally patient and understanding with Danny. It hurt to discover that he wasn't all that she'd imagined.

"You go upstairs. Call Mrs. Fontenot and apologize. Then set up a time to take that test, even if it's after school. Do you understand me?"

"Yes, sir," Danny replied meekly.

"You're also grounded for the weekend," Nick added angrily.

Danny uttered a grunt of protest. "But you said I could go to John's tonight."

"No way, pal," he said firmly.

Danny grumbled and started toward the living room. "What about the crawfish boil tomorrow? Can I go to that?

Aunt Dixie and the kids will be there.'' His voice held a belligerent note.

"Watch your attitude, young man," Nick warned, "or you won't go tomorrow. As it stands now, you can go to the crawfish boil and the game on Sunday. That's all. But if you don't toe the line, I'll put your backside in your room, and you'll stay there till school on Monday. You get my point?"

With a mumbled but respectful "Yes, sir," Danny disappeared into the other room. DeShea could hear him stomping angrily up the stairs. Her heart ached for the boy and she turned to Nick, expecting him to follow and offer some apology—a hug—some gesture of affection like she'd seen before. But he was planted firmly in the kitchen and showed no signs of moving. His face was stormy and his eyes were dark.

"I'm sure he didn't mean to do anything wrong."

"He lied to me," he stated flatly, shrugging out of his suit coat and draping it over the kitchen chair.

"He's just a little boy. Maybe you should have talked to him calmly and quietly and discussed your reasons for being angry."

Nick rolled back the cuffs on his dress shirt with quick, angry motions. "He's *not* a little boy. He's a young man, and he needs to know what is acceptable behavior in this house and what isn't. I'll tolerate a great many things from him, but *not* lying."

"Maybe he had a good reason. Maybe he was afraid of your... temper." Part of her mind warned her that she was interfering in something that was not her concern, but she couldn't help herself. She was trying to protect the only family she had left.

"My temper is a fact of life here. When I'm angry, I yell, I shout. Sometimes I cuss. Danny knows that. He also knows I only reach that point when I'm pushed beyond the limits. He made a mistake and he's paying the consequences." Nick turned his back and walked away.

DeShea moved to follow. "I think it might have been—"

Nick whirled and faced her. "What you think, DeShea, isn't important here. It's what *I* think that counts. Danny is my responsibility."

DeShea knew when to bide her time. Trying to discuss the matter further when Nick was so incensed was futile. Gathering her dignity, she returned Nick's fierce glare with a level gaze. "If you'll excuse me, I need to get dressed," she said quietly, then walked past him and up the stairs.

Nick watched her go and felt his insides sink like a stone. Idiot. He had no reason to lash out at DeShea. She'd been right. He had overreacted with Danny. There'd been no need to shout and curse at the boy. While it was true he was prone to raising his voice, he didn't usually get ugly in the process. He'd have to apologize to them both—to Danny for being so harsh and to DeShea for telling her to mind her own business. He'd seen her disapproval and taken offense. She couldn't be expected to understand the finer points of child rearing. To someone outside the family, his behavior probably looked worse than it actually was.

Shutting his bedroom door, Nick vowed to talk to both of them this evening over dinner. He had to repair the damage his temper had done. Strange, but he hadn't gotten that angry in a long, long time.

The door to Danny's room was open when DeShea walked by a short while later. She stopped, listening closely, but didn't hear any sounds of crying or anger from within. After a moment's hesitation she peeked in. Danny was stretched out on his side on the bed, reading. "Mind if I come in?"

"No, ma'am," he said, sitting up.

DeShea sat down beside him. "Are you okay?"

"I guess." He shrugged. "I really screwed up this time. Uncle Nick is really ticked."

"Everyone makes mistakes from time to time," she said softly. She was thinking of herself and how much she'd lost in her life to her own mistakes.

Danny stared at the floor, then reached down and picked up the soft ball he always played with.

"I shouldn't have lied about that test," he admitted, his expression contrite. "I just wanted to get to Houston. I hate English."

DeShea reached out and smoothed his hair back. It felt soft and silky, and she was filled with a powerful urge to hold him close to her heart and protect him from all the harsh realities of life. Instead she smiled and said, "Maybe I could help you. I used to be very good in English."

Danny screwed up his face. "It's literature. Stories and stuff. We're talking megaboring here."

"Oh, good," she enthused. "That's what I'm best at. I even write stories and some poetry now and again."

"You do?" Wide brown eyes studied her closely as if inspecting the new data.

She nodded. "In fact, I'll tell you a secret. I've sent a story to a publisher friend of mine, and I'm waiting to see if she will buy it for her magazine."

"Really? Awesome." Danny was obviously impressed. "I never knew anyone who had a story published."

"Well, don't tell anyone," she urged. "I'm not sure it'll sell, and if I'm rejected, well, I'd rather only you and I had to know, okay?"

"Sure. Can I read some of your stuff? What do you write about? Sports, or is it that gooey stuff?"

"A little of both." She chuckled. "Mostly I try to portray feelings and emotions, people I see or know, places I've been to. Whatever touches me."

"Did you write about me?"

"As a matter of fact, I did. I wrote a little story about you. I'll let you read it soon."

"Cool." He smiled, getting up. "Can I tell Uncle Nick? Just that you write stories, I mean. Not about the magazine."

DeShea almost gave him permission, but then she remembered her mother's scathing criticism and the humiliation that had followed and changed her mind. She didn't know Nick well enough yet to confide her secret. Not until she was sure he wouldn't laugh or ridicule her. "No. Not right now," she replied. "Maybe later."

"Okay. But I'll bet he'll be real surprised." Dropping the ball to the floor, he began to dribble it across the room. "I'd better go help with supper."

Danny wandered out into the hall, and DeShea stood and followed slowly behind him. She hadn't intended to tell him about her writing, but now that she had, it felt good to share her dream with someone. Her nephew had been interested, even excited, by her foray into the professional realm of writing. But what would Nick say? Would he scoff, or worse yet, would he even care?

Irked that she even considered his opinion, she stepped out into the hallway. As she glanced over the wooden railing to the living room below, she noticed Nick standing near the sofa. When Danny came into the room, he opened his arms and smiled. Danny went to him eagerly, and the two embraced for a long moment. Nick ruffled the boy's hair, his arm resting affectionately across the young shoulders as they retreated to the kitchen.

The touching scene filled DeShea's heart with a deep feeling of tenderness. She also felt a rush of profound relief. Nick wasn't as arbitrary as she'd feared. It was obvious from their affectionate attitudes that there were layers to the relationship she knew nothing about. The smile on his face, the open arms, were an apology to Danny, a sign that underneath the loud words was love.

It was something she would have to think through carefully. Perhaps she'd been wrong to question Nick's methods. She'd never doubted that he had the boy's best interest at heart, and from what she'd just witnessed, apparently Danny knew and understood Nick's volatile moods. Perhaps Nick knew what was best. The incident deepened her feelings for him, and she warned herself sternly that it was dangerous to care too much for him. Unfortunately, she doubted if she could stop what was already in motion.

When she crossed the living room and entered the kitchen, Danny and Nick were busy preparing supper, joking and laughing as if nothing had happened. They put her to work on some simple tasks and soon they were all seated at the table enjoying a hearty home-cooked meal. Nick teased her about the fast-food binge they'd been on all week, and even Danny admitted he'd gotten tired of pizza and burgers.

The rest of the evening passed pleasantly, and before DeShea realized it, it was ten o'clock. Danny trotted off to bed, and DeShea decided to follow. Nick could probably use some quiet time to himself. She knew how stressful house guests could be. She said good-night and started from the room, turning at the foot of the stairs when Nick called her name.

As he came toward her, DeShea couldn't help but admire his physique. The light, faded jeans he wore hugged every muscle as he walked with a confident swagger that stimulated her imagination.

"DeShea, I owe you an apology for this afternoon," he said softly. "I was out of line about Danny, and I was rude to you. I had no right to get so angry with either of you."

"You were right, though," she said quickly. "I'm hardly an authority on child discipline. I shouldn't have interfered."

Nick shook his head. "You're entitled to your opinion. The whole thing just caught me by surprise. Danny's never done this before, and I was very disappointed." He raised one corner of his mouth in a lopsided grin. "Didn't do my ego any good, either. Fate has a way of dropping these embarrassing moments on a parent's head just to remind us that we're not quite as smart as we'd like everyone to believe."

"No, please don't think that," DeShea urged earnestly. "I saw how quickly you two made up. It was very reassuring to me. Danny loves you, and he seems to understand you. That's all that really matters."

DeShea's grasp of the situation both pleased and surprised Nick. He hadn't realized how perceptive she was. He looked into her amethyst eyes and felt that odd sensation again, as if they were connected, as if there was total empathy between them. It was unlike anything he'd ever felt before. "Danny mentioned the crawfish boil tomorrow. Would you like to come? It's a family thing, very informal."

"I'd love to," she said, unable to hold back the smile of delight his invitation brought. "I heard about your family. I'm looking forward to meeting all of them."

"Good." He smiled in return. "We'll leave early, about eight o'clock. Good night, DeShea."

Chapter Seven

The four walls of Nick's office seemed to close in tighter and tighter on him with each passing moment. Sighing heavily, he rose and walked out into the reception area and back toward the small kitchen in the far corner. It was Saturday. He was supposed to be at his sister's enjoying a crawfish boil with his family.

Instead he was stuck at the office waiting for a company representative who might or might not drop in to verify the yearly inventory. His lead salesman was supposed to be baby-sitting the office, but he'd had a family emergency and it had fallen to Nick to take up the slack. Being the boss, it was his responsibility, and it wasn't the first time this had happened. But for some reason, today it filled him with resentment.

Retrieving a cold drink from the small refrigerator, he popped the top and took a big swallow. Danny had been disappointed at the change in plans. But Hugh had stepped in, offering to show DeShea the ropes and introduce her to the Couvillion clan. Nick should have been grateful. But he wasn't. He felt a certain responsibility for DeShea. She was, after all, his guest, and Hugh, despite his good intentions, could be dense at times. He hoped his brother didn't throw DeShea to the wolves. Not that his family was unkind. Quite the contrary. They were warm, friendly people who would go out of their way to make DeShea feel at home. Still, meeting forty or fifty strangers all at once would be a bit overwhelming, even to someone used to it, and DeShea had never been exposed to a large family. And what about the crawfish boil? Outside of southern Louisiana, it was a pretty obscure experience. Who would show her how to peel the crawfish, which ones not to eat? Would they warn her of how spicy hot they would be?

He reminded himself that both Danny and Hugh would be there. But Danny would be off with his cousins, and Hugh would be busy cooking the mud bugs. Would De-Shea have anything in common with his sisters? He really should have been there, he admonished himself again. She didn't know anyone but him.

As he took another swig of his now lukewarm soda, he suddenly realized where his thoughts were heading. It was more than a feeling of responsibility. He wanted to be there to show her around, introduce her to his family. He wanted to watch her reaction to it all and be there if she felt awkward. That was a stupid idea, he told himself. If anyone could handle a group of people, DeShea could. She ran a worldwide company. She was cool and controlled and sophisticated. Why didn't that fact comfort him?

Returning to his office, he leaned back in his chair and propped his feet up, thinking about last night and how relieved he'd been when DeShea had accepted his apology so readily. It was only now in the quiet, clear daylight that he could see why DeShea's disapproving attitude had rankled. He had wanted to seem infallible in her eyes. The perfect guardian.

Why he should care what she thought of him he didn't know. He shouldn't feel a need to make her understand him and his position, and he certainly didn't need any approval or support.

When Nick arrived home late in the afternoon, his confusion over his unaccustomed need for acceptance was only compounded, fueled with irritation. The company representative had never appeared, which meant he'd wasted an entire day in an empty office.

Laughter and giggles filled the air as he entered the large living room, and he looked up to see Danny in the loft. A small black-and-white ball sailed over the railing and landed in the middle of the room. As Nick scooped it up, a voice chimed, "I'll get it!"

He watched as a young girl bounced down the stairs. She was dressed in jeans and a plaid shirt, her blond hair hanging loose about her shoulders and tucked carelessly behind her ears. Her face was flushed and her violet eyes glowing. She stopped at the foot of the stairs and smiled at him, and he realized with a jolt that it was DeShea.

"Hi," she said between rapid breaths. "Danny is teaching me how to kick the soccer ball."

Nick stared dumbfounded, unable to speak. She was the most enchanting thing he'd ever seen. Vibrant, animated and absolutely radiant.

"I'm not very good at it yet," she went on when he didn't speak. "I spend more time running after the ball than kicking it." She giggled nervously.

"It just takes practice," he finally said, walking toward her. He felt dazed, drawn to her by some invisible, compelling force. His eyes met hers, and the air between them vibrated softly, quietly.

When he stood only a foot away, he held out the ball, unable to wrest his eyes away from hers. They seemed warm, inviting, and he fought the urge to let go and lose himself in the bright violet sunshine.

DeShea reached out her hand and grasped the small vinyl ball, only to find her fingers touching his. The contact made her tremble, and she thought she saw an answering surge of emotion in Nick's brown eyes. Then the phone rang and the moment was broken.

The bell sounded three full rings before Nick could pull himself into motion. Turning, he walked away feeling vaguely disoriented.

DeShea took a deep breath, willing her senses to return to normal. The current of awareness that passed between them had left her shaken and a bit puzzled.

"Don't forget the other balls, Aunt DeShea," Danny called, leaning over the railing.

Mechanically she moved around the room collecting the four or five balls they'd been practicing with. When she picked up the last one, she was near the kitchen and could just catch the end of Nick's conversation.

"No, I won't forget, Tiffany. I made reservations at Joey's." He laughed. "I'm glad you're impressed.... Yeah. Me, too." He laughed again. "Monday night should be...productive. Our meetings are usually very stimulating.... Not me. I'm always good.... Right.... No, I won't forget.... Me, too. Bye."

Nick replaced the receiver and glanced up to see DeShea looking at him with a strange expression. The light in the wisteria eyes had clouded, her smile was gone, and she looked strangely disappointed. He couldn't for the life of him find a reason for that. He was about to ask her when she turned and went back up to the loft and continued her game with Danny.

Puzzled by the sudden change, Nick went to his room to change clothes. When he returned Danny was on the sofa and DeShea was nowhere to be seen. Danny said she'd "remembered some important work she had to do."

Nick felt the knot in his gut again. Just when he'd come to think DeShea was like Marette after all, just when she'd seemed real and exciting, she'd withdrawn again behind that

Ice Princess facade. "I was going to see if she'd like to come to the game tomorrow, but I guess she'll be too busy for that."

"Oh, she's coming," Danny said, munching a handful of chips. "I already asked her."

Nick could only reply with a soft, humble "Oh."

Seven o'clock seemed to come awfully early. But that was probably because DeShea hadn't gotten to sleep until the wee hours of the morning. She'd spent the early evening checking on details of Clotilles's financial status with Howard. It had kept her mind fully occupied. But the hours after were filled with a raw disappointment that seemed to eat away at her insides. The phone call she'd overheard was obviously about a dinner date for Monday night with a woman named Tiffany. DeShea could easily imagine what she would look like—a tall, stunning redhead with flashing green eyes and sensual figure—the kind of lusty, electrifying woman men found irresistible.

It had never occurred to her that there might be a woman in his life. A ridiculous assumption. A man like Nick would have no trouble finding female companionship. It was perfectly normal. But what bothered her more than Nick's date with the unknown Tiffany was her own fierce jealousy. Her feelings toward him were growing too possessive. He was in her thoughts continuously. She was beginning to care for him, more than was safe. But there didn't seem to be any way to stop her growing attachment.

Pulling on her jeans, she tugged up the zipper, then slid her head and arms into a pale green sweater. She brushed her hair and positioned two small green barrettes to hold the thick tresses out of her eyes. The woman in the mirror smiled back at her. Quite a change from last week. She was becoming a totally different person inwardly and outwardly.

The change pleased her. Coming to Baton Rouge was the best thing that had ever happened to her. Finally free from

Natalie's influence, she was shedding the carefully constructed executive image and emerging as just plain De-Shea, a person she'd lost touch with since her divorce from Eric.

Danny, Nick and Hugh all had a hand in her metamorphosis. That was probably why it was happening so quickly. She'd feared the process of rediscovering who she was would be a long, arduous road. Instead, it had been shamefully easy to toss aside Natalie's ersatz image and learn to like herself again. Watching Danny and Nick together had taught her a lot about love. The little things they did, the looks that passed between them, the consideration they showed each other in small, almost imperceptible ways. She was learning about patience, about tolerance and about guiding a young mind toward maturity. She was also learning about devotion and selflessness in the way Nick treated his nephew.

If she could only stay here forever, happy, contented... But there were obstacles. Nick and her deepening feelings for him were the largest. Common sense told her falling in love with Nick was pointless and foolhardy. At best, she would be setting herself up for a serious emotional fall. She'd never been successful with close relationships.

Nick's kindness was for Danny's sake. He would be as accommodating to anyone who was part of the boy's life. She needed to be sensible. To even hope for more than friendship from him was futile. But futile or not, reckless or not, she was quickly realizing that Nick Couvillion was a man worth loving. He possessed all the qualities she most admired. Thoughtfulness, devotion to family, tenderness, kindness and strength of character. But how did she get a man like that to become interested in her? How did she attract his attention? What kind of woman did he like? Apparently ones named Tiffany. And where did that leave her? That puzzle danced through her dreams the rest of the night.

The interior of the van was silent as Nick maneuvered through Baton Rouge and onto I-10. When the vehicle assumed a steady speed, DeShea glanced over at him and said, "You have a wonderful family. Everyone was so nice to me yesterday. Especially your mother."

"I'm glad you think so." Nick grinned slightly. "I was afraid you might be a little overwhelmed."

"I was a bit at first. But they were all so sweet and friendly. Your mother made me feel like family from the moment I met her."

"She's a remarkable woman," he replied, his voice filled with affection. "It wasn't easy raising a family without a husband."

"She's very proud of you."

A small grin touched one corner of Nick's mouth. "What she's proud of are her nine grandchildren."

"That would explain why she is so anxious to see you and Hugh married," DeShea commented. "The first thing she asked me was whether or not I was spoken for."

"She's always matchmaking. Even when it's obvious the woman is all wrong."

DeShea flinched at the words. She *was* wrong for him, but it hurt to have it pointed out so bluntly.

"I think it's something in her Italian blood," Nick said. "She won't feel totally fulfilled until she has at least an even dozen."

DeShea stared out the window and added softly, "It must be wonderful having so many people who love you and care about you."

The wistful note in her voice sliced into Nick's conscience. He tended to take his large family for granted. Having his mother only a phone call away, his brother and sisters and brothers-in-law dropping in from time to time, was such a way of life that he rarely thought about those who had no relatives.

He wondered what DeShea had done for holidays, vacations, even weekends. Was her whole world centered on Clotilles? For the first time, he considered the possibility that her career might not have been so much a choice as a means to fill the long hours. "It is," he answered. "They are a very important part of my life."

"I'm glad Marette found that. She always wanted a big family. It was hard sometimes with just the two of us."

"No grandparents? Cousins?"

"Not that we ever saw. My father left when we were very young, and we never saw him again. I don't even know if he had brothers or sisters. My mother's parents lived in upstate New York, but we only saw them once or twice in our whole lives."

Nick struggled to understand a family that never communicated and felt himself beginning to get a better understanding of DeShea. "Staying with us must be a shock to you. We lead a rather haphazard life."

"Oh, no, I'm enjoying it, really. It's opened up a whole new world for me. It's so different from what Marette and I had growing up. There's so much love and affection in your family. There's this beautiful balance between your life and Danny's that's wonderful to see. The balance in our family was always weighted heavily toward our mother's side." She glanced at him briefly, realizing she'd revealed too much. "I'm sure you know that Marette and I had a rather limited childhood."

"Marette told me some of it but I still find your mother's attitude hard to understand."

She answered after a long pause. "My mother had a very precise format for raising children. I think she looked upon us as an investment in the future of Clotilles, small companies that she had to turn into profitable businesses. We were always told to be productive in anything we did, and she hired the best people in their respective fields to restructure us."

Nick had a sudden vision of Marette and DeShea as little girls, forbidden to run and play like other children, raised with the unemotional detachment of a "business," not the warm support of a loving family. DeShea had grown up an isolated, lonely child. "It must have been very difficult for you when Marette left."

DeShea looked at him, surprised at his sudden show of compassion. He'd always been rather cold regarding her personal life. "Yes," she said quietly. "Very difficult."

"I used to wonder how Marette maintained her sense of humor about her childhood."

DeShea felt resentment surface. "Probably because she was always the rebel. She was the leader, the one who defied authority—who said what she thought and demanded things her way, or no way at all. Sometimes she'd rebel just to show Mother she couldn't be forced to do anything."

"That sounds like my Marette."

The little trickle of resentment swelled at the affection she heard for Marette in Nick's voice. "Marette was Mother's favorite. But she ran away." I was the one who stayed, but I was the child she never wanted, she added silently.

Nick had never considered the price DeShea might have paid for Marette's leaving. Had she borne the backlash of Natalie's pain and resentment?

"What about you?" he asked.

The gentleness in his voice made DeShea aware that she'd revealed far more than she'd intended. But it was so easy to talk to him when he was being kind and thoughtful. It was when he was emotional that she froze up. The raised voice and scowling expression reminded her vividly of Natalie, and she would instantly withdraw, her protective mask firmly in place. Daring a glance, she saw only compassion in the brown eyes and felt her resentment vanish.

"I was the quiet one. I followed Marette everywhere. She was the only friend I had growing up. We were never allowed to play with other children, except for school, of course. We used to pretend we had lots of brothers and sisters so we could go to ball games and the zoo or have picnics. My mother was too busy to bother with those things. Her whole life was wrapped up in Clotilles. Marette and I were sort of an inconvenience."

"Strange, isn't it?" Nick commented. "You didn't have enough family, and I often think I have too much. Sometimes I feel like the world is made up of nothing but Couvillions and that I can never go far enough away to get out of their influence."

"I'd gladly change places with you. Being alone is not quite so enviable a position as you might think."

"I guess the grass is always greener, huh?" Nick watched the sadness in her eyes and began to understand why she'd come to Baton Rouge. "What about later on? No special boyfriend, husband?"

"Not really. I was married briefly several years ago. But he . . . we're divorced."

"You were married?" Danny asked, leaning forward in his seat.

Nick had almost forgotten his nephew. He'd assumed the long silence was because Danny had his ears plugged up to his tape deck, but apparently he'd been listening to the adults' conversation with relish. "Danny," he said by way of warning. But the boy was completely unaware of the tension his question had created.

"What happened?" he asked.

"He fell in love with someone else," DeShea answered before Nick could reprimand his nephew more forcefully. There was nothing to be gained by withholding the truth. "We've been divorced three years now, but we've remained good friends just the same."

"Gosh, that's too bad. I'll bet she wasn't as pretty as you."

"Thank you, Danny." DeShea smiled. "But the important thing is that Eric loved her and they are very happy together."

Nick glanced at her but could read nothing in the impassive expression on her face. "You're still friends with the guy?"

"Yes, of course. We were always good friends."

A look of skepticism appeared on Nick's face. "I've heard of relationships like that, but I've never believed they really existed. Sounds unusual."

"Our marriage was unusual," she said bluntly, turning her face away. A marriage with no passion, only deep abiding affection. To a passionate man like Nick, someone who felt every emotion deeply, fiercely, her relationship with Eric would be unfathomable.

Nick heard sadness in her voice and dared a glance. Her face was averted, so he couldn't read anything in her expression. But it was clear DeShea didn't want to discuss her marriage any further. He turned the conversation back to safer topics.

"So how did you like the crawfish?" he asked and was rewarded with a smile so bright he had to force his eyes back to the road. The desire to lose himself in her smile was overwhelming.

"It was delicious. Messy, but good."

Nick chuckled softly. "Not too hot for you?"

"A little," she admitted. "I know I didn't eat as much as everyone else. I was too slow at peeling them."

"There's a knack to it. You'll get better."

"I hope so." She laughed. "Or I'd probably starve. I couldn't believe that all those crawfish were eaten. It looked like tons when they dumped them on the table."

"Only 150 pounds," Nick replied.

"I'm so sorry you couldn't be there yesterday."

"Are you?" he asked softly, meeting her honest glance. The eyes didn't flinch. "Yes."

He felt an absurd sense of delight race through him at her admission. "So was I. I felt like it was my place to show you the ropes."

DeShea's heart sank. Nick wasn't sorry he missed the gathering because he also missed her, only because he felt responsible.

"I suppose Hugh did the honors," he said without thinking, surprised to hear a hard edge creep into his voice.

"No, sir, I did," Danny piped up from the back. "She learned quick. I didn't think she was going to touch them at first, though," he added with a chuckle. "She had that look."

Nick chuckled, too, and DeShea felt her cheeks warm.

"Didn't like the looks of those red critters, huh?" he teased.

"Well, you have to admit, they're pretty ugly," she said, wrinkling her nose.

"But delicious," he said with a smirk.

"Yes, very. Once you get over the idea of pulling off legs and heads and . . . ooh." She shivered.

The sound of Nick's deep laughter reverberated through the van. "Just try and think of them as baby lobsters."

"Now why didn't I think of that?"

The companionable silence that settled between them filled DeShea with a warm contentment. At least they were becoming friends. It was better than enemies.

Not as good as lovers, though. Her thought sent a rush of blood to her face, and she turned toward the window to hide it. Why did she keep having these fantasies about Nick? Their relationship was purely platonic and likely to stay that way. It was the best she could hope for. Anything else was pure nonsense and the sooner she realized it, the better. She should be grateful that he was no longer hostile toward her. It was a vast improvement from the first day she'd arrived. Stealing a glance at his strong profile, she struggled to get her emotions into a manageable state. It was perfectly all right to admire Nick, to respect him, and even to like him both as a man and a person, but anything more was unwise.

"Where exactly are we going in New Orleans?" she asked, proud of the casual tone she'd achieved.

"Lafreniere Park. It's out in Metairie, one of the suburbs. They have a strong select program there. It should be a couple of good games. Oh, and by the way," he said over his shoulder, "Dan, you'd better get after that homework."

A low groan drifted forward, and DeShea looked back at the grimace on Danny's face.

"Can't I do it on the way home?"

"No. You'll be tired and sore," his uncle told him firmly.

With a deep sigh, Danny reached for the stack of books on the seat beside him and started to work.

"Does he always do his homework in the car?" DeShea asked.

Nick nodded. "When we've got out-of-town games. Might as well put the time to good use." He looked at her sharply. "You don't approve?"

"On the contrary. I think it's an excellent idea."

The warm brown eyes smiled. "Thanks."

As they rode along, Nick pointed out several points of interest. The Bonnet Carré Spillway that linked the Mississippi River and Lake Pontchartrain, the twelve-mile bridge that crossed the swamp between LaPlace and Kenner, and Lake Maurepas. What fascinated DeShea the most, however, was the way the freeway was at treetop level, with a commanding view of the wetlands below. It felt like flying on solid ground.

"Aunt DeShea, remember when you said you'd help me with English?" Danny asked, leaning over the seat.

"Yes. What are you studying?"

"Vocabulary. What a bummer," he grumbled. "What's the definition of prudent?"

"Modest," she replied promptly. She could hear the pen scratching as he wrote that down. "Do you have a dictionary with you?"

"Yes, ma'am."

"Then look it up and see if I'm right," she suggested.

"Don't you know?"

"Maybe. Maybe not."

The sound of rustling pages told her he was following her suggestion. "Hey! That's not what it means at all."

"Oh? Well, then you've learned something today. Never accept someone else's word on something. Check it out for yourself."

A low groan drifted up from the back seat. "I get the point. Do my own work."

DeShea turned around and smiled. "But I'd be happy to help you if you don't understand the definition. But only *after* you've looked it up first."

"Yes, ma'am."

Nick looked over at DeShea. "You seem to have a real rapport with Danny. It reminds me a lot of Marette. They had a very special relationship."

His kind words filled DeShea with a rush of gratitude. "Thank you. That means a lot to me."

When Nick pulled into the park, DeShea was surprised at its size. There was a huge lake and several soccer fields, as well as a playground and picnic areas. Nick explained that it used to be a horse racetrack.

After he parked the van, they made their way across the road to the playing field. Nick and Danny introduced her to several parents they encountered along the way, and she filed the names in her memory.

Once at the field, she was left to fend for herself on the sidelines while Nick and Danny began the pregame warm-up. She sat quietly in the small bleachers, watching and wishing she knew more about the game. During the several years she'd lived in London, she had never attended a game of football—as the British called soccer.

Her gaze moved back and forth between Danny darting around the field, kicking the ball in a complicated drill, and Nick, who stood like a centurion, directing the energetic boys through their strenuous maneuvers.

When the game finally started, DeShea turned her main attention on her nephew, who seemed to be the smallest player on the field. He took up a position in front of the goalie, and DeShea tried to gain at least a cursory under-standing of the game—beyond the obvious purpose of putting the ball in the net, that was. But after twenty minutes she gave up and settled for just watching. The action was nonstop, ever-changing and fast-paced. The boys were constantly on the move, and the ball had a mind of its own.

A friendly parent sitting beside her helped by explaining a few key points, but her overall impression was that the game was much rougher than she'd expected. Danny had talked of skill and quickness, but she was unprepared for the sight of players being tripped, shoved and sent flying through the air. The parents seated with her didn't seem too concerned, however, so she held her tongue. But she couldn't stop her mounting concern for Danny. It seemed to her as if every big boy on the field was deliberately assaulting him.

It was over lunch between the games that DeShea had an opportunity to voice her feelings.

"So what did you think of the game?" Danny asked. "Pretty hairy, huh? We almost lost that one."

"Well, to tell the truth," she said slowly, "it was a lot more physical than I expected. The other boys were so rough."

"No more than most," Nick explained with a careless shrug.

"But isn't Danny too small to be playing with boys so much bigger? He could get hurt."

Danny shook his head. "Nah. I'm little, but I'm quick and I *love* to stick those big guys."

"Stick?" DeShea asked, puzzled by the term.

"Steal the ball, make 'em look sad, unskilled," Nick offered. "Danny is good at it. Because he's small, they don't expect him to be a problem. He usually brings them down a peg or two."

"But isn't it dangerous—" DeShea frowned, not placated with Nick's answer "—putting him up against boys twice his size?"

"They're all the same age," Nick said firmly. "What Dan lacks in size he makes up in skill. Trust me. Dan knows what he's doing out there, and he can take care of himself."

DeShea wasn't entirely reassured, but she didn't press the matter. She was, after all, a novice. Best leave these things to Danny and Nick. They surely knew the limits of her nephew's ability.

The second game was more exciting—fierce and high scoring. DeShea found herself being drawn into the competition, hoping that Danny's team would win. She was fully engrossed in the game, seated on the end of the lower level of the bleachers, watching as Danny maneuvered the ball around two other players, then passed off to the side. Her gaze darted to Nick, who was smiling with pride and approval at his nephew's expertise.

Suddenly a shout went up, but before DeShea could react, she was knocked unceremoniously to the ground. Dazed, she sat up and blinked, rubbing her left shoulder.

Nick was kneeling in front of her, his dark eyes filled with concern. "Are you all right?"

DeShea looked up at him and the crowd of parents that ringed her. "What hit me?" She grinned, offering her hand to Nick and getting to her feet.

"The ball," Nick said, keeping an arm around her waist. "Are you sure you're not hurt?"

"Yes, just stunned," she assured him. "I'm fine. Really." Brushing off her backside, she smiled at the little circle of people. "I know one thing I learned about soccer today."

"What's that?" Nick asked.

"The next time I hear 'heads up,' I'll be sure and duck."

A round of chuckles went up, and the parents slowly returned to the bleachers. Nick smiled into her eyes. "No broken bones?"

She shook her head. "Just bruised pride."

"Well—" he grinned wickedly "—you did look rather comical sailing off the end of the bench that way."

A laugh gurgled up from her throat. "But was it a lady-like fall? That's what I want to know."

"Oh, yes. Very feminine. Plop. Onto the ground like a sack of potatoes." He laughed.

DeShea joined in, feeling lighthearted and happy and, strangely, real. A person in her own right. Not just a shadow of her mother.

Nick took his arm from her waist and pointed to the bleachers. "Now see if you can keep your seat for the rest of the game."

"Yes, sir."

DeShea had no further run-ins with the soccer ball, but unfortunately the score at game's end was Lafreniere 7, Baton Rouge 5. And it was a dejected team of boys that walked off the field.

The ride home had a much more subdued tone than the trip out. DeShea sat silently listening while Nick recounted in great detail each of Danny's mistakes during the two games.

After about forty-five minutes, she could no longer hold her tongue. It seemed such an unnecessary attack on Danny's playing ability. "Didn't he do something right today, even something small?"

Nick tightened his grip on the steering wheel. "He did a lot right. He did a lot wrong, and he won't learn to correct his mistakes unless they're pointed out to him."

"It's just a game," she said quickly.

Dark eyes snapped in her direction. "No. It's not. If we don't win enough games, we won't be in the state tournament. And these boys are the best in the state. They deserve to win it. But they've got to work at it."

"Is being state champions really that important?" she asked skeptically.

"Why don't you ask Dan?"

"Yes, ma'am, it is," the boy answered earnestly. "We almost won it two years ago. We all really want it this time.

Besides, if we win state then we get to go to regionals, and that's where the college coaches get to see us."

"What do you mean?"

"If Dan wants to get a scholarship to college, he has to be seen by the coaches. He's got to get exposure. Louisiana doesn't have a strong soccer program like Texas and Florida. So our guys have to work harder."

"And I want to be on a national team someday, and being state champs would help a lot," Danny explained, positioning the headset over his ears again and stretching out on the back seat.

DeShea nodded. "I think I see."

"I'm not really some macho, obsessed coach who wants to win at all costs. All we're having here is an after-game discussion about how we played, what we did wrong and what we need to work on. I'm not trying to tear Danny down or make him feel like a failure." He looked over at her with an understanding smile. "Even though it might look that way."

"I'm sorry."

"Don't be. I appreciate your concern for Danny. It shows that you care. But maybe we should have a pact in the future?"

"Oh?" DeShea studied his profile, admiring the strength she saw there.

"Any time you have a question about my decisions regarding Danny's behavior or his discipline, just ask. I'd be happy to explain my reason to you. I usually have a good one for everything I do. I can't promise I'll change my mind just because you have a different viewpoint, but I will promise to at least listen to your suggestions. Fair?"

"Very fair," she said, apology in her voice.

"I don't claim to know it all, either." Nick smiled, his eyes warm and friendly. "Sometimes I make it up as I go along. Other times, I pick up the phone and yell for help from Mom. You know," he said quietly, holding her gaze, "it's not easy raising a boy alone."

"But you won't always be—I mean, you'll marry one day and then you'll be a family again."

Nick sighed heavily. "Sometimes I wonder if there's anyone out there for me. At least, not one who could accept my life the way it is now. She'd not only have to love me but Danny as well. We're a package deal. But most of the women I meet aren't willing to take on a ready-made family. I guess it is asking a lot."

"I don't think so," she said. "I'm sure there's a woman somewhere who would have no trouble loving both of you."

"I don't know," he drawled. "I just want a woman who will put us first, someone who believes in marriage and commitment—but I think that's a qualification that has become extinct." He glanced over at DeShea and saw an odd expression on her face. Pinched, as if she were unhappy or displeased. A woman like DeShea probably didn't appreciate his chauvinistic attitudes. He suddenly realized what he'd been doing and understood. Nick wasn't accustomed to confiding in others; he was the one his family confided in. He'd certainly never intended to confess his feelings to DeShea, but something about her was warm and sympathetic, and he found himself speaking before he realized it. Confiding in her had seemed as natural as breathing. "Sorry, DeShea. I didn't mean to unload on you like that."

"Please don't apologize," she said quietly, avoiding his eyes. "We all need someone to talk to from time to time. I'm a very good listener, remember?"

Chapter Eight

By Monday afternoon, life in the Couvillion house was beginning to fall into a comfortable pattern, and DeShea found a kind of peace and contentment in the predictable routine. Yesterday had not only been enjoyable and fun, it had also marked a major turning point in her relationship with Nick. Her unexpected run-in with the errant soccer ball had chased away the lingering awkwardness between them. She didn't understand why, exactly, but Nick was much more approachable now. Even their disagreement over Danny had ended well, and she wasn't about to look the proverbial gift horse in the mouth.

Nick's mother, Millie, stopped by in the morning to see if she was doing all right, and Hugh and his sister Jessie both phoned to say hello. It made DeShea feel accepted, and part of the family. So when the phone rang later in the afternoon, it seemed the most natural thing in the world to hear Nick's deep, vibrant voice on the other end.

Dare you escape into a world of excitement, passion and pure joy?

With four FREE Desires and two FREE gifts from Silhouette

Silhouette Desires capture *all* the love and warmth of modern relationships. Share moments of intimacy, moments of intensity, moments of ecstasy ... and more.

To introduce to you this highly charged series, we'll send you four Silhouette Desires, a cuddly Teddy Bear plus a Mystery Gift, absolutely FREE when you complete and return this card. At the same time we'll reserve a subscription for you which means that you could enjoy:

- **SIX SILHOUETTE DESIRES** - sent direct to you every month.

- **FREE POSTAGE AND PACKAGING** - we pay all the extras.

- **FREE MONTHLY NEWSLETTER** - packed with competitions, author news, horoscopes and much more.

- **SPECIAL OFFERS** - selected exclusively for our readers.

Simply fill in the claim overleaf for your free books and gifts.

Free Books and Gifts claim

Yes Please send me my four FREE Silhouette Desires together with my FREE Gifts. Please also reserve a special Reader Service Subscription for me. If I decide to subscribe, each month I shall receive six superb new titles for just £9.60 postage and packing FREE. If I decide not to subscribe I shall write to you within 10 days. The FREE books and Gifts will be mine to keep in any case. I understand that I am under no obligation whatsoever. I may cancel or suspend my subscription at any time simply by writing to you. I am over 18 years of age.

3S2SD

Mrs/Miss/Mr —————————————————————

Address —————————————————————

————————————————————————————

————————————————————————————

————————————————— Postcode ——————————

Signature —————————————————————

Reader Service
FREEPOST
P.O. Box 236
Croydon
Surrey CR9 9EL

NO STAMP NEEDED

Send NO money now

"Just wanted to remind you I won't be home for supper. I have a dinner engagement."

"Yes, I remember," she answered, trying to keep the disappointment from her voice. The only sour note in the entire day was the impending dinner date Nick had with the lovely Tiffany.

"Do what you think best for supper. If you'd like to go out, feel free to use the van, or I'm sure my mother and Cherie wouldn't mind you eating there."

"Your mother already invited us over, but I've got supper all planned. Don't worry."

"Okay. Don't wait up. I don't know how late I'll be."

"All right. Have a good time."

Nick replaced the receiver, but DeShea's musical voice lingered in his ears. He liked the idea of her being on the other end of the phone, at home, watching over Danny and him. It would be nice to have someone to take care of him for a change. He thought about how she'd looked that morning, making coffee, getting Dan ready for school.... Strange how quickly she seemed to have become part of his life. She barely resembled the cool, indifferent Ice Princess who had greeted him on the porch that day. Though she was still a puzzle to him in many ways, he had at least begun to find the real woman behind that cool exterior.

The truth was, he'd been forced to revise his opinion considerably in the past few days. She was more like Marette than he'd first thought. But there was a wistful quality about DeShea that intrigued him, as if there was something private, some secret, that she was afraid to share.

Perhaps it was the outward change, as well, that helped to dispel that cold image. The snug-fitting blue jeans and loose shirts and sweaters she'd taken to wearing the past few days were somehow more provocative than the thin silk blouses she'd worn before. She seemed real now, approachable and, heaven help him, desirable.

When had she switched from unwelcome intruder to desirable woman? More important, what was he going to do about it? Nothing, he decided promptly. This attraction was purely physical and certainly unthinkable in the present conditions. Besides, DeShea would probably be leaving shortly. Her job at Clotilles would demand her return soon and then temptation would be removed. End of problem.

Spaghetti happened to be one of Danny's favorite meals. It also happened to be the one dish at which DeShea excelled. Yet even her triumph at the supper table failed to completely dispel her somber mood, caused by the knowledge that Nick was out with Tiffany. She wished he'd been home tonight so he could see how handy she was around the house as well as around a business office. While she wasn't exactly Julia Child, thanks to Eric she could at least fix a basic and nutritious meal.

So consumed was she with her own feelings that she failed to notice Danny's quiet mood as soon as she should have. He was toying with his leftovers, staring down at his plate. "What's bothering you, Danny?" she asked quietly. "Schoolwork again?"

"I don't know," he mumbled, keeping his eyes lowered. He sounded so forlorn her heart ached for him.

"Would you like to tell me about it? Maybe I can help."

He was quiet a long time, as if debating whether or not to confide in her. Brown eyes looked at her pleadingly. "Do you ever feel like you're jinxed?"

There it was. Like a bolt out of the blue. Her first major test with Danny. He was asking her for advice. From the tone of his voice, she knew it was serious, a turning point for them both. Here was an opportunity to really help her nephew in a significant way.

The responsibility was awesome. What she said to him now could affect him for the rest of his life. Doubt washed over her like a tidal wave. She had no knowledge of children. She couldn't presume to advise him on anything so important. In just one moment she'd gained a whole new perspective and level of admiration for Nick and what he'd undertaken in raising Danny. Looking over at him, she saw he was staring at her, waiting for a response. "What do you mean?" she asked softly.

He looked down again, taking a long ragged breath. "Like you've been cursed and that's why everyone you love goes away."

DeShea's heart froze in her chest. The poor child. He'd lost everyone he cared for, and he felt as if he were somehow to blame. It was a subject she was more than qualified to answer. She understood only too well the loneliness Danny was feeling. She'd lived with it most of her life. Her doubts about offering sound advice faded. "Yes, Danny. I've often felt that way."

His wide brown eyes met hers as she continued. "As a child, I used to think I'd done something awful and was being punished for it. I believed for a long time that there was something wrong with me, inside, and that's why no one loved me." She took a deep breath. "But now, as an adult, I know that none of it was my fault. Not really. It's just the way things were."

"Do you have this ache inside that never goes away?" he asked, staring at his small hands.

"Yes. All the time," she admitted, fighting back her own tears.

"Sometimes I feel like I'm the only person in the whole wide world. Like I'm floating away all by myself. Like those balloons you get when you're little, ya know? And when you let go they go up and up and then burst because they don't have anyone to hold them down and bring 'em back safe."

Reaching over, DeShea took his cool fingers in her hand. "I know. You feel as if no one else understands that hurt you have inside—the fear that says you're all alone."

Huge tears rolled down Danny's cheeks. "Why does everyone go away?"

DeShea hesitated a moment, then went to him and pulled him into her arms, holding him close. He felt very small and warm against her bosom. "It feels like that sometimes, doesn't it? But not everyone goes away. You have Uncle Nick. He loves you very, *very* much, as if you were his own son.''

"But what if Uncle Nick goes away?" he sobbed.

"He won't. He'll be right here for you always." DeShea felt her own tears streaming down her cheeks. "You have so many people who love you, including me, and that's very important. You may not realize it now, but you will someday." Danny hugged her tighter as he cried softly. "You're so lucky, Danny," she said. "Luckier than I was."

"How?"

"I didn't have anyone. No uncle or grandma. After your mother left, I was alone all the time."

"What about Grandma Ballard? Didn't you have her?"

"Not really. She was always gone or busy." DeShea closed her eyes against the memories, but they still filled her mind. "But you have a lot of people, a whole big family. That's a special gift. Always cherish it, and never take it for granted."

Danny looked up and rubbed his eyes. "That's what Mom always said."

"Your mom always wished for a family." DeShea smiled, dabbing at her own eyes. "I'm so glad she found it. She was very lucky, too."

"She was a great mom."

DeShea smiled. "I'm sure she was. Playing house was her favorite game when we were little. She always had four or five dolls as her kids, and she'd take them to all sorts of imaginary places. We used to pretend the library was the movies and the sun room was the zoo. I remember once we..."

DeShea and Danny spent the evening reminiscing. The bond between them strengthened, deepened, and she began to realize how difficult it would be to leave her nephew when the time came. But she shoved that unpleasant inevitability aside for the time being. Right now she was living moment to moment and day to day.

After Danny went to bed, DeShea took a quick shower and slipped into her thick terry robe. Wandering downstairs, she perused the extensive collection of books, selecting one about the plantations of Louisiana, and curled up on the couch to read. Usually she read in her room, since the living room seemed to be Nick's acknowledged territory. But tonight she wanted to claim it for herself. It was such a cozy, relaxing place. Besides, Nick wouldn't be home for hours yet. She would look through the book for a little while, then go up to bed.

The clock on the dash read 10:45 when Nick pulled the Stingray into the carport. Dinner had ended earlier than he'd figured, much to his delight. He'd found it difficult to keep his mind focused on business when visions of DeShea kept intruding. He wanted to be home with her and Danny, not sitting in an expensive steak house with his boss on a Monday night.

Locking the back door behind him, he was surprised to see lights still on in the living room. Dan should have been in bed long ago, and DeShea usually turned in early as well.

The moment he stepped onto the carpet, he saw her. She was curled up on the sofa, sound asleep. One slender calf and foot were exposed. The terry robe gaped slightly over her chest. Blond hair tumbled around her face and across her throat like silk sunshine.

Slowly he walked toward the sofa, unable to take his eyes from the lovely picture she made. Captivated by the look of childlike innocence on her face, he reached out and gently touched her hair. She didn't stir, and he lowered himself onto the edge of the coffee table, content to watch her sleep. She looked angelic, ethereal, and he wanted to sit and watch her forever.

"DeShea." He whispered the name softly.

She stirred, turning her head and sending the silken strands in motion. The opening of the robe at her throat widened, giving him a tantalizing view of the swell of her right breast. The man in him wanted to feast his eyes upon the lovely sight. The gentleman in him decided he'd better rouse her before she embarrassed them both.

"DeShea" he said again, gently touching her shoulder. Her face was turned toward him, and he gave in to the impulse to rest his palm against her cheek. If felt like warm satin, soft, delicate, and he wondered if the rest of her skin was as soft and how it would feel against his own. "Shea, it's late. You need to go to bed." The words emerged as a ragged whisper.

Her eyes opened, but they were clouded with sleep. "Nick?" she mumbled.

"Yeah, come on, Sunshine, you'd better go upstairs." DeShea closed her eyes again, snuggling into the sofa. "Come on, Shea. You need to get to bed." Taking her arm, he tugged her to a sitting position. "Wake up."

"What time is it?" she mumbled, frowning at him.

"Nearly eleven."

"You're early."

"I am?"

She nodded loosely as he lifted her feet and placed them on the floor, draping the robe over the generous expanse of leg he'd uncovered.

"Did you have a nice dinner?" she asked. Her speech was slightly slurred.

"Terrific," he answered as he pulled her to her feet. She drooped against him, and he slipped his arm around her waist.

Resting her head against his chest, she sighed loudly. "I'm tired."

"I know. Let's get you upstairs and you can go to sleep."

"Was she lusty?" she asked as they slowly climbed the steps.

"Who?"

"Tiffany."

"I wasn't with Tiffany," he said, giving her a questioning glance. Her eyes were dreamy, fogged with drowsiness. Apparently she was still half-asleep.

"Beautiful Tiffany," she said with a pout.

"No, Shea, I was with a portly old gentleman. My regional manager. He is neither lusty nor beautiful. Tiffany is his secretary."

At the top of the stairs, DeShea turned toward him and looked up into his eyes. "You weren't on a date?"

"No."

A silly smile spread across her face, and she dropped her forehead onto his chest. "Oh, good."

Nick was no match for the force of longing that filled him at her closeness. But his conscience stirred. DeShea wasn't fully aware of what she was doing. He shouldn't take advantage. But she felt so warm, so soft and desirable in his arms. She smelled sweet, like baby powder and wildflowers. He cradled her close, inhaling her special fragrance deeply into his lungs, burying his face in the tangle of golden curls.

When he opened his eyes, he saw Danny's door standing slightly ajar, and common sense prevailed. Gently he pushed DeShea away and steered her toward her bedroom door.

Inside the room he glanced at the neatly made bed, and for a brief second imagined making love to the woman beside him. Never in his whole life had he wanted something, someone, as desperately as he did DeShea at this moment.

Abruptly he dropped his hands from around her waist as if he'd been burned. "Uh, you'd better get into bed," he said quickly, stepping back.

DeShea nodded and tugged at the sash holding her robe at the waist. "G'night," she muttered.

Nick grunted in response and turned away, determined to be out of the room when the robe hit the floor. "I'll see you in the morning."

Not waiting for a reply, he made a hasty retreat, shutting the door firmly behind him. As he headed downstairs he released a ragged breath. Safe in his own room at last, he went straight to the bathroom and turned on the shower.

He couldn't let this desire for DeShea get out of hand. True, she was a very attractive woman. Any man would be drawn to her. But he wasn't just any man. He was Danny's guardian, and besides, it was pointless to even think about DeShea in any way other than as Danny's aunt. She was everything he *didn't* want: career-oriented, ultrasophisticated and aloof.

But she hadn't seemed aloof tonight. She'd seemed warm and soft and sweetly feminine. He remembered her little-girl pout, and her delight when she found out he'd not been on a date. Had she been jealous? Ridiculous assumption.

Even if she was, it didn't change the facts. DeShea was too unemotional to be content with the rigors of family life. What sort of emotional support could she provide for her children, especially with Natalie as a role model?

DeShea was about as unqualified to be a wife and mother as anyone he'd ever met. So why did he keep seeing her in his mind's eye sitting at the table each night, waiting for him at the front door, lying beside him in bed? It was pure madness. He'd better get a handle on his libido quickly or he might be making an appointment with a counselor himself.

Unfortunately, Nick's good intentions were worthless. Falling asleep was practically impossible. His mind was tormented by the vision of DeShea he'd seen and the temptation she'd presented in her sleepy, adorable state. It had been easy to maintain his detachment when he perceived her as a cold, unfeeling woman with no emotions. That DeShea he could dismiss with some honest anger and resentment.

But this new woman he saw emerging, the soft, sensitive DeShea—she wouldn't be so easy to dismiss or ignore.

By morning he'd convinced himself that his attraction to DeShea last night had been caused partly by fatigue, partly by alcohol, and he was determined to maintain his composure from now on. It was a fluke, circumstance, nothing more. Pure male/female attraction based on physical chemistry. What else could it be? They had nothing in common other than Danny.

Fortunately, he didn't have to put his new resolve to the test, because DeShea was nowhere to be seen when he came downstairs next morning.

DeShea awoke with a smile on her face. Stretching like a contented cat, she reveled in the sunlight that streaked through the window. She tossed off the covers and sat on the edge of the bed, scooping her hair off her neck and sighing happily. It was going to be a glorious day, a wonderful day. Today was...

The smile slid into a frown. What was today? Her hair tumbled back around her shoulders as her hand came down to rest on the mattress. Why was she so happy this morning? Yesterday she'd been depressed, disappointed, today almost giddy, and there was absolutely no reason, unless... There was that dream. DeShea closed her eyes, struggling to recapture the elusive threads of her dream. She was lying on soft grass—no, the sofa downstairs—and Nick was there. He was speaking softly to her, and his words made her feel ridiculously happy. Then they were walking close together, and she felt warm and safe. They were close, very close, then the dream ended.

But was it a dream? She'd been curled up on the sofa last night reading, enjoying the solitude while Nick was at dinner. Tiffany. She remembered asking Nick about her, but was that in the dream or had it really happened? She couldn't remember coming to bed. Yet she'd obviously slept in it.

With a shake of her head, she rose and moved to the bathroom. Maybe she'd filled her small wineglass one too many times last night, though it wasn't her usual habit. Perhaps it would all make sense when she was fully awake. If she'd fallen asleep on the couch, Nick would say something about it. But by the time she'd dressed and gone downstairs, Nick and Danny were already gone for the day, and she was left to sort out the dream-versus-reality puzzle on her own.

It was the next evening when DeShea's good mood deteriorated, and try as she would she couldn't stop the downward plunge.

She helped prepare supper, listening while Nick and Danny shared various details of their day, then Danny hurried off to Boy Scouts, leaving his aunt and uncle alone. The camaraderie Nick and Danny had shared over supper, while thoroughly enjoyable, had left DeShea feeling envious and depressed. Nick and Danny had gone out of their way to include her, but their effort only seemed to point up how isolated she really was. They had a vocabulary all their own, derived from living together and sharing the same experiences. They had countless little inside jokes that lost their humor when explained to DeShea and were then dismissed with a glance and a shrug that said, "You had to be there."

She'd never be a part of that past. There was too much between them, too much she didn't understand. No matter how hard she tried to fit in, there would always be a large part of their life from which she'd be forever excluded.

In some ways, though, that wasn't so different from what she was used to. She'd always felt like a supporting player in her own life.

The comfortable atmosphere that had been growing between her and Nick was strained again, and she took full responsibility. She suspected Nick was getting irritated with her drastic swings in temperament. She couldn't blame him. She was irritated with herself. But how did she stop them when her mind was such a jumble of conflicting emotions? She almost longed for the days back at Clotilles when all she had to do was play her one well-defined role. No, despite the turbulent state of her emotions now, she far preferred this to the cold void she'd lived in for so long. All she needed was practice at dealing with and sorting out these new feelings.

The soft, mellow tone of the piano reached through her introspection, drawing her into the living room. Nick was seated on the bench, his long, artistic fingers lightly caressing the keys. She went and stood beside the baby grand, mesmerized by the seductive way he manipulated the ivories. The tune he was playing eluded her, but she knew it was an old one, hauntingly beautiful, and each note seemed to reverberate on her already tender nerve endings. She listened for a long time, but when the melody began to sink deep into her soul, she had to wrench herself away.

"I didn't know you played," she said softly.

"We all had lessons when we were kids. I don't play as often as I'd like. Marette was the one who loved the piano. She'd sit and play for hours."

Resentment filled her throat. She didn't want Marette to intrude on the moment. "She always wanted to learn as a child. But our mother never considered it a worthwhile pursuit."

"And what about you, DeShea?" Nick asked, his brown eyes warm and probing. "What did you always want to learn to do?"

She grinned shyly and stared out the window. She was tempted to tell him about her writing, but didn't. "Oh, I don't know. Nothing really. I'm a good business manager, I guess, but that's not the same thing, is it?"

Nick turned his eyes back to the piano and began to softly play an old Gershwin tune, his thoughts drifting with the melody back to his sister-in-law and the times he'd dropped by to find her engrossed in her music, totally absorbed and happy. "Your sister had a real zest for life. She was so full of curiosity and enthusiasm, she would carry you off on her latest project before you knew what hit you. My mom used to call her Hurricane Marette because she'd swoop into the house and breeze out again before you could say hello.

"She was interested in everything, almost hungry for information. She absorbed it like a sponge. Maybe that's why she was so easy to talk to. She was knowledgeable on so many different subjects. I really miss having her to talk to. When Marette was alive, everything seemed more exciting and fun. René was such a lucky man. I always envied him. There aren't many women like Marette. Was she always that way—effervescent and full of life?''

DeShea nodded, then turned away from the piano. Nick's fingers were moving gracefully over the keys, evoking a sweet melancholy tune from the beautiful instrument, and her heart felt as if it were being ripped open with each touch on the ivory. His deep voice droned on in a lovely eulogy, an eerie counterpoint to the music. She'd broken free of Natalie's shadow, only to step into Marette's.

She should have felt good about all the wonderful things Nick was saying about Marette, but all she could feel at the moment was resentment and anger. What did Nick know about Marette? He only knew the woman. DeShea had known the child who broke her promise and left her little sister to fend for herself. The pain from so long ago began to swell up inside, and she choked it back, going to stand in front of the window. The music Nick was creating seemed to pierce her heart, and she fought to hold back the tears.

''She talked about you a lot and how close you were as kids. It's too bad you couldn't have gotten together before she died. She loved you very much, and I know you felt the same way.''

DeShea's mood shifted and she plunged into a chasm of hurt and anger long-buried. She turned away, her jaw working nervously. Her eyes were dry, yet stinging with tears. The pain shot up hot and quick through her insides, and she spoke before she'd consciously formed the words. ''I hated her.'' DeShea felt her heart chill as she realized she had actually vocalized the thought.

Nick stopped playing and looked over at her, a deep frown on his face. ''What?'' he asked, unable to believe that he'd heard her right.

''I hated her,'' DeShea repeated loudly, shocked that she'd finally admitted her guilty secret, but powerless to stop the force once it had started. The words tumbled out and she realized she was crying, hot angry tears that had been stored up for far too long. The sorrow was painful, yet somehow also felt welcome.

"She went off and left me all alone. She deserted me. Walked out of the house, and I never saw her again. I never talked to her, never got a letter, nothing. She just vanished. She never thought about me, about what would happen to me after she left. I had no one to talk to, no one to go to for help, no one to hold me when I was scared and alone. Then when I have a chance to find her, she dies. No, I hated her for what she'd done to me." The tears began to flow freely down her cheeks, and she brushed them angrily aside.

Nick rested his palms on his thighs and leaned forward, staring at DeShea's back. When he saw her brush at her cheeks, he realized that she was crying. "DeShea?" he said softly, uncertain whether to leave her alone or go to her and offer comfort.

"No, I didn't really hate her," she amended softly. "I loved her. But I hated her for leaving me. Why didn't she take me with her? I was old enough. Why did she go off and leave me with no one at all?"

The plaintive note in DeShea's voice gripped his heart, and he rose from the piano bench and went quickly to her side, pulling her around to face him. Her violet eyes were brimming with tears, her cheeks wet. Without a conscious thought, he drew her close, pressing her head against his chest and resting his chin on her soft hair.

"It's all right," he murmured. "Marette loved you. You have to believe that. She didn't mean to hurt you when she left."

"I know, I know, but I missed her so much and now it's too late." DeShea's last measure of control crumbled, and she let her unhappiness burst forth, crying against the solid comfort of Nick's chest. It felt like a dam bursting. The resentment, the heartache held in check for so many years, finally broke free, and she was swept away.

Through it all Nick held her gently, stroking her back and cooing softly. When her sobbing eased she lifted her head and tried to look into his eyes but glanced quickly away again when she realized she'd revealed a part of herself to him no one else had ever seen. "I'm sorry. I didn't mean to get so emotional."

Nick tilted her face upward and smiled into her eyes, the thumbs of his hands brushing away the dampness on her cheeks. "There's nothing to apologize for. I understand. I felt the same way when my father died and when René died. It's a natural part of grieving. When Marette left it seemed to you as if she'd died, too. Of course you were angry with her. But believe me when I tell you that she loved you very much."

"Did she? Oh, I wish I could have heard her say it just once. I wish I could have found her before she..."

Nick's heart ached for her. The violet eyes were so filled with sadness that he felt an overpowering surge of protectiveness swell inside him. He wanted to comfort her, to keep her safe and let her know he understood. But it went deeper than that, much deeper. He felt himself being drawn to her again, fiercely, inexorably, and he knew he was powerless against it this time. Slowly, as if guided by some unseen force, he lowered his head, his eyes fixed upon the full pouting lips that tempted him beyond reason.

She came to him willingly, tasting sweet, fresh and slightly salty from tears. Her kiss was timid, uncertain, and he increased his pressure, testing, fascinated by the innocence he found in her lips. He wasn't sure what he'd expected. Resistance, perhaps, cool indifference, something to match the Ice Princess image he still recalled. But what he found was vulnerability, and it fueled his craving.

Had her defenses been in place, DeShea might have been able to withstand Nick's sincere concern and tender comfort. But her barriers were weakened, and the first whisper of his breath against her lips had collapsed the fragile walls.

She needed him, needed to feel safe, to cling to someone, just for a moment.

She met his lips with shy anticipation, uncertain of what she would find. Her emotions swirled together, resentment mixing with tenderness, loneliness entwined with desire. She felt confusion slide into an unfamiliar kind of need.

DeShea's hesitancy was like a potent wine to Nick. He pulled her closer, giving in to the rising swell of longing that was building deep inside. He urged her into a deeper kiss, his lips exploring the corners of her mouth, his tongue dancing over her lips in invitation.

It was the need, a deep, age-old hunger that finally emerged from her jumbled emotions. Instinctively she sought to appease that basic need and gave herself over to the one sure source of fulfillment. Nick.

He felt the subtle difference the moment she melted into him. She was so soft and warm in his arms. He felt himself losing control, drawn into the surprisingly intoxicating mixture of innocence and passion that DeShea gave him. His arms tightened, crushing her close. Her breasts pressed against his chest; her soft curves fitted enticingly to his body. With a grunt of satisfaction, he invaded her mouth with his tongue and let himself be carried away on the glory of her kiss.

When Nick's arms tightened around her, DeShea no longer knew where he began and she ended. The flood of emotions he'd unleashed was gaining momentum. She'd always kept her feelings firmly tamped down, a safe distance below the surface, so she hadn't anticipated the power that would be released if those emotions were set free. She clung to him with no choice but to abandon her hold and ride out the storm. Nothing mattered but his lips, his tongue, and the sensations that were so exciting and new to her, exciting but not frightening.

Desire, raw and white-hot as lightning, burst upon her, and she heard him grunt deep in the back of his throat. With a recklessness she hadn't known she possessed she returned his kiss with abandon, heedless of everything but the sheer perfection of this feeling. She was home, she was full, she was part of life. She had substance. She existed.

The jolt of passion struck Nick without warning, engulfing him with the blinding intensity of the sun. She turned them into heat and light and made them one totally new being. It was the overpowering force of her response that shocked him and sent a strange kind of fear into his heart. He pulled away and stared down at her, unable to reconcile the woman he saw with the one he'd imagined. Where was the Ice Princess, the shy maiden, the pathetic lonely child? They were all there in front of him, yet none of them held a hint of the passionate woman he'd just kissed. He stared at her intrigued, bewildered.

The violet eyes widened, clouded, then were suddenly hidden behind long lashes. She turned in his arms and stepped away. Before he could touch her again to bring her back, the door opened and Danny burst into the room.

"Hiya, guys," he called, jogging through the room and up the stairs without so much as a glance at his aunt and uncle. "Got homework to do."

With a heavy sigh, Nick looked ceilingward, dragging a hand over his mouth as he attempted to get control of his emotions and sort out what had just happened between them. "DeShea..."

DeShea's knees nearly buckled under the mortification she felt about her brazenness. His sudden withdrawal, the astonished look in his eyes had told her how he felt. He'd been repulsed by her unrestrained response. He made it abundantly clear that he considered her unqualified for any real place in his life. Things were awkward enough between them. She wouldn't make matters worse by bestowing unwanted affections upon him.

With the ability of long practice, she masked her emotions behind a strained but composed smile. "Don't worry about it, Nick," she said softly, anxious to spare him any further humiliation. "I appreciate your trying to comfort me. I shouldn't have burdened you with this. As for the... other, as far as I'm concerned, it never happened.''

Nick couldn't believe his ears. Had he totally misread that kiss? Was he so out of touch that he was imagining emotions that weren't there? No. He'd felt her need, and it matched his own. But that response was gone now. DeShea was posting a no-trespassing sign, telling him she didn't want to get involved.

DeShea brushed past him and was up the stairs before he found the motivation to move. He heard the soft click of her door shutting him out. Bewildered, he retreated to his study and shut the door himself.

Why couldn't he figure her out? Why was she such a mystery to him? And why, in God's name, had he allowed himself to kiss her? It was a stupid, disastrous impulse, because now that he'd kissed her, his worst suspicions had been confirmed. His attraction for DeShea went far beyond mere curiosity, beyond mere physical appreciation. Deeper feelings were now coming into play. He wanted more than just a few stolen kisses, he wanted to make love with her and that was something he couldn't afford. Loving DeShea would be the worst possible thing that could happen to him at this point in his life. Of all the women in the city he could have built a nice solid relationship with, he had to find himself drawn to a woman who didn't want his affections and with whom he had little or nothing in common.

Curled up in the rocker in her room, DeShea stared at the door as if something threatening loomed on the other side. But the real threat was inside the room, inside her. Tonight had only proved that her feelings for Nick were out of control. He was in her thoughts all the time. She couldn't keep her eyes off him when he was around. Her dreams were filled with his likeness, her daydreams consumed with impossible fantasies that centered around him.

For one moment, as he held her in his arms, she'd believed those idle dreams might come true. That perhaps her destiny, like Marette's, could be found in a man named Couvillion. But when she'd given in to the belief, he'd rebuffed her, reminding her that he didn't want her in his life permanently.

She pushed herself out of the chair and walked to the mirror. "What did you expect?" her reflection asked of her. Nick wanted someone strong and exciting, like Marette. Not a shy, nondescript copy like herself. He wanted someone who excelled at everything, who rose to every occasion. All she'd ever excelled at was being a clone of her mother.

Marette. The perfect woman. That hadn't changed. Her sister was everything she wanted to be. Her idol. But she'd never quite measured up. The face in the mirror contorted in pain and she turned away. That was what she got for letting her emotions get out of control. But what did she know about love? She had to face the fact that she was developing deep feelings for Nick. Well, she'd just have to live with that fact, keep her secret. It was her own inexperience in these matters that was at fault. She'd have to find the strength to go on and act like business as usual.

Chapter Nine

DeShea was already up and fixing coffee when Nick entered the kitchen the next morning. She smiled and said good-morning as if nothing had happened between them last night, and he clamped down fiercely on the anger that rose in him.

If that was the way she wanted to play it, then that was fine with him. He could be as indifferent as the next guy. It was easy to say but not quite so easy to put into practice. When Danny strolled into the kitchen, the room seemed to shrink, and no matter where Nick moved he bumped into DeShea. Apparently unaffected by the closeness, she laughed and talked as if it was all rather amusing, which only fueled his irritation.

Seeking a safe barrier between them, he retreated to the bar stool but was unable to keep his mind from thinking of her or his eyes from watching. Last night, he'd thought their relationship had turned a new corner when DeShea confessed her resentment toward Marette. The tears she'd shed, the kiss they'd shared had seemed to ease the uncharacteristic tendency he'd developed to being judgmental. Where DeShea was concerned he was either black or white, hot or cold. He either felt relaxed in her company or angry and defensive.

Last night, when she cried, when he saw how deeply Marette's leaving had scarred her, he'd thought he'd found some middle ground in his feelings, a touchstone for understanding her. He remembered the vulnerable woman he'd held last night, the one with the passion like a scorching summer sun. There were traces of her in the room now. This DeShea was natural, sensitive and feminine. There was no sign of the remote, indifferent woman who had emerged after his kiss and dismissed him with a haughty flick of her wrist. He felt as if he was back at square one—no closer to understanding her now than he had been before.

When the phone rang, Nick moved to get it, but Danny's voice bellowed through the house that he had it under control. Assuming it would be for him anyway and needing to escape, Nick rose and started toward the study.

"Aunt DeShea, it's for you."

Hurriedly she wiped her hands on a towel and sent a guarded glance in Nick's direction. "Excuse me."

He watched her go, his jaw working nervously, then set down his cup and gathered up his briefcase. After sending Danny on his way, he started out the door, then remembered his price book was still on the table in the study. DeShea was using that phone, but he could slip in and retrieve it without disturbing her.

She was seated at the desk when he stepped into the room, the phone cradled in one hand, head bowed as the fingers of her other hand rested against her forehead in concentration. She seemed oblivious to his presence. As he moved forward, her words reached him and he stopped, a cold chill invading his blood as he listened.

"Only three million? Howard, that's not nearly enough. No, I can't accept that.... I understand, Howard, but it's ludicrous. I couldn't possibly manage on that amount. Do you?... Yes, I know. Talk to them again. Please. See if you can get them up another quarter of a million, then get back to me. I want this settled as soon as possible. It's dragged on much too long, and I'm ready for it to be over.''

Nick must have moved or made a sound because she raised her head abruptly and looked directly into his eyes with the cold violet gaze of the Ice Princess. His heart thudded in his chest. Without a word, he grabbed his price book, turned and walked out of the room. He had to get to work, after all.

Nick wasn't sure whom he was angrier with, himself or DeShea. What a jerk he was to keep being suckered in by her sweet smile and pretty face. Just when he began to think he'd found the real DeShea, someone warm and real, she would remind him in no uncertain terms that she was first and foremost a career-motivated businesswoman.

Her conversation echoed in his mind. She had sat at that desk, cool as ice, stating in no uncertain terms that she couldn't possibly manage on three million dollars, pleading with her associate to up the ante.

Three million dollars. He'd never see that much in his lifetime. In two lifetimes. Her pretty face kept blinding him to the truth—DeShea was merely on holiday, some sort of unusual vacation getaway. "Enjoy a fun-filled trip to Baton Rouge, three weeks of ordinary family life." What a bargain. Next season she could take her R and R at a ski resort or on a safari. This visit was nothing more than a temporary diversion. They were worlds apart in every way that mattered. He couldn't see her with 2.5 kids and a station wagon, carpooling to Boy Scouts and ball games. She'd said herself that she and Marette were total opposites. He'd do well to remember that.

When the doorbell rang in midafternoon, DeShea half expected to find Hugh standing on the porch. He'd mentioned he might stop by, although he usually walked right in. She pulled the door open and saw the messenger.

"Special delivery for DeShea Ballard," he said.

"I'm Ms. Ballard," she replied, taking the envelope and signing her name to the record sheet.

Back in the living room, she opened the large folder and pulled out a letter. It was from her friend, the publisher of *Uptown Magazine,* and it took three readings before DeShea could comprehend the words. The letter was filled with glowing compliments and friendly excitement. Her friend wanted to know if she had more stories, and if so would she please send them immediately. The magazine was interested in everything she had. The sum they offered was very generous. While it wouldn't support her in and of itself, with her house in Galena and her personal savings she could live modestly enough. Provided, of course, she could continue to write and sell her work.

As the realisation filtered through, she began to smile, and a warm feeling of accomplishment filled her until she was nearly drunk with giddiness. The letter she held in her hand was more than her declaration of independence. It was her deliverance, her diploma, her passport into the real world. This one insignificant literary effort was the first thing in her life she'd done totally on her own, from her own resources and her own heart and soul.

She could make a new life now, one with purpose, fulfillment. She felt validated, as if she was actually worth something, something more than a well-trained shadow of her mother. Now she had a personality of her own, a life of her own. It felt glorious, intoxicating, and she laughed out loud, twirling around in the living room.

Everything was perfect now. Blissfully, gloriously perfect. She stopped. Well, almost. It would be perfect if Nick could return her feelings. She glanced at the letter again, and thought of the way she'd felt in his arms. She was falling in love, hopelessly, irrevocably, unwisely in love. It made her feel deliriously happy and chillingly terrified all at the same time. She'd learned early that such happiness was fleeting. Good things always came with a price tag. There would be a toll exacted for her achievement. She could have independence and a career of her own but not Nick. It had been like that for as long as she could remember. She could have a mother but not a father or a sister, a husband but not love.

The letter crackled in her hand as she started to ball up her fist and she looked down at it. She couldn't let herself drown in such pessimism. She'd also learned that you did the best with what you were given. Nick wanted someone like Marette. But that was impossible. She could never be like her sister. But she could make the most of her time here, and when it was over she knew Danny would keep in touch. At least now she had a future and that was a lot to be grateful for. Smiling, she looked at the letter again.

"You just win the daily double or something?"

DeShea looked up to see Hugh. She dashed toward him, waving the envelope, her words tumbling out incoherently.

"Whoa, DeeDee, slow down." He chuckled. "Let me see that." He scanned the letter and grinned. "So you're a big-time author now, huh? Congratulations. That's great."

"Isn't it wonderful? I can hardly believe it."

"So what're you going to do with your earnings? Buy a beach house in Malibu? A chalet in St. Moritz?"

"No." She grinned. "This is my new career. I've got to support myself now, don't forget."

"Oh, yeah," he said, nodding and slipping his hands in his pockets. "How's it going with Clotilles?"

"Not good. I've had one offer to buy, but the figure is ridiculously low. I'd still have a huge debt to pay off. I've made a counteroffer, but I haven't heard if it's been accepted or not."

"And when it's gone, when you're out from under this burden, then what?"

Something in Hugh's voice made her look at him more closely, her smile fading. "Then I go home and start a new life, hopefully by writing more stories. Maybe I'll even try a novel."

"Alone?"

"Yes," she said, averting her eyes. Hugh was too perceptive at times. "Don't you know writers do their best work alone? It's tradition. All that solitude makes them more creative or something."

"I just thought maybe there was someone you'd like to share your new life with. Someone you've come to know and perhaps love?"

She smiled, but refused to rise to the bait. "Yes, of course. Danny."

Nick was still in a dark mood when he arrived home that evening. He'd spent the day trying to sort out his conflicting emotions about DeShea and wondering why it was so all fired important anyway. Everything would make sense if he'd just keep the image of the Ice Princess firmly fixed in his mind.

When he walked into the house she was waiting for him, smiling and relaxed, and he felt the battle start all over again. She'd cut a multimillion-dollar deal before breakfast and then had the audacity to look at home in his kitchen, as if she had a right to be there.

"Hi," she said brightly.

"Hi." Setting his briefcase on the floor he tried to remember all the reasons to steer clear of this woman. "Any messages?"

"No. Well," she said with a small gesture of her hand, "not for you."

Nick steeled himself and glanced over at her. She looked positively radiant, lit from within. He felt a rush of warmth in his veins that he promptly squelched. Three million dollars would light up damn near anyone.

"You look happy," he observed, picking up the stack of mail and sorting through the envelopes.

"I am. I got some wonderful news today," she said, leaning toward him across the counter. "Something that might change my whole future."

Nick felt his gut tighten and he tossed the mail down onto the desk. It was always the same. When he was near De-Shea he forgot the differences between them—until she brought him to his senses again. "Yeah, I heard you on the phone this morning. Congratulations. Guess you won't have to worry about overdue bills like the rest of us poor slobs, huh? Not that you ever did," he added, yanking at his tie.

The light in DeShea's eyes vanished so quickly that Nick felt a jolt of painful surprise. She looked hurt and disappointed. Was he mistaken? Was there something else she had wanted to tell him? Suddenly he felt like a heel for snapping at her. Just because he was in a foul mood didn't mean he had to take it out on her. "Uh, DeShea—"

"Hey, Uncle Nick, you seen my soccer shoes?" Danny asked as he skidded into the kitchen.

Nick turned and frowned at his nephew. "You interrupted me."

"I'm sorry," he said with a contrite expression. "But I can't find my shoes and it's time to go to practice."

Nick looked at his watch and silently cursed when he saw that they were already ten minutes late. "Could you fix the water jug, DeShea?" he asked as he spun on his heel and started out of the room. His conscience wouldn't let him go quite so easily, however. Jamming his hands in his pockets, he turned around but found it difficult to meet her eyes. "Would you like to come?"

"No, thank you," she said coolly. "I think I'll start getting things ready for the Dallas trip."

Nick chewed the inside of his mouth, knowing he'd hurt her feelings yet finding it hard to apologize. "Was there something else you wanted to tell me about?" he finally asked when the silence between them grew uncomfortable.

DeShea lifted her head and met his gaze with unflinching calm. "No. Nothing at all."

* * *

After Nick and Danny left, DeShea swallowed her disappointment and returned to her room. She'd been so anxious to tell Nick about selling her story. She'd even kept up her courage when she saw the frown on his face as he came through the door. It wasn't until he'd made his comment about Clotilles that she'd had second thoughts. There'd been such a hard edge of disapproval to his voice that she'd immediately retreated.

She hated herself for being so fainthearted, but sometimes, when he looked so angry and critical, she wasn't sure how to deal with him.

Telling Danny about her writing had been easy. She'd wanted to let him know she understood and that she could help him with his schoolwork. Hugh had just happened to come to the house right after the letter arrived or she probably wouldn't have told him. She didn't really care what Hugh thought of her accomplishment. But she cared very much what Nick thought. She wanted his encouragement and acceptance. But until she was certain how he felt about her she didn't want to risk creating any more problems. He already thought she was cold and withdrawn. If he found out she was a writer he might take that as one more reason to dislike her.

It was just one more way in which she and her sister were opposites. Marette had played the piano, a very conspicuous hobby shared by anyone within hearing distance. It invited people to gather round, and listen and participate.

Writing, on the other hand, was a personal and private endeavor, created alone, and read alone. It was like herself, solitary and internal.

Her eyes traveled to the nightstand and the letter lying there. She picked it up and folded it, slipping it into the drawer. Maybe it was just as well she hadn't told Nick. All she'd really done was sell one insignificant story. The magazine had requested more, but that was no guarantee they would buy them. Maybe she'd wait until the story was actually in print. That would be more impressive anyway. It would be out in the open.

Curling up in the rocker, she started a list of things she needed for the big soccer tournament. They would be leaving for Dallas this weekend, and there was a lot to do to get ready. Infected by Danny's excitement, she was looking forward to the tournament eagerly, though she couldn't quite decide whether her nephew was excited about the trip or the fact that he would be off school for Easter vacation. The reason behind her own excitement she understood clearly. What she was looking forward to the most was spending a whole week with Nick.

Throughout the next day, Nick found himself remembering the excitement on DeShea's face and wondering about her "wonderful" news. He rubbed his forehead, remembering how effectively he'd killed that excitement. He could still see the disappointment that had filled her eyes. What if her good news hadn't been about Clotilles and the three million? What if it was something else? He had to admit she rarely talked about her business, not nearly as much as he'd expected.

In fact, if she was as career-oriented as he first thought, then why had she stayed here so long? Wouldn't she have rushed back to New York after finding her nephew and spending a few days? She didn't seem in any hurry to leave, as far as he could tell. She hadn't even mentioned it.

Planting his elbows on the desktop, he clasped his hands in front of his mouth and thought back to the previous night. He'd wanted to ask her about her news when he got back from practice, but between helping Danny with his homework, business and soccer-related phone calls, it had been impossible for him to get her alone. He realized now that he should have made a stronger effort to do so.

Maybe he could make it up to her somehow. Picking up the phone, he dialed his home and waited anxiously as it rang in his ear. The sound of DeShea's voice felt like a soothing balm on his senses, caressing him through the wires, and his mind filled with an image of her, soft and dreamy, swaying against him, of the way she had felt in his arms, tasted on his lips. Afraid that she would refuse to talk to him, he quickly suggested dinner that evening. His heart stopped beating until she accepted his invitation, then kicked in with a vengeance when her voice smiled through the phone at him.

He made a quick call to his mother to make arrangements for Dan to spend the evening with her, then he checked the clock on the wall. He hoped the afternoon would pass quickly.

Nick and DeShea were already on their way to their table that evening when he realized he'd made a poor choice in restaurants. He'd picked Mulate's, a widely renowned and excellent Cajun place. The atmosphere was open and friendly, the food spicy and authentic. A live band was playing near the dance floor where the patrons could work up an appetite. It was his favorite spot to eat, and he was anxious to introduce DeShea to authentic Cajun cuisine.

But he knew now that what he really wanted was a nice, dark, romantic location where they could sit in the shadows and talk. Strange how easy she was to talk to, how he found himself almost compelled to confide in her. It was something he was still trying to grasp.

One look at DeShea, however, and his regret eased. Her eyes were bright, and she cast them around the room like a delighted child, taking in every detail. Her uninhibited pleasure touched him in a way he wasn't sure he even understood. That someone like her, raised in luxury, the world's treasures at her fingertips, could be pleased by the simple trappings of the restaurant added another layer to her complex personality. Apparently he'd misread a great deal about DeShea.

The wide-open arrangement of Mulate's made intimate conversation difficult, but they still managed to discuss the menu and the band in between talk about Danny. After Nick placed their order, DeShea turned her attention toward the men on the platform, thoroughly entertained by the infectious music. She asked questions about the songs, which were sung in Cajun French, and about the Cajun people, and Nick took immense delight in explaining it all to her.

They watched the couples whirling around the floor, and Nick was captivated by the sheer enjoyment reflected in her violet eyes. When one of the waiters invited her to dance, she hesitated, her cheeks flushed and her eyes uncertain. It was part of the custom for the waiters to lure patrons onto the dance floor, but Nick could see DeShea was reluctant. Suddenly, he wanted more than anything to hold her in his arms. Not that the folk dances were akin to ballroom dancing, where he could have held her close against him and felt her supple body move and sway. They were more like square dances with a little rock and roll mingled in. But it was better than nothing.

Reaching out, he rested his fingers on her hand. "Would you try it with me?"

The lavender eyes clouded, then warmed, and she nodded. He led her to the floor, his arm around her waist. Standing at her side, he proceeded to execute the Cajun two-step. DeShea picked it up quickly, and by the second number Nick was adding spins and twirls and DeShea was laughing gaily.

The evening was still young when they left Mulate's, and Nick was strangely unwilling to see it end. He wanted to go somewhere else, to stretch out the night a little longer, but he couldn't quite decide where to go. A bar seemed inappropriate, as did a movie or a comedy club. The night air was unusually balmy for this time of year, and he finally decided to take advantage of it.

"You haven't seen much of Baton Rouge, have you?"

"No. Though I have been looking through the papers, and it seems like there is an enormous amount to do here.

I'd love to see some of the plantations and visit Cajun country.''

"Well, for now, how about a tour of downtown and a walk on the levee?"

"That would be nice." She smiled.

A short trip on the freeway brought them to Florida Boulevard, and Nick made a sweep of the downtown area before parking the car in front of the Naval History Museum and helping DeShea from her seat. They strolled leisurely through Riverfront Park, climbing the steps through the water garden upward to the crest of the levee that separated the city from the Mississippi River. In front of them, the USS *Kidd* and the new Riverfront Landing dominated the water's edge. Upriver, the thousand points of light that marked the location of the huge refinery there resembled a vast twinkling fairyland in the darkness.

"You never did tell me about your good news," he said as they sat below the symbolic *baton rouge,* the Red Stick sculpture that was the focal point of the park and from which the city had taken its name. "You mentioned Clotilles. Business must be going well."

"No, quite the contrary," she replied, watching the river sliding slowly past. "Business is very bad. But part of the good news is that I think I've found a buyer. And I have you to thank."

"Me?"

"Yes. You helped me make the decision. I felt so guilty at the thought of getting rid of the business my mother dedicated her life to that I was wearing myself out looking for ways to save it. But after you told me about your family business, it gave me the courage to do what was necessary—what I wanted to do."

Nick was stunned. He remembered the conversation and how she'd dashed off to make a phone call. He also remembered the assumption he'd made, that business was her main purpose in life. "I had no idea you were considering selling the salons."

"The business has been declining for years," DeShea said. "But when my mother died, Clotilles died with her."

"I'm sorry. I know how involved you've been in it. What are you going to do now?"

Her voice took on a wistful tone when she spoke. "I'm not sure. With Clotilles gone I'm in limbo. I have a chance at a new career but it's risky at the moment." For some reason she shied away from telling Nick about her writing.

Nick felt a jolt of disappointment. Without missing a beat DeShea shed one career and picked up another. "I'm sure it'll all work out."

"I suppose. It's a sobering prospect having no solid future. For thirty years my every move and thought were planned out. Each day scheduled down to the minute. Even my marriage was arranged."

"Your mother picked him?" Nick said, incredulous that Natalie Ballard was truly capable of such a thing.

"It's not quite the way it sounds. I loved him. She just aided the relationship. Eric was an up-and-coming young executive, and Mother thought that our merged talents would be an asset to her company."

"What kind of man would agree to that?"

"An ambitious one. And a very understanding one. I know how it sounds, but Eric was the best thing that ever happened to me. We were very happy until he..." She shrugged slightly.

"You loved him very much?"

Had she? She'd thought so at the time. Now she wasn't as sure. In spite of her deep feelings for Eric, she'd been afraid to open her heart completely and say the words that might have kept him at her side. "Not like I should have."

"He loved you?"

"As best he could, I suppose."

Nick nodded. Having Natalie Ballard as a mother-in-law would be a strain on the best of men. "Is he still with Clotilles?"

"No." She laughed ruefully. "No one is now. Not even me. It's still a bit scary not knowing your direction in life. I always wished I was brave like Marette. She was the one who dared to defy our mother, to risk punishment to get her own way. I used to wish I could be more like her. Then I would have had the courage and strength to turn my back and walk away, to start over with nothing but my wits and determination." She laughed softly and stared up at the darkening sky. "I guess I'll get my chance now, won't I? My mother is gone. My job is gone. All I need now is the bravery."

"You already have that, DeShea," Nick said softly. "It took courage to come down here and confront your sister, it took courage to stay and claim your rights with Danny. Coming down here was like braving a new frontier. This is a totally foreign environment, and yet you've adjusted quickly. I'm not sure I could have adapted as easily to your world as you have to ours."

"No." She shook her head. "That wasn't courage, or adaptability, merely selfish desire to find Marette."

"You're wrong. I think it took bravery to stay and learn to cope with your mother's overbearing ways. Marette ran away. You found a way to balance her excesses with your own abilities. You became good at your job, successful despite her. And from the little you've told me, it sounds like you held the company together the past few years while your mother was ill."

"That wasn't bravery, Nick, that was weakness. It was an easy solution to a complicated problem, and I'm here now because I was forced to change. I didn't leave of my own accord. My mother died. I didn't have a hand in the new direction my life is taking. I came here to find Marette because she was the only family I had left and I was afraid of being alone."

"No one wants to be alone," he said softly.

"Exactly. That's why I'm so glad Danny has you and your family. He'll know what love is, what belonging is.

He'll be part of an ongoing unit, a circle of love and support."

Nick shook his head. "Right at this moment, I'd give the whole lot to you with no strings attached," he groaned softly, getting to his feet.

DeShea joined him, strolling slowly along the levee. "Why? What's wrong?"

"I don't know. It seems like lately, every time I turn around someone is hounding me for advice. Dixie called about a business she wants to get into and then Mom called about the same thing. Then Hugh pestered me over lunch yesterday about some job offer he's gotten, wanting to know whether I thought it was a good deal or not." He rubbed his forehead. "I suppose I'm just tired. It's been a rough couple of weeks, what with inventory and Danny's school problems and strange relatives dropping in...." He looked up, realizing what he was saying, and was surprised to find DeShea smiling.

"It's okay. I understand. Really," she said quietly. "I was a big disruption in your life. That's a strain on anyone."

He shrugged and straightened his back. "I'm usually more than willing to listen to everyone's troubles and offer my opinion. But lately it seems like they're all pulling at me, looking to me for answers to every little thing, and I'm beginning to resent it."

"And that makes you feel guilty?"

"Yes," he said quickly. "I shouldn't. I never did before. They're my family. If they need my help, I should be more than glad to help, but..."

"You feel like you're being torn apart piece by piece, and there's nowhere for you to go, no one to turn to for replenishment."

"Exactly," he said, stunned at her total understanding. "How did you know?"

"I've been in a similar position most of my life. When I was younger, I was the mediator between Marette and my mother. I was cursed with this awful ability to see both sides

of a situation. At Clotilles I was the only person in authority who could deal with Mother when she went on one of her
rampages. Howard could handle her sometimes, but usually it came back to me. Everyone was always coming to me
for help and advice, asking me for my opinion on how best
to approach Mother about a problem or asking me to inter-
vene on their behalf.''

Turning her face toward him, she sighed softly. ''But no
one ever offered to act as go-between on *my* behalf when
Mother and I were at odds. I sometimes felt as if I'd given
every little part of me away and nothing was left but the
shell.'' She realized she'd said way too much, more than
she'd ever told anyone with the exception of Eric, her one
confidant. ''That's why I envy you your family. Your
mother, sisters and Hugh. Maybe you need to talk to one of
them.''

''That's just it. I can't and it's probably my own fault,''
he admitted sadly. ''I set myself up as the patriarch. The
man with all the answers. Now they think I'm infallible, an
all-wise Solomon.'' He shook his head. ''I sometimes feel
like I was forced to grow up too fast after Dad died. I didn't
get enough time to be just a kid. I was always the dependable one. Good old Nick. Mom even sought my advice before René's. I used to be glad of that, even proud. But now
I feel...burdened. For the first time in my life, I wish I could
get away from the family. Then I feel *really* guilty. They
need me.''

''But you have needs too, Nick,'' she pointed out, one
hand touching his arm lightly. ''You have a right to your
own life. Could it be you've made yourself too available, too
accessible? Perhaps they've all come to take you for granted.
You need to let them manage their own lives and take time
to nurture your own.''

''Maybe I'm just greedy, huh? I mean, I have so much.
Good job, great kid, a family that's supportive. Most people would give fortunes for that.''

"But somehow it's not enough, is it?" DeShea stated quietly, thinking of her own greed—wanting her freedom and Nick and Danny, too.

Nick's dark eyes probed deeply into hers. "How did you get to be so wise? You're too young to have discovered such deep truths."

"I spent most of my life alone. I've been an observer of life more than a participant. It was safer to listen and learn from other's mistakes. Less painful, too. I had lots of time to figure things out—like all the whys and wherefores and who and what I am. And because of that I developed a lot of common sense. I learned about people and the way they react to things. But there are still far too many situations that I find myself in that I have no idea how to deal with."

"If only there were some sort of handbook," he said, staring out across the river. "Something that outlined the direction a person is supposed to go in life, that held clearly defined solutions to complex situations and reasons for the odd feelings that seem to grow out of nowhere and eat away at your guts."

"The hollow sensation," she said softly, more to herself than to him.

Nick glanced at her sharply. "Yes. I sometimes feel like there's this hole inside me that I can't ever seem to fill up."

"The hungry heart." She looked at him and saw the puzzlement in his dark eyes. "The heart that's hungry for love and emotional fulfillment."

"You mean love between a man and a woman?" There was a hint of skepticism in his voice.

"Partly," she replied. "I think there's two parts to it. One is filled with yourself. You have to like yourself first, then you have to find something that fulfills you, a creation of your own. The other part is filled by a special someone, a husband, a wife, a child."

Nick sat down on the rim of the fountain pool at the top of the park. "But I have that, Shea. I have a job I truly love, and I have Dan. But it's still not enough. Something is missing.''

DeShea sat down and looked away, hiding the thrill that had raced trough her at the nickname he'd bestowed upon her so casually.

Nick thought for a moment. "Like Marette and René. The family didn't think their marriage would work. Everything pointed against them because they were so different. Yet, they seemed to complement each other. It shouldn't have worked, but it did. They proved us all wrong. I guess that's what I'm looking for. Someone to be my friend and partner as well as lover.''

"Someone to complete who you are," she added.

"Yes. Exactly." He felt again that strange sense of bonding, of understanding between them.

"I know this sounds clichéd, but she's out there. Someplace. The right woman for you does exist, Nick. You'll just have to keep looking.''

"I have a feeling I'm looking in all the wrong places." He sighed loudly.

"Maybe you are.''

He hadn't expected that response. "What do you mean?''

DeShea hesitated a moment, debating whether to express her honest opinion or remain silent. Deciding that she'd already said more than she'd planned, she forged ahead. "Maybe it's time to break away from your family and spread your wings a little. You might be surprised at what you discover about yourself.''

She was thinking of herself. If she'd never been set free of her own bonds, she'd never have tried to sell her story or have found Nick. The only difference was he, at least, had hope of finding someone. She'd found the man of her dreams, but he was clearly not meant for her.

"Is that what you were doing when you came here, Shea?" he asked. "Spreading your wings?''

"Yes, I suppose," she answered, shifting uncomfortably on the concrete seat.

She'd meant to keep the conversation directed at Nick's problems, not her own. Talking about herself always made her feel awkward. It was much easier to listen and offer comfort to others, to be their sounding board, than to have to examine her own insecurities and faults. But she hadn't counted on Nick's perception.

"I guess we're a lot alike in some ways," she said. "I hope you have better luck than I did. What I found at the end of my journey was more unhappiness."

The sadness in her voice created an ache deep in Nick's chest. She sounded so forlorn, so alone. Her violet eyes were deep purple now, like the night sky, and the sorrow he saw in their depths was so real he felt as if he could reach out and hold it in one of his hands. He watched her as the moonlight kissed her pale skin and caressed her fine, lustrous hair. She was so beautiful, so fragile, like a wraith, an ethereal being perched at his side who needed to be touched by a mortal hand or else she'd fade into the mist.

He didn't remember saying her name, but he must have, for the dark purple eyes were looking at him, looking deep inside, touching him in a way he'd never been touched before, replacing the cold hollow in his heart with warmth and light and sweetness. He reached for her, drawing her against him, sinking into the warmth and the beauty that washed over him when he touched her. A delicate fragrance filled his nostrils, permeating his senses with its loveliness. His hands slid around her back, his fingers tingling at the heat radiating from her body.

When his lips met hers, he found them moist and parted, and surprisingly pure. He felt as if he was traversing unspoiled territory, virginal ground, breathing life into a young goddess. Barely had that thought been born when the goddess awoke. Her soft whimper was filled with fire, her lips parted in urgent invitation, and the innocence was gone. In its place he found the passion of a woman, one who knew the joys of love.

The intensity of DeShea's response was exhilarating and alarming. His own needs had burst full force upon him, consuming him like an eternal flame. And he knew beyond a doubt that the only one capable of dousing it was De-Shea. He didn't understand it, didn't understand why the unfathomable Ice Princess should hold such power over him, but at that moment he didn't care. He plundered her mouth as if it were his only chance at survival and found her pliant and equally urgent.

Perhaps her mind was more easily controlled or her needs less urgent. But just as suddenly as it had begun it was over, and he found himself looking at deep-purple eyes that were troubled and slightly frightened.

His voice was husky and strained when he spoke. "I don't understand this. It shouldn't be happening."

How could he possibly be feeling so much for this woman? He didn't understand this compelling attraction for someone he knew was all wrong for him. He shouldn't be feeling so good—so *right*—whenever they were together.

DeShea swallowed the hurt in her heart. For one second she'd allowed herself to consider telling him how she felt. To hope that maybe he was beginning to feel something, too. But she couldn't tell him now. She'd have to let him think it was pure chemistry between them. Nothing more, nothing he need be concerned about.

"Sometimes when people are lonely they reach out to the person closest, for reassurance, to feel solid and real," she said quietly.

He slowly slid his hands down her arms, as if reluctant to let go. His eyes were lit by the faint glow of the light overhead. "I guess I have been feeling that way lately—searching, aimless. And I know you must be feeling especially vulnerable."

She forced a faint smile on her face, gratified that she was so well practiced at masking her real feelings, because otherwise the hurt would have been clearly visible at that moment. "Yes. More than you know."

"But it's more than that, Shea. There's an attraction there, only..."

"You're not sure what's attraction and what's loneliness."

"Whether it's you that's created this hunger in me, or something else and you just happen to be here." He dropped her hands and rubbed his forehead. "Sorry. That's not very complimentary, is it?"

"I understand," she assured him. "We're strangers who happen to have the same problem. It's hard to know if we're drawn to each other through need or genuine interest."

"Maybe it would be easier if we were more alike," he commented, brushing a stray wisp of hair from her cheek.

"Do you think we're so different?"

"We're worlds apart, Shea. We want different things. You've been raised to be in command. Your life is focused on a career. You've run a worldwide business, come and gone as you pleased. I'm not a worldly man, Shea. My roots are blue-collar, simple. I'm happiest at home, being with the family, taking a vacation once a year. I'm very middle class. You come from a life of wealth and privilege, accustomed to having the best of everything. We don't want the same things."

Was he right? She and Eric had been compatible, with endless interests in common, and their marriage had failed. How could she and Nick ever have a relationship when they were so different?

"Maybe not," she replied softly, thinking that she wanted him and he wanted... "What do you want, Nick?"

"Someone to care, to share my life. Someone like Marette who would be a partner, a friend, as well as a wife." As always, his eyes softened with affection when he spoke of his sister-in-law.

"Did you love my sister?" The question was as much a surprise to DeShea as it was to Nick.

"No," he said firmly, after a brief pause. "Not the way you mean. I loved her, yes, but I wasn't in love with her.

Though I suppose it looks that way since I'm always singing her praises.

"Actually, Marette wasn't as perfect as I may have led you to believe. She had faults like everyone else. She was much too strict with Daniel, and too tolerant of René. She was a perfectionist. Everything had to be just right. It used to drive my brother crazy because he was just the opposite. But they loved each other and that made all the other things work out."

"Then we're not so different," she said. "We both want someone to care for us. To love us. It's only human nature to want to be loved and accepted."

"I suppose so."

"Perhaps the transition from one way of life to another isn't as hard as you think, if a person really wants to change and if the motivation is strong enough. Marette adjusted to a different kind of life."

Was his motivation strong enough? Nick wondered as they walked back to the car. Could he learn to live in Shea's world? Wasn't that what she was hinting?

Chapter Ten

"Dallas, Texas. All right!" Danny peered eagerly between the front seats at the looming skyline ahead. "How much longer?"

"Twenty or thirty minutes," his uncle replied, as he maneuvered the van onto the Outer Belt. "Keep your eyes peeled for the Coit Road exit."

"You ever been here before?" Danny asked his aunt.

"Once. When I was about seventeen. My mother was here negotiating the possible site of a Clotilles, but the plans never materialized. We were only here a few days, so I didn't get to see much."

"The only thing I really want to see is a Sidekicks game," Danny announced, scooting back into his seat.

DeShea turned her eyes toward the window, the landscape a blur as nervousness churned in her stomach. Now that the trip was under way, her excitement had been replaced with serious misgivings. Her visit to Dallas this time was from a totally different and somewhat bewildering perspective. Marette's home had become a familiar environment. A place where she felt secure and comfortable. If the occasion had been a business conference she would have had no qualms at all. But a week in a hotel with a soccer team and the boys' parents, most of whom she barely knew, was different. It made her feel uncomfortable and insecure. She had no idea what would be expected of her, how she should behave or even what to talk about.

"You okay?" Nick asked, reaching over and touching her clenched hands gently.

The lie was on her lips but suddenly she didn't want to pretend anymore. "I'm a little nervous, that's all," she admitted.

"About this trip?"

She nodded, keeping her eyes focused straight ahead. Sharing her fears with someone else was not an ability she'd ever mastered, and she was already regretting her confession. Nick already had a poor opinion of her. This would only add to it.

Nick's strong features reflected his surprise. He wouldn't have thought a sophisticated woman like DeShea could be nervous. But he liked it. Her insecurity made her seem more human. He found that very reassuring.

"Anything in particular?" he asked gently, his fingers still resting on hers.

"It's nothing, really."

"Nothing wouldn't have your teeth gnawing on your bottom lip. Come on, tell Uncle Nick," he teased.

His attitude eased her reluctance. "It suddenly dawned on me that I won't be with you and Danny all week. I don't know why I didn't realize it sooner. I mean, you'll be busy coaching and he'll be with his friends." She shrugged. "That leaves me with only the other mothers to talk to, and I don't think we have a whole lot in common."

"I see what you mean." Nick nodded thoughtfully.

"What do we talk about? I'm sure they don't care about my problems with Clotilles, and I can't discuss the ins and outs of parenting. And as far as soccer is concerned—" she shook her head "—I've learned a little by sheer osmosis but not nearly enough to conduct an intelligent conversation."

"I wouldn't worry too much. You've met Rona and Frances before, and they're both easy to talk to. And you can always come to practices with us if you'd like. I want you to have a good time here. Maybe you could sign up at the hotel for some of the city tours. You said you didn't get to see much when you were here before."

"Alone?"

Nick looked over at her sharply. There was a strange note in her voice. He saw her lavender eyes were wide and filled with an incredible sadness, and realized he'd seen the look before. A jolt of understanding rocketed through him. Sadness. That was what he'd seen in her eyes all those times. The look he had so smugly termed as cold. Hugh had tried to tell him, but he wouldn't listen. And now he had blithely suggested that she see Dallas alone. Lord knew, she had reason enough to be sad. Marette had been full of tales about Natalie, none of them good; she had been forced to turn her back on her family in order to find happiness.

"No, of course not alone," he said quickly. "I wasn't thinking."

She smiled apologetically. "I'm sorry. I'm being selfish. The most important thing is that you and Danny have fun. I'm really just along for the ride. I'll be just fine. Really."

DeShea was relieved that further conversation was made difficult by the increasing traffic. The trip had been pleasant, and Nick had been congenial and charming, but the encounter on the levee had created a new kind of tension between them. There had been no opportunity to discuss the question of attraction or loneliness. Though for DeShea the answer was simple. She'd been falling in love with Nick from the first day. Each moment she was near him only strengthened that. But what about Nick's feelings? Was it his loneliness that drew him to her? Was she merely a sympathetic and convenient source of solace?

She didn't want to believe that. Nick wasn't the type to use people, women, as a panacea for loneliness. But if he *was* attracted to her? What then? She already knew the answer.

Nick wanted a woman like Marette. Someone warm and loving, someone who knew how to nurture and comfort.

How could she offer those things to Nick, to anyone, when she'd never known them herself? Working at Clotilles was all she knew. Nick had all but said he found it hard to believe that she and Marette were related. Marette had been the risk taker, the one who stood up and told the world what she wanted and then went out and got it. She, on the other hand, was more comfortable in the background, content to go quietly about her business, making sure her mother's commands were carried out with as little friction as possible.

From somewhere in the back of her mind the words of her mantra echoed forth. *What do you want to do?* How easy it was to fall into old patterns of thought. She had made a promise to herself when she came to Baton Rouge that she would start to take control of her life. To assert her wishes. But so far she hadn't done much. She had managed to tell Danny how much she loved him. That was a start. As for Nick, she wasn't ready to wear her heart on her sleeve, but she could at least begin to show him that she was capable of change.

She might not be well versed in the intricacies of family life, but she sure as hell could learn. If she ever got the chance. So far all he seemed to want of her was a friendly ear. At least he would accept that from her. But it wasn't what DeShea wanted. What she wanted was out of her reach. And how did she stop her heart from wanting something it was hungry for?

They had no trouble finding the hotel, but there was a moment of anxiety when they checked in. The management had inadvertently reserved only one room instead of two. Since the hotel was also tournament headquarters, there were few extra rooms available. Nick offered to find her accommodations elsewhere, but the idea of being alone—not to mention the inconvenience of their being in two locations—seemed unnecessary. Eventually the hotel offered to provide a suite in place of a double room. It had a spacious bedroom with two queen-size beds and a large closet, and a living room, which held the usual assortment of furniture, including a sofa bed where DeShea could sleep. Both the bath and the door to the corridor opened from this main area, which gave equal access to everyone, although DeShea felt a little awkward at the intimacy this would entail. Still, there *was* sufficient space to move about without continually bumping against Nick, and it would have to do.

Now it was after eleven o'clock the first evening, and she was waiting for Danny and Nick to return from a team meeting. She'd taken advantage of the time alone to settle in and come to grips with the week ahead. The trip had tired her more than she'd realized, and she was already in bed when she heard the sound of a key turning in the door lock. Slipping deeper under the covers, she feigned sleep, listening to the rustle of their movements and Nick's whispered command to ''not wake your aunt.''

Danny disappeared into the bathroom and through the safety of the dim light, she saw Nick moving about preparing for bed. She felt an odd restlessness between her legs as she watched him.

He laid his coach's binder on the desk and piled some other items on top. Then he reached into his pockets and pulled out a handful of change. The wallet was next, then he turned and walked toward the bedroom, pulling off his lightweight jacket as he went. A few minutes later he came back, and DeShea found herself following his every move. He unbuttoned his shirt, tugging it from the waistband of his slacks, then bent and retrieved a canned drink from the refrigerator and took a long swallow.

The dim light from the bath was enough to give DeShea a view of his well-developed chest and the dark hair that splayed across his chest and down the trim, taut stomach. He hefted the can again, and the shadows caressed the angles of his body, the square, firm chin, the thick throat and the well-defined pectorals and narrow waist.

The ache in her center was fierce. She clenched her teeth at the surge of desire the sight of him had created. Fortunately, Danny emerged from the bath at that moment, breaking the spell, and Nick claimed his turn in the lavatory.

She was barely aware of Danny as he retrieved a bag from the storehouse of snacks they'd brought with them. She was still trying to overcome the intense need Nick had given birth to. Just when she felt she had it mastered, he emerged from the bath and went toward the bedroom. She heard him say a soft good-night to Danny then place a quick call to the desk, asking to be awakened at seven o'clock.

The door to the bedroom was open, and from her position in the living room DeShea could easily see Nick as he turned down the sheets and began to undress. DeShea closed her eyes, knowing the sight of him would be her undoing. But even so his movements were still detectable to her ears. The rasp of the zipper on his trousers, the whoosh as he pulled them from his legs and the soft bump as the belt was draped over a chair.

Daring a peek, she opened her eyes slightly, but found only darkness. After a few moments her pupils adjusted, and she could just make out his form in the faint light that filtered in around the draperies. He was standing in the bedroom, his body partially shielded by the door, watching her.

What was he thinking? Suddenly, as if she'd read his thoughts, she knew the answer. He was standing there wanting her as much as she wanted him. She could feel his gaze across the distance, knew that if the light were on, their eyes would be locked. A wave of longing built deep inside, gathering strength, rolling along each nerve. It took all her willpower to keep perfectly still when what she really wanted was to turn away and bury her head under the sheets. She could hear each breath he took, smell him, could almost feel him reaching for her, touching her. Squeezing her eyes tightly closed, she prayed for a release from the tension between them. Finally, after an eternity, she heard Nick softly close the door. After a long moment, she allowed herself the luxury of movement. Clutching her pillow tightly, she sought sleep.

Sunday passed in a whirlwind of activity as the team registered and assembled for a short practice, then rehearsed for the elaborate opening ceremonies. DeShea felt like a fish out of water. Nothing in her previous experience had prepared her for the chaos that seemed to pervade the hotel and tournament events.

The restaurant was always packed with boys. Teams from Ireland, England, Brazil and Germany clogged the elevators and halls. At any given moment, a team would either be leaving in clean uniforms or returning muddied, bandaged and bruised—a fact that gave DeShea some serious concern.

"What are you thinking about?" Nick asked as they finished an early supper in the hotel dining room. "You have a very strange look on your face."

"My mother," she said with a faint smile, failing to notice the sudden stiffening of Nick's jaw.

"Oh?"

"She would be appalled by all this."

"You mean the tournament?"

"All of it. Especially seeing the boys kicking soccer balls in the hallways, running up and down the stairs, lounging all over the lobby...." She glanced over at him. "My mother was an advocate of the children-should-be-seen-and-not-heard school of thought, and seeing the adults encouraging and even amused by such behavior would have horrified her.''

"How do you feel about it?'' he asked, a slight defensive edge to his voice.

Her eyes met his in a look of puzzlement. "I don't know. As far as I can see they are all polite, clean and, while a bit rambunctious, not destructive or belligerent, but..."

"So you don't approve?''

"Oh, no, I'm not saying that,'' she clarified quickly. "But it is a concept that takes some getting used to.'' She didn't add that it made her realize just how out of touch with the real world she really was.

Natalie Ballard would have been even more appalled at the behavior of some of the adults, DeShea thought later that evening as she stepped off the elevator. The parents of the boys on Danny's team were all seated on the floor of one of the many open areas, busily at work. Some of the mothers were painting signs; others had huge piles of plastic beads in front of them. Fathers were lounging around, laughing and talking about the skill of the competition. She was about to go on her way when one of the mothers invited her to help, and after a moment of hesitation she agreed.

"We're painting signs to hold up at the ceremonies tonight,'' Frances explained.

"And these are to exchange with the other teams,'' Rona added, holding up a fistful of bright necklaces. "It's traditional for each team to exchange some token of its home state or country.''

DeShea's puzzlement over their choice of tokens must have been clearly written on her face, for Margaret smiled and added, "Since we're from south Louisiana, we thought it would be fun to trade the beads and doubloons that are tossed from the floats during Mardi Gras parades.''

"It looks like you have enough for all 120 teams,'' De-Shea observed with a grin.

"What we don't need to trade with the teams we're going to give to the boys to throw up into the crowd this evening during the opening ceremonies."

By the time DeShea had helped sort out sixteen bundles for each boy for each of their three opposing teams, she felt like a real "team Mom."

As she sat in the stadium later, she felt an excitement and camaraderie she'd never known before. The ceremonies were similar to those that opened the Olympics—bands, dance teams, balloons, fireworks and speeches, followed by the long-awaited presentation of each of the 120 participating teams. When the Baton Rouge United Thunder was announced, DeShea felt her heart swell with a love and pride that brought tears to her eyes. Nick looked handsome and very proud as he waved to the crowd. Danny was grinning from ear to ear, tossing his trinkets up into the waving hands of the people.

The feeling lingered on after the ceremonies were over and she was back at the hotel waiting anxiously for Nick and Danny to return. Her heart was beating erratically and a faint flush colored her cheeks. She couldn't wait to see them and tell them how proud she was. A huge smile lit her face when she saw them coming down the hallway. Danny trotted toward her, his face beaming.

"Wasn't that too smooth?" he asked. "Just like the Olympics."

"I was so proud of you," she said, reaching out and touching her nephew's hair gently. *Proud* was such an inadequate word for the way she was feeling. Watching Nick and Danny coming onto the field with young players from all over the world, being a part of something so worthwhile, had given her a profound sense of satisfaction and fulfillment unlike anything she'd ever known. She wanted desperately to tell Nick how she felt, but even after all she had shared with them, her painfully learned reticence seemed impossible to overcome.

Danny smiled and stepped closer, wrapping his arms around her in a hug. "I'm glad you came, Aunt DeShea."

Surprised and somewhat awkward with his affectionate gesture, DeShea hesitated, her arms held stiffly out from her body. Then slowly, she enfolded the slender form. Her heart filled with a beautiful tranquility.

"I tried to find you in the stands," Danny said, pulling out of the embrace, "but I couldn't. Did you see us throwing the beads? Some of those people didn't know what we were doing," he said with a laugh.

"Yes, I did," she replied, her eyes drinking in his smiling face. "I was sitting with the Russells on the far end. I waved, but there were a lot of people in the stadium."

Nick came and stood beside his nephew, resting one hand on the boy's shoulder. "Quite a thrill, wasn't it?" His words were directed at Daniel, but his eyes were focused on DeShea's clear lavender ones.

"Yes, sir. Can I go and find John and Ted? I won't stay long."

DeShea, her heart bursting with love and pride, watched as the boy jogged down the hallway. Suddenly, as if a curtain had been lifted from her mind, she knew what life was all about. It was these small beautiful events, the little moments shared with those you love. Not what you wear or where you live or who you know. It was watching your child in the school band, shopping together after school, quiet talks over the kitchen table. That was a kind of fulfillment no career on earth could provide. Fighting back the moisture that formed in her eyes, she turned and went back into the room.

"What's wrong?" Nick asked.

Wrapping her arms around her waist, she walked to the window, shaking her head slowly. "When I was working at Clotilles and I achieved some new goal, I always expected a feeling of accomplishment, of achievement. It never came and I didn't know why. But this—" She closed her eyes briefly, unable to express her emotions. She couldn't explain the disappointment, the vague is-that-all-there-is feeling, but she still struggled to communicate with Nick. "I've learned so much being here, seeing you and Danny together day to day. I'm very grateful to you for allowing me to stay and be a part of it."

Nick felt the now familiar chill drifting over him. This was all still a field trip to her. An excursion into another way of life. She spoke dry-eyed of accomplishments at Clotilles and of learning. Not one word about how she felt or whether she had come to care. "I don't want your gratitude," he said tersely.

DeShea flinched, realizing that her words must sound as if she were trying to take credit for something she had no hand in. She longed to explain to him the things she'd just realized, to tell him how deeply she was beginning to care for Danny and everyone in her sister's family. But expressing her love, opening her heart was something she had never been able to do. She knew it was the main reason Eric had found someone else. She had been unable to tell him how she cared, unable to say the words he needed to hear. And she was unable to tell Nick the way she felt right now. So her only choice was to endure this peculiar kind of torture, of being part of a family but only from the threshold.

Despite her difficulties expressing herself to Nick, De-Shea was becoming more at ease with the other mothers. It was after breakfast the next morning that she found herself elected to an unexpected position on the Thunder team.

"Aunt DeShea, can you speak French?" Danny asked.

Somewhat startled by the question, she blinked and replied, "Yes, I can. Why?"

Two of Danny's teammates were eating with them, and Ted posed the next question. "How about Italian?"

She nodded as Ethan started inquiring excitedly about other languages. "I speak French, Italian, Spanish and a little German. Why?"

"Well, you see, we brought our old team shirts, and we want to trade them with the guys on the Italian team," Danny explained.

"And the French team," Ted added.

"Yeah, but we can't talk to them," came Ethan's enlightening statement.

"And their English sounds weird."

"Can't understand them."

"Could you come and be our interpreter?" Danny begged.

Their request softened her heart, and she was more than happy to help them out. It felt good to be included, not just as a gesture but because she was truly needed. So Aunt DeShea became the team-shirt broker of the tournament and, thanks to her business savvy, negotiated some tough trade-offs. It was the most fun she'd had in her life.

And so the following two days passed quickly. When she saw Nick, it was usually in a group, and the talk centered entirely on the games and which teams were likely to make it to the qualifying rounds.

DeShea stepped out of the shower and dried herself slowly with one of the thick towels, then glanced in the mirror and saw a guilty frown on her lips. The Thunder families had all gone to dinner together, and she was supposed to go along. Nick had arranged it, though he couldn't go himself. A business meeting, something connected with Beller Electronics, had called him away for most of the evening. He'd apologized for his work intruding into the trip but said it couldn't be helped.

At the last minute, DeShea had begged off on the pretense of not feeling well and had stayed behind, sending Danny with the Langlois family. It wasn't entirely a lie. She was troubled and needed some time alone to think.

Her enthusiasm for the tournament had palled considerably. Thunder had won their first game against Mexico on Monday and tied France this afternoon, but after watching those games, she was beginning to have serious doubts about Danny's participation. His small stature seemed woefully inadequate against the speed and size of the other boys his age. Two of the members of Danny's team had been injured today. One had broken his arm; the other had pulled muscles.

Her concern for her nephew had risen sharply after that, but when she'd mentioned it to Nick, he had smiled patiently and dismissed her fears. Only slightly pacified by his reassurance, she nonetheless withheld further comment. Thunder would have to beat the Dallas team tomorrow in order to remain in the tournament. If they lost, they would all be going home and she found herself hoping, somewhat guiltily, that Danny's team would lose. She would like to get him back home in one piece.

Home. It had such a lovely sound to it. Her reflection smiled back at her. The three of them had become closer these past few days. With every passing hour, each minor event, she felt more and more like part of a real family. It was almost as if she were destined to belong to Nick and Danny. Sometimes, alone in the dark, late at night, she would allow herself to pretend that it was true. It was a dangerous habit to get into because it was something that would never happen. But as long as Nick didn't know what she was thinking, what harm could it do? The only one hurt by her imaginings would be herself.

Reaching into the closet, she touched her robe, brushing against one of Nick's shirts in the process. Tenderly she stroked the fabric, bringing the sleeve to her lips and inhaling the lingering scent of him. If she couldn't have him close, then she could at least wrap herself in his aroma. On impulse, she slipped the striped shirt from the hanger and pulled it on as she let her imagination carry her away.

She smiled into the mirror. The shirt swallowed her. She rolled up the sleeves and adjusted the large collar. Even with the first button fastened, it gaped nearly to her breasts. The hem dipped low in front but left a healthy expanse of thigh

revealed on the sides. She started to unbutton the cool, soft
folds and replace it on the hanger, then decided to indulge
herself a while longer. Nick wouldn't be back until after
midnight, and she'd have changed into her nightgown and
gone to bed long before that.

As she brushed her hair up into a ponytail she remembered the way he'd looked during the parade today, and dug
out her notebook. Curling up on the bed, she began to write.
She had the whole evening to herself. Nick needn't know
until morning that she hadn't gone to dinner with the others.

Nick guided his van onto the LBJ Freeway, loosened his
tie and breathed a heartfelt sigh of relief. His business had
been conducted in a quarter of the time he'd expected, and
now he was free to put it behind him and enjoy the rest of
the trip. He thought briefly about going to the restaurant
and catching up with the team for dinner, but decided a
quiet evening alone might be more beneficial. The trip
wasn't turning out the way he'd hoped.

Thunder was doing well and the guys were having a great
time. In that regard, the tournament was a huge success.
What wasn't so successful was his relationship with De-
Shea. He'd hoped to find some time alone to sort out the
feelings of loneliness they had both admitted to. But with his
coaching duties, her translator jobs and the general ebb and
flow of parents and kids, it had been impossible.

Sometime during the past few days he'd sensed a subtle
shift in their relationship. DeShea had become his friend.
Someone who understood his point of view, his feelings,
and didn't expect him to have all the answers. It was a re-
freshing change from his family. She asked nothing in return, merely offered a strong shoulder and a willing ear. He
found himself drawn to her in a way he'd never been to other
women. It was more than her physical appearance, though
she was beautiful in a delicate angelic way. She stirred his

protective instincts, which didn't make sense because De-Shea was nothing if not self-sufficient.

But it was even more than that. There was a link, some undercurrent that bound them, a connection of some kind on a deep, mysterious level, that he didn't fully understand.

Nick rubbed his upper lip in contemplation. That made no sense at all. Other than Danny, what common ground could he and Shea possibly have? Perhaps it was just his own unsettled mental state that was at fault here. He had a lovely, unattached female living in his house. He was lonely. She was pretty. Ergo, he was attracted. Nothing mystical about it. Man plus woman equals sexual desire.

So if it was that normal, why did he feel so abnormal?

The question dogged him as he parked the van and made his way through the hotel to his room. Still without a satisfactory answer, he opened the door with more force than necessary and forged into the room, only to be brought up short by the sight before him. DeShea was lying on her stomach across her pulled-out sofa bed, ankles crossed in the air. She was propped up on her elbows, a notebook in front of her and a pencil clenched in her teeth. Her only clothing was one of his shirts, rolled up at the sleeves and draped rather sparingly over her body. Her silky golden hair was pulled high on her head in a saucy ponytail, and she looked for all the world like a young teenage girl.

She looked up at him with surprise on her face, then flushed crimson with embarrassment. He tried to find his voice, but it was lodged in his chest somewhere. All he was conscious of was the sweetness of her, the fresh, innocent vulnerability that she presented.

She watched with wide amethyst eyes, then said softly, "I didn't expect you back so soon."

He could only stare as a tightness began to coil inside. Suddenly he was consumed with a need to feel her against him, to hold her, to run his hands over the satin contours and explore every curve and hollow of that luscious, inviting form. His eyes met hers, and he felt his own needs answered in the smoky lavender depths.

"I finished sooner than I expected," he muttered, unable to move.

DeShea's mind was a whirlwind of disjointed thoughts. She knew she should move, should explain why she was here and not at dinner, why she was dressed in his shirt. What must he be thinking? She was stretched out on the bed in his clothes, barely covered, her hair in a tail, writing poems about her feelings for him. She tried to find some reproach in his eyes, but she could only see admiration and hunger.

He walked toward her, and she felt an undercurrent vibrate between them, something strong and hot that made her quiver in anticipation. Unable to wrest her gaze from his, she knew she should break the spell, stop the inevitable. It could only complicate matters between them. But she didn't want to. Couldn't. She wasn't strong enough, and she wanted it so badly. The reasons for saying no seemed insignificant when faced with the smoldering eyes caressing her, the raw masculinity, the promise of fulfillment in his arms. Even if the magic time was only one night in heaven, never to be repeated, better heaven once than not at all. To have someone care so much, even for a brief moment, was worth any price.

There was no way to throttle the hunger building within him. Nick felt as if he moved in a daze, slowly, not of his own volition, but compelled by some outside force.

DeShea looked young and romantic, a woman-child, so vulnerable, innocent, yet ripe for the love of a man. Her peach-hued skin glowed in the soft light as if she'd just scrubbed herself. Her hair was wispy strands of sunshine. The shirttail draped her sweetly rounded derriere, exposing her long slender legs and the sensitive arch of her foot. Her eyes were wide, limpid, yet he could read a trace of concern. He'd have to be careful, very careful. They could both be hurt by what was about to happen. And it would happen. He had no doubt. He knew it. She knew it. Both wanted it. Both needed it. Whatever the consequences, tonight would belong to some separate universe.

"Shea," he said softly when he stood beside the bed. She hadn't moved. Her elbows were still holding her up, her ankles were crossed in the air. He could see the rapid pulse in her throat now and the faint tremor on her lips. "God, you are so lovely. So incredibly lovely."

His words seemed to break the spell. DeShea sat up on the bed. She looked deep into his eyes. The brown depths were smoldering, stirring an intense heat in her center. As if in a trance, she watched as his hand moved toward her and gently traced the line of her jaw, then dipped down to caress the side of her neck. Her skin was aflame, and she held her breath, afraid the intoxicating feeling would vanish if she dared to move. His hand came to rest on her shoulder, and he eased her onto her feet, bringing her close against him.

The large shirt dipped low over one shoulder, and he caressed the bare skin with his eyes before pressing his lips against the firm flesh in a feather-light but lingering kiss. Then he raised his head and looked down at her while his fingers touched her face, her cheeks, as if inspecting a fragile piece of porcelain. The faint trembling of those long fingers, indication of her power over him, stole the strength from her knees.

"Shea, I want you," Nick murmured. "I've wanted you for so long." He looked into her eyes for the answer and felt her sway against him in reply. "If you don't want this, tell me now before it's too late."

His eager hands circled her back, exploring the sloping curves of her spine, the sweetly rounded behind, pinning her hips against his own.

Her answer was the slow entwining of her arms around his neck. With a grunt of hunger, he crushed her to him, his mouth devouring hers.

DeShea felt as if every nerve and vein in her body was burning, boiling with liquid desire. Nothing mattered but

the need to be in his arms, to feast upon the love he was offering and partake of the nourishment he gave.

She wanted to fill her senses with him. To taste him, touch
him and breathe in his scent. Her hands slid down his neck
and over his shoulders, urging the heavy suit coat from the
hard angles. He shrugged it off, holding her against him,
unwilling to let go even a fraction of an inch.

The need for air forced him apart from her, and he looked
into the purple eyes and saw a new DeShea. No Ice Princess, no young teenager, no vulnerable child. This was the
look of a passionate woman, a woman who wanted a man.
There were no restraints. She was coming to him eagerly,
simply, in the same way she offered her friendship.

He tugged at his tie, his impatience matched only by the
eagerness of DeShea's fingers as she worked the buttons on
his shirt. The belt was discarded, the slacks unzipped, then
he sucked in sharply as her warm hands slid under his shirt
and caressed the flesh beneath.

Quickly he discarded the remainder of his clothing and
turned his attention to the few buttons on the shirt she wore.
Never again would he be able to cover his body with that
garment and not think of how it sheathed hers. As the last
fastener was undone, he opened the striped fabric and took
his first look at her. He'd imagined her many times in his
mind, shamelessly picturing her breasts, but never had he
imagined such perfection. Full, rounded, with pink tips,
they stood proudly, invitingly. "You're more perfect than
anything I've ever dreamed."

DeShea knew the look in his eyes was worth whatever
penalty she might be forced to pay later. To have him think
her lovely, perfect, was the ultimate in happiness.

His lips covered hers with an urgency that fueled her own.
In one instant she understood the hunger, the longing she'd
been feeling. She'd wanted him, intimately, fiercely, in a way
that was frightening and exciting at the same time. Loving
Eric had been an easy, gentle joining. Her need for Nick was
like an open flame, bold and unstoppable.

He pressed her body against his and the feel of his hot length stole the strength from her limbs. She clung to his neck, grunting in satisfaction as his tongue filled her mouth, dancing over her teeth in a symbolic prelude to what was to come.

She felt a subtle shifting and the cool sheets against her back. His searing flesh was beside her and she turned toward him instinctively. Her fingers slid along the nape of his neck, burrowing into the thick dark hair that covered his skull.

Her body began the slow rhythmic undulation that knew its own source. Strong, incredibly gentle hands caressed her sides, venturing slowly upward and encircling her breasts. The anticipation was deliciously painful, and she arched toward him, inviting more intimate exploration. His thumb gently danced over her nipple, bringing it to aching fullness. She silently begged him to continue. Deft fingers teased the other breast until she felt sure she would explode with the pleasure.

DeShea gave herself over to his gentle ministrations, his tenderness unlocking doors long bolted shut by loneliness and insecurity. Her heart absorbed his love, soaking it in like a sponge, feasting upon it. This went beyond the needs of the body. He began to seep slowly into cold hollows of her mind and offer nourishment to a starving soul. But those chambers had been closed too long to throw wide the doors now. Still, she couldn't prevent him from warming the empty place in her heart as he showed her a new world of passion.

A fresh sensation drew a gasp from her passion-shrouded senses when he gently drew the sensitive tip of her breast into his mouth and slowly laved it with his tongue. She was mindless with the new sensations he was giving her, weak as a kitten, totally at his mercy. She could only writhe in the age-old rhythm of passion as the need for him swelled.

His tongue still teased her nipple, teeth nipping at the hard bud, while his hand moved downward, fingers probing her warm core. Shock and excitement pushed her near the precipice of release and she cried out his name, fingers digging into his back. He covered her body with his own, and smoothly parted her thighs.

There was no time to go slowly, their mutual need was too urgent, too out of control. He thrust inward and she soared off the edge of the world, suspended in air as he moved inside her, faster and faster, lifting her higher toward the sun, until finally it shattered and she was a hot, clear ray of sunshine, drifting earthward.

For the first time in her life she felt connected, a part of something. Her sense of being adrift, without roots, had been replaced with a feeling of completeness.

Later, cradled against him, she savored the feeling of wholeness, of belonging, that lingered in her heart. Somewhere, deep in the back of her mind, a small ray of hope was born that perhaps, just perhaps, Nick might be starting to care for her as much as she cared for him. A tiny voice tried to remind her that this feeling would never come again. It was only a temporary shelter, a brief respite from the real world.

Nick rolled onto his side, head propped on the heel of his hand and gazed into her eyes. "I've never known anyone like you before, Shea. You're like a small sun trapped in a block of ice. On the outside you look crystal clear, smooth, unblemished and cool to the touch." His hand trailed up her arm slowly. "But on the inside you're hot, dazzling, a beam of sunshine that's so intense it frightens me."

She looked away, uncertain if he was bestowing a compliment or expressing his disapproval of her sexual abandon. His strong fingers gently urged her face toward him again.

"Who are you, Sunshine? What's going on in that little head of yours? I can never read your thoughts through your eyes. Why won't they talk to me?"

She wanted to tell him how confused she felt, how uncertain she was of what was ahead. Until now it had all been a fantasy played out in her heart and mind. But the reality of being in his arms had changed everything. "Words don't come easily to me," she said softly. "Especially now."

"Tell me what you're feeling," he whispered, his hand caressing her neck.

If only she could find the courage to say the words, to release that final hold her mother seemed to have and tell him what she was feeling. "I don't know," she finally whispered. "I've never felt like this before."

"And how is that, Sunshine?"

Her mind raced through the words, trying to find the right one. Cherished, precious, fulfilled, complete, whole. But they all seemed too personal, too possessive. She might be unskilled in the ways of love, but she knew enough to understand that one night in bed didn't necessarily mean commitment. Finally she settled on the emotion that seemed to sum up all of her feelings at the moment. "Contented."

The warm sable color of Nick's eyes deepened as a wave of disappointment washed through him. He'd hoped for something more revealing, more personal. She might as well have said "satisfied." "Is that all?" he asked quietly, unwilling to accept that response.

DeShea traced his jaw with her fingertips, then touched his chest. She quivered at the sensation she felt. For her, actions always spoke louder than words. Her hands strayed lower. She couldn't say what she felt but she could show him, let him draw his own conclusions. She pressed herself against him and sought his mouth, tongue invading, seductively expressing her desire the only way she knew how. Surely he would understand. Her hands skimmed his torso and slid down to his aroused manhood, and she felt him respond.

Nick wanted to hear her answer, wanted to hear the words. But she pressed against him and the need for her blocked out all other considerations.

The loud ringing of the phone ended the blissful evening, and Nick reached over and lifted the receiver. "Yeah."

He glanced at DeShea and mouthed the name Danny, smiling when he saw her blush. "Got done a little early... Aunt DeShea? She's in bed." He grinned wickedly. "Yes, she's feeling much better now. An evening in bed did wonders for her.... Okay. See ya soon." He cradled the phone and said, "He's on his way back."

"What will we tell him?" she wondered, her lavender eyes filled with concern.

"I don't think we need to tell him anything yet, until we have a chance to make sense of this," he said, fingering her soft hair.

DeShea rested her hand against his cheek, feeling the scratchy stubble against her palm. "Yes, I suppose that's best."

He kissed her lips gently, then said, "We'd better get dressed. Danny called from the Hard Rock Café. They'll be back in about forty-five minutes."

She watched as he gathered up his clothes, then disappeared into the bathroom. As she collected her nightgown and robe, she reluctantly hung his shirt back in the closet. He hadn't said anything about her wearing it. Perhaps he hadn't noticed. Now that reality was settling in, she was plagued with doubts.

Nick came up behind her and gathered the golden locks in his hands, lifting them to allow his mouth access to the soft nape of her neck. His kisses were lingering, and she felt the subtle coilings begin in her center.

"Why didn't you go to dinner tonight?" he asked softly.

"I wanted to be alone. I had some things to think over."

"What things, DeShea?" he asked softly.

"Just things." Should she tell him the truth, that she wanted to sort out her feelings for him? She wasn't sure she could say the words even if she wanted to. "Danny," she finally answered.

"What else?" he urged gently.

Steeling herself, she replied, "You."

Chapter Eleven

It looked as if it was all over. United Thunder would be going home. The French team was proving to be a fearsome adversary and was ahead of Baton Rouge seven goals to one. Faster, rougher and brutally physical, the opposing team had already sent two Thunder players to the bench with injuries. DeShea watched anxiously from the bleachers as the game wound down. There was only eight minutes left and then it would be over. She had to admit, she was eager to get her nephew off the field. One of the players from the other side had been particularly bad about shoving and tripping. As she completed that thought she waited in horror as that same player threw his body into her nephew's. Hit from behind, Danny sailed into the air, landing hard on his stomach. He didn't move.

DeShea's anger had been building during the course of the game, but now it exploded with the power of a nuclear blast. Suddenly she was filled with an all-consuming fury, with a fierce blinding rage directed at the boy who had deliberately hurt Danny. Unaware of her actions she rose from her seat and stomped out of the bleachers. She was on the ground preparing to walk onto the field before she realized what she was about to do. Sanity returned with cold chilling clarity, and her face filled with scalding humiliation. She had actually wanted to hit the child, to do physical harm to him. The magnitude of her anger horrified her. There was no way she could justify this kind of behavior. Nothing in her life had prepared her for it. To lose control so thoroughly that she wasn't even aware of doing it, to lust for revenge with such intensity was abhorrent to her.

So consumed was she with self-loathing that she didn't see Nick approaching until he touched her shoulders. "He's all right, Shea. Don't look so terrified. He just had the wind knocked out of him."

She was unable to speak around the relief that roared through her. Nick smiled and turned her around, gently urging her back toward the bleachers. She moved, but away from the spectators and toward the parking lot.

The sight of Nick had brought something else into focus for her. The only other time she'd lost total control over her emotions was with Nick. Passion had consumed her then, the way rage had just now.

Nick had been right about her. She wasn't suited to family life. Her behavior now proved that. Surely these extremes were unhealthy. Her unwarranted hatred of the other young player was unforgivable. Thank God she'd stopped herself before she acted upon that instinct. But what if she couldn't control it next time? Or worse, what if it was directed at Danny and she didn't stop as she had today?

Marette would never have done this. She'd been an exceptional wife and mother. So what did that make DeShea?

A chorus of shouts distracted her from answering that question. The game was over and the boys were coming off the field.

Nick was gathering the parents together. DeShea joined them but stayed in the background, only half-listening as

Nick gave his farewell speech. While their win-loss record was a good one for such a large tournament, they had not done well enough to advance to the next level.

As the parents and boys dispersed, several of them stopped to speak to DeShea. She just wanted to be alone, but that was impossible at the moment. So she called up her business face and went through the motions anyway, for Danny's sake. But her demeaning behavior festered in her mind throughout the evening, preventing her from enjoying the party the team had put together.

When they finally returned to the hotel room, she kept her mind occupied by gathering up clothes and packing for the trip home. She couldn't wait to get back. Maybe there, in the cozy house, things wouldn't seem so horrible. Her newest fear was that she'd be forced to stay away from Danny in case her rage took hold again. The mere thought sent shock waves through her system. If she could hang on until bedtime, when it was dark and she was alone, then she would find a way to come to grips with it. But right now she had to stay busy and keep her mind on fundamentals.

Turning to Nick, she asked, "What time do you want to leave in the morning?"

"Between eight and nine, I guess," he replied, tucking the player passes into his binder. "That'll put us back in Baton Rouge around suppertime tomorrow night."

DeShea picked up one of Danny's shirts and started to place it in his satchel.

"Oh, I forgot to tell you—" Nick grinned sheepishly "—Danny's not going home with us. He's going to spend the rest of the week here with the Langloises. They're going to do some sight-seeing. You know, take in Six Flags, visit Fort Worth, maybe go to a Sidekicks' game. Frances asked me earlier today if he could go, and I said it was okay."

She nodded and put the shirt back on the chair. For an insane moment she wondered if Nick had guessed her guilty secret and was trying to keep Danny out of her way. She dismissed that idea immediately, but the thought did little to ease her concern.

Nick watched as DeShea drew the cool marble shell around her again. He felt as if someone had punched him in the gut. Damn the woman. Why wouldn't she talk to him? He didn't think he would ever understand DeShea the way he had her sister. Marette had poured her heart out to him, told him things René hadn't known. She had worn her feelings on her sleeve, and those she kept inside were still accessible with a little persuasion. But DeShea, she kept her feelings in cold storage. How was he to interpret the icy indifference that had come over her once again? Did it mean she was unaffected by everything? Was she angry? Hurt? Pouting? Was she playing coy and trying to get him to coax her to talk? Well, if that was her game, she was in for a long wait because he intended to ignore her.

He even managed to do it. For about an hour. Then he looked over at her and saw the wisteria eyes filled with sadness. He couldn't ignore her any longer.

Walking over to the sofa, he sat down beside her, his fingertips brushing her arm lightly. "What's wrong, Sunshine? Homesick?" he asked, taking a stab in the dark.

DeShea looked into his warm brown eyes and for a fleeting second thought of telling him the truth. But she didn't. It was safer to let him think he had guessed the reason for her withdrawal. "A little."

"Did you enjoy this trip?" he asked.

"Yes. Very much."

When she fell silent again, Nick tried a more direct approach. "You've been so quiet and thoughtful all evening. What are you thinking about?"

She wanted to tell him, wanted to believe he would understand. Maybe if she told him part of it, just to see what his reaction would be. "About that last game with France," she finally answered. "I had some feelings, some...strong feelings that I've never felt before."

Nick smiled. "I know. So did I."

"You did?" Her heart swelled with hope.

"Yeah, when the two teams posed together under the Baton Rouge banner and then started to cheer for each other... Man," he said softly, shaking his head in wonderment. "I think the spirit of the whole tournament came together for me in that moment. Thirty boys, from two different countries, all pursuing a common purpose—to play soccer, just for the love of the game. It makes you believe in the future."

DeShea swallowed her disappointment. He didn't understand. She, too, had been moved by the sight he described. But that had been before the game. Her problems had surfaced later. "Yes, it was a very special moment."

"I'm glad we were accepted for this tournament. It's a chance of a lifetime for these kids. The experience they gained here couldn't have been attained in six seasons in Louisiana. How many boys can say they played Mexico and France, or even that they participated in the Dallas Cup? This is something they'll remember for the rest of their lives."

DeShea wouldn't have spoiled the joy in his brown eyes for anything. Especially not by asking him to deal with her inadequacies. "I'm glad I came," she recited.

"So am I." He leaned toward her, his intentions clear, but the sharp click of the door lock jerked them apart. Danny was back.

Later, as she lay in the protective darkness, DeShea relived again her shameful behavior. Only now when she replayed the emotions, they didn't seem quite so violent. The horror had faded.

The doubts, however, still bubbled below the surface, ready to greet her on awakening. Leaving Danny behind with the Langloises the next morning didn't help, either. She brooded all the way to the Louisiana state line.

DeShea's silence had steadily eaten away at Nick, so that he felt a series of emotions. At first he was understanding.

He'd seen the moisture in her eyes when she said goodbye to Dan, and it pleased him to know she was going to miss the boy. When her silence dragged on, he told himself she was probably tired. It had been a long, crazy week and a whole new experience for her. Now that it was all over she was undoubtedly exhausted.

But when a second hour of silence wore on he began to take it personally. Since he couldn't think of a thing he might have said or done that would have created such a state of wintry isolation, this thought roused his anger.

When the anger passed, and it passed quickly, he remembered something she had said to him: *words don't come easily to me.* At the time he'd thought she meant at that moment, after their lovemaking. He'd felt a bit overwhelmed himself. But what if she had meant all the time? What if she meant she had trouble expressing herself—the way Dan had for a while after Marette's death?

He glanced over at her and knew he had to at least try to get her to open up and talk to him. Only where did he start? He still didn't know how to approach her when she reverted to being the Ice Princess. Maybe if he stuck to safe topics and saw where things went from there...

"Are you hungry? We'll be in Shreveport soon, and it's our last chance to eat for a while."

DeShea turned to him briefly but refused to meet his eyes. "Yes, that would be fine."

So much for that topic. Maybe something a little more personal would draw her out. "I think Marette would be pleased to know you were here with Danny in her place. She loved to travel with the team, loved watching Dan play. I think she was Thunder's biggest fan." He smiled over at DeShea, relieved to find she was at least listening to him. "She really got caught up in the game. She was like a one-woman cheering section. I'd never seen anyone with so much enthusiasm."

DeShea realized Nick was attempting to draw her into conversation, but his words had the opposite effect. Marette had been enthusiastic, a cheerleader for the team, not an enraged animal intent on harming a child. Marette understood children and what was needed to raise them. She'd been born to it. Fate had not blessed her little sister with the necessary intuition for that task. Nick had said Marette would be happy DeShea was in her place. But he was wrong. She could never fill Marette's shoes.

Nick didn't have to see DeShea to feel her withdrawing inside herself even more. Impulsively, he reached over and took her hand, trying to keep her from slipping farther away. "Shea, what is it? What's bothering you?"

She shook her head. "Nothing."

"Shea, talk to me. I know something is wrong. I can feel you shutting yourself off from me. Whatever it is, I'll try and understand." He squeezed her hand encouragingly. "Please."

DeShea felt the warmth of his hand and the strength behind it. Should she risk admitting her disgraceful feelings and ask for his help? Would he understand? Or would he be repulsed and horrified and decide she was unfit to remain with him and Danny?

Nick saw her uncertainty and pressed his advantage, filling his voice with all the reassurance he had. "You know, I'm pretty experienced with a wide range of problems. Most of my life has been spent sorting out other people's messes. I don't think there's anything new you could throw at me that I haven't dealt with before."

Was that true? Had he run across this sort of thing before? She held on to his hand a little tighter, trying to draw courage from his strength and kindness. Dared she risk it? Should she jeopardize what progress they'd made?

She thought back to the night Nick had held her while she cried, releasing her long-buried resentment toward Marette. It had felt good to get that out in the open. It would be a relief to unload this burden as well. She looked over at him and he smiled.

"Sunshine?"

Taking every ounce of courage into her hands, she made the first step. "Yesterday, when Danny got hurt . . . I . . . got very upset." It was harder than she imagined.

Nick waited patiently, his thumb rubbing the back of her hand, with steady reassurance.

"It was more than upset. I got . . . I felt angry at that boy."

"You mean the one who tripped him?" he asked quietly.

She nodded, then tilted her head back against the seat as it all came tumbling out. "He did it on purpose. I saw it. And then Danny was on the ground, not moving. I was furious. No, I was inflamed with rage. I wanted to take that boy and shake him, rip his vicious heart out. I even jumped off the bleachers to go after him. Then I realized what I'd been about to do and stopped."

Inhaling deeply, she continued. "I've never, ever felt such blind rage. It was terrifying. I didn't know I had such intense feelings. I don't understand where it came from. But I know it was wrong, and I know it's dangerous. It's something Danny shouldn't be exposed to."

She closed her eyes and waited. The die was cast. What would the result be? She expected many reactions—a soft chuckle wasn't one of them. Her eyes flew open, and she turned to Nick as he picked up her hand and pulled it over to kiss it.

"Sunshine, don't be so hard on yourself. You've just experienced the same fierce emotions every mother feels when her child is injured or threatened."

"No," she replied, afraid to believe the gentle understanding in his eyes. "This was insanity, unhealthy. . . ."

"And perfectly normal."

She couldn't accept it. "Marette would never have reacted that way."

Nick's laughter reverberated through the van. "Shea, I've seen your sister so mad over a bad call by the ref that she was absolutely livid. And the call didn't even involve Dan. A couple times she even got red-carded for harassing the ref and got thrown out of the stands."

She tried to absorb that. It seemed in character for Marette, but arguing with a referee wasn't the same thing as wanting to hurt another player. "No, you don't understand the way I felt."

"You wanted blood," he said casually. "You wanted to grab that kid and punch his lights out, then give him a swift kick on his backside, maybe take out a few teeth for good measure."

He really did understand and he wasn't the least bit shocked. "You've felt that way?"

"You betcha. All the time. It's the mother lion syndrome. Protect the cub at all costs."

Surely it couldn't be that simple. Could it? Didn't there have to be more? "But it was such an overpowering anger. What if I got that angry at Danny someday? What if I couldn't stop? What if . . ."

Nick squeezed her hand. "Did you follow through on your intentions? Did you attack the boy?"

"Almost. I wanted to."

"Did you do it?"

"No."

"Then there's your answer. That's what makes the difference. Knowing when to stop. Kids will do some incredibly dumb and irritating things. And they usually pick the day you feel least like dealing with it. Sometimes you want to just sell them to the first Gypsy wagon that rolls by. But you love them too much, so you don't. Because you also know that the next minute they'll do something so sweet that your heart will melt." Nick could see DeShea pondering that idea. "Give yourself some time. You'll get used to all of this."

"I don't think I'll ever get used to seeing Danny knocked down and pushed by those bigger boys. I was hoping his team would lose that last game. I wanted him off the field. I hate this game. It's too rough. Maybe . . . maybe you shouldn't let him play. He should concentrate more on his schoolwork. I still wonder about him missing tests."

"Select soccer was Dan's idea, Shea. Not mine, not his parents'. He really loves it. He's talented and eager to learn. He's too dedicated and too serious to be satisfied with a rec team where the kids don't care if they win or lose. He wants to be good, he wants to improve, and he works at it, hard. He's a very competitive kid, and he's playing where he'll be happiest and where he'll learn, develop."

"He's so small compared to the other boys. He could get hurt."

"Yes, he could," Nick agreed, "He could get hurt at school or on a Boy Scout trip, too. But it's part of growing up. You can't lock kids in a bubble and keep them safe until they're grown and then turn them loose. How will they learn to deal with the real world? They have to adjust to the ups and downs as they go along. All parents can do is be there to pick them up when they fall and point out the right direction when they get lost." He glanced over at her. "Danny means everything to me. I promise you I won't place him in jeopardy."

"Not deliberately, but . . ."

"I know there's a lot that you don't understand about Danny and how I handle things, but that's because you're working without the whole picture. Your perspective is hampered by ignorance. I don't mean that unkindly, but it's like coming into a movie in the middle. It won't make much sense if you don't know what the plot is all about. As for his schoolwork, I can assure you Dan's a solid A and B student. I'll show you his report card. This thing with English is just a personality problem with the teacher that we've been working on all year. It'll be all right. I promise."

Obviously she had a lot to learn about raising kids. "I just get scared when I see him out there with the other boys. Whenever he falls, I feel my blood turn to ice, my knees buckle. Seeing someone I love hurt—" she took a deep breath "—it's a terrifying feeling."

"What makes you think I don't feel the same way?"

She looked at him sharply. "You do?" He'd seemed so cool and unruffled by the whole thing.

"Of course. It's not a new sensation. A parent feels that way each time their child falls learning to walk, bumps its head, cuts a finger or scrapes a knee. It's part of the job."

"How do you stand it?" Her voice was laced with bewilderment.

Nick smiled. "You learn to put things in the proper perspective. You develop a type of detachment."

"I don't know if I could do that. Danny is all that I have."

Nick looked over at her, his dark eyes warm and intimate. "You have me."

"I do?" she asked breathlessly as a glorious warmth invaded her heart.

"Yes, of course. We're family."

Bitter disappointment prevented her from responding.

The house was strangely empty when they got back, and Danny's absence was acutely felt. The comfortable rapport they'd shared on the long ride home was gone, replaced with awkward tension. It was as if that couple who spent the night together in Dallas had been someone else, not the real Nick and DeShea.

After a hastily mumbled excuse, DeShea retreated to her room and unpacked, hoping the mindless routine would help her gain some insight into the way things were supposed to be between them now. How did one act after sharing a man's bed? Casual? Seductive? Or did one merely ignore it? She lingered in her room much longer than necessary until she realized that her continued absence would only aggravate the situation. Gathering up her courage, she returned downstairs to find Hugh seated in the living room. The sight of his friendly face was wonderfully welcome.

"Hi, DeeDee," he said, rising and coming to give her a big hug. "Welcome home. Did you survive the tournament?"

He released her hand, and she sat on the edge of the sofa near Nick. "Yes, of course. I had a wonderful time."

Hugh's eyebrows rose skeptically. "You're kidding, right? Nick paid you to say that."

"No." She smiled and shook her head. "Really. It was fun."

"Nah, I'm not buying this," Hugh scoffed. "No one could have fun in Dallas for five days surrounded by a hundred teams of sweaty, dirty, obnoxious boys. Uh-uh. Not on your life."

"But I did," she insisted.

"Shea was the official team interpreter," Nick said proudly. His eyes smiled over at her.

Hugh's eyebrows climbed higher at the nickname and his brother's possessive attitude, but he didn't comment. "Oh, yeah? This I gotta hear." He settled back in the recliner, instructing them to fill him in on the trip.

When Hugh left, the awkwardness that had been present earlier had been replaced with a strange sense of familiarity. Nick walked DeShea back to the living room, one arm resting comfortably around her waist. "You really did enjoy this trip, didn't you?"

"Yes, I did, and I think I've found a whole new career."

"Linguistics?" he guessed.

She nodded and smiled at him. "They were all so cute trying to swap those shirts. I didn't know I had a talent for bartering."

He turned her against his chest. "Care to do a little bartering with me?"

DeShea looked up into his beautiful brown eyes and felt the air leave her lungs. He was so dear, so wonderful, and she loved him so much. She knew she was on a dead-end street but there was no way to turn back now, either. This glorious feeling of belonging, of being loved would never come her way again, and she was going to immerse herself in it as long as it was available. She wanted him to love her, body and soul. He only wanted one part of her. But for now that was enough.

"What are we bartering for?" she asked.

"Something personal," he whispered against her ear. "Intimate."

His hot breath on her neck stole all coherent thought from her mind, and she swayed against him, inviting his kiss. When he captured her mouth, she gave herself over to it with relish, greedy for the taste of him.

Time became meaningless. Existence was the touch of his lips. Reality, the strength in his arms. She didn't even realize she needed air until Nick released her and smiled. Slowly he guided her down the hall and into his room, keeping her hand firmly in his as he stretched out on the bed.

DeShea wasn't sure where the thought came from, probably from somewhere deep in her subconscious. But one minute she was lost in the heady world of Nick's seductive gaze, the next staring fearfully at the king-size bed. What surprised her most, however, was that Nick was able to read her mind. "Shea, this is my bed. Not Marette's. Her furniture is in storage."

She sighed in relief. "I'm sorry. That was silly."

"No, not at all. Come here." He pulled her down beside him and held her close, one hand stroking her hair gently. "I know we need to talk, to find out what's happening, but when you're so close, my common sense disappears and all I have are feelings and needs. I want to love you, Shea."

His hand came down to rest tenderly against the side of her neck. His thumb stroked the throbbing column as his eyes probed deeply into hers. "Your eyes remind me of wisteria, soft and moist and dreamy. I like that color. But when you're annoyed or disapproving they turn a dark purple, like a summer storm cloud and I want to run for cover."

DeShea smiled and placed her fingertips on his bottom lip, tracing the sensuous fullness lightly. "I don't want you to run."

"Good." He smiled, pulling her close. "Because I like you this way—soft, sweet and fresh, like sunlight in my arms."

His sweet words were almost as erotic as his touch. She encircled his neck with her arms, pulling him down to receive her kiss. His lips set off an explosion of desire, fierce and hot and so overwhelming it frightened her. She'd never wanted —*needed*—anyone this much in her life.

Nick felt the surge of desire engulf him and struggled against it, gently releasing her hungry lips and cradling her face in his palms. She whispered his name, but he hushed her into silence. "I know, Sunshine. I know. But I want to go slowly. I want to savor every morsel of you, memorize every inch of your lovely body." He felt her shudder with the intensity of her need and caressed her cheek. "Relax, enjoy. Let me show you the way."

He touched her lips with his feather-light kiss, then moved on to her eyes and forehead. He burrowed his fingers into her golden locks and cradled her scalp, tilting her head back to taste the slim line of her throat. She clutched his arms, then slowly began to relax as he persisted in this slow, gentle exploration.

She was hypnotized, so fully under the spell of his kisses that she was hardly aware of her blouse being removed or her skirt unfastened. Her hands moved as if by instinct, blindly seeking the buttons on his shirt. Her palms slid up his warm torso, her fingers skimming through the thick, coarse hair that covered his broad chest. Her body arched against him, the churning need deep within her beginning to swell again.

A smile formed in Nick's eyes as he watched DeShea's desire ebb and flow like a raging tide. She was a passionate little sunbeam, dazzling and full of sparks. But he wanted to teach her the pleasure of restraint, how to savor the sweet sensation they could give to each other.

Their first night together had been urgent, almost desperate. The long-pent-up tensions that had grown between them over the weeks had needed to be released, their sudden and surprising feelings for each other to be met and addressed. Their joining had been an explosion of great longing.

This time he wanted to reach inside, to touch the inner woman, the one who held the intense passion he'd experienced in her arms, the one she kept deeply buried except in the throes of passion. If he could release that woman, bring her forth into the daylight, then he was sure there was a future for them together.

DeShea felt the tightness in her center grow with each caress, and she pressed against him eagerly. She urged him closer but he drew back, a smile curling one side of his mouth.

"Shh..." he whispered in her ear, easing her onto her back, speaking softly, steadily turning down the bright yellow flame of desire to a low, smoldering blue heat. Then he gently took her wrists and drew them upward beside her head. Immobile, and unable to touch him, she whimpered, but he silenced her with a kiss—a slow, sensuous inspection punctuated with teasing thrusts from his tongue. She gave herself over to him eagerly.

Nick turned his attention to her throbbing temples, kissing each one in turn gently, lingeringly. Her eyes were next, her cheeks, the moist corners of her parted lips, then the sensitive underside of her jaw.

Hypnotized by the new sensations, she could only savor the delicious feel of his lips as he explored. He dallied over her neck and throat, tasting each pulsating inch, then moved lower, over the firm mounds that thrust upward, urgent for his attention. He teased the edges, kissing the soft undersides but deliberately avoiding the tender tips.

DeShea moaned as the slow torment stoked the smoldering fire inside to hotter flames. His tongue flicked over her nipple, and she gave a cry of pleasure. She tugged at her arms, but he held them firmly in his hands.

His wet tongue moved languidly over its prize, then bestowed the same gift on its eager mate, drawing it deeply into his mouth.

DeShea found the anticipation almost unbearable as he worked his way lower. He shifted again, keeping both wrists in one hand now as he explored her rib cage and the slope of her stomach where it dipped between her hips. When his tongue gently urged her legs apart, her mind became a maelstrom of exquisite pain.

Even as her body opened to him, she felt her soul opening as well. The cold emptiness that had always lived inside her begin to warm and fill with glowing love for Nick. There was a flash of alarm in her mind, of trepidation at exposing a part of her that had been closed and vacant for so long, but the security and fulfillment she found in Nick's arms quickly dispelled it. She released that last fragile hold and opened herself wholly to him.

And in that instant Nick knew he was lost. There was no holding back now, no hope of restraining his need any longer. She became like liquid sunshine in his hands, bright, blinding hot and pure. He arched above her and heard her gasp out his name, and his mind exploded like a white-hot star. He plunged deeply into her molten center, reveling in the dazzling light and the innocence he found there. The depth of her emotion, of her passion, was profound and all-consuming. Then the sunlight engulfed them both, and they shattered into the air, a thousand burning rays of love.

When Nick opened his eyes, he was afraid the sunshine would be gone, but she was there, entwined with him, her golden hair a yellow tangle on his chest and between his fingers. Clear violet eyes gazed at him lovingly, and he felt a need to say the words he'd never said before. But he was confused, and questioned if it was because he cared or merely an aftermath of the special time they'd just shared.

"Talk to me, Shea," he said. "Tell me what you're thinking behind those deep-purple eyes." He needed reassurance that what they'd shared was more than just an exceptionally good sexual encounter. He wanted to know that she'd felt the same specialness he had.

Why couldn't she say the words to Nick? She'd said them to Danny and never even given it a thought. But with Nick she was tongue-tied, unable to speak her feelings for fear of rejection, for fear she'd fail at it the way she'd failed Eric. Resting her ear against his chest, she smoothed her hand over his stomach. "I'd rather just listen to your heart beating. It's such a wonderful sound."

Nick smiled and wrapped her more closely in his arms. "Aren't you glad Danny stayed in Dallas?"

"Oh, yes." She smiled sweetly. Did people who had this every day—the security and the closeness—realize how rare and precious a gift they'd been given? Did they know how lucky they were?

"We need to talk, Shea. To sort things out between us," he said quietly.

"Here?" she asked in anticipation.

"No!" he yelped with a grin. "I was thinking more along the lines of making some coffee and then snuggling on the couch. We won't get that opportunity when Danny is around."

"All right." DeShea rested her head on his chest, trying to hide her nervousness. It was confession time, and the thought was distressing. Talking about her feelings for Danny was one thing. They had a mutual desire to see him happy. But telling Nick that she loved him, that was different. What if he didn't feel the same way? But after tonight, Nick would expect some words—words she didn't know how to express. Where was she going to find the courage to tell him what he wanted to hear?

Nick saw her eyes darken and felt her slight withdrawal. He tried not to read anything ominous into it, but it still made him feel uncomfortable. "I'll grab a shower first. By the time you're finished, the coffee should be ready, okay?" He leaned over and kissed her, watching her eyes lighten. He smiled, then rose from the bed.

As the hot water pounded down upon him Nick began to feel the old worries creep back in. He was falling in love with DeShea. That night in Dallas, he'd thought he was lonely, thought he needed someone to hold, someone to make him feel connected. But he'd gotten more than he'd expected, much more than mere physical release. He'd been replenished.

The realization set off alarms in his head. He was asking for trouble if he let his emotions get any more entangled with DeShea. She wasn't his type. She was too private, too reticent. She kept her feelings shielded behind those violet eyes, never letting anyone see her emotions. If there was anything in her to share. He still had some doubts. True, she had adjusted to their lives better than he'd expected, helping around the house, becoming involved with the team, but it was all new to her still. What about the long term? Did she have staying power? Once she'd gotten her fill of family life, would she be anxious to shed the mundane and often thankless role? Was he willing to take such a risk?

But he couldn't shake the memory of how right they felt together. Maybe it was his imagination; maybe abstinence had distorted his recollection of what a night in a woman's arms was really like. Tonight in bed he'd had no doubts that she felt as strongly as he did. She was passionate and giving. He had felt closer to her, not just in the physical sense but spiritually. Yet she'd never said she cared, never admitted that her feelings were anything other than attraction. Maybe that was all it was. An affair, a nice romantic encounter while she visited Baton Rouge.

Somehow he couldn't bring himself to believe that. He didn't see her as a woman who took lovers carelessly. If only she'd said something, anything, to let him know their nights together were important to her, too. He wanted to believe she had strong feelings for him, feelings that went beyond mere sexual need. But she'd dismissed it as a mutual need of two lonely people without a hint of her real feelings about him.

He felt as if he were missing some vital part of the puzzle, the secret password that would open up DeShea's heart and let the words he wanted to hear emerge. He couldn't go on like this, not without some reassurance. He thought she was afraid to talk, but with a little patience he could change that. But what did he really have to go on besides intense passions in bed? Hell, maybe his male ego was just badly bruised. Yet he refused to accept that she didn't care.

There was, of course, the possibility that she didn't love him. Not enough to think of a future. But she did care for Daniel. Could he use her love for their nephew to further his own plans?

God, he must be desperate to even think of such a thing!

Turning off the shower he stepped out and dried himself vigorously.

After Nick left, DeShea showered and slipped on her jeans and shirt. As she fastened the buttons she tried not to let her fears get the better of her. What if she was reading more into Nick's attentions than he intended? Maybe it would be wise not to get her hopes up. It would just be asking for heartache. There were a million things in the universe she could have and a million things she couldn't. Nick could be one of the things she couldn't have.

Nick was spooning sugar into the coffee mugs when she came out into the kitchen. He looked up and smiled, and she felt her heart warm with love. He handed her a cup and then they walked into the living room and sat on the sofa. DeShea curled into his arms as if she were meant to be there.

Nick was silent for a while. Finally, he set down his mug and trailed his fingers along her thigh. "I'm glad you came to Baton Rouge, Shea," he said softly.

She looked into his eyes, her heart suspended in breathless anticipation for his next words. "Why?"

"Because you've become important to me. Important to both Danny and me."

For a moment, DeShea allowed herself to believe he was hinting at a future for them, that she'd finally found someone to love her, care for her, someone she loved in return. The old notion of being unloved, of being doomed to grow old alone, lifted, allowing the shining light that was Nick to seep through. Dared she believe it, or was it too soon? A chill touched her heart. It was too perfect.

"Don't go back to New York, Shea. Stay here, with us. Give us all a chance to work this out."

Her heart swelled, and she felt her courage rising. Now. Now was the moment to tell him, to set aside the fear and say the words. Yet they refused to come. "All right," she agreed softly.

"I want to settle that question of loneliness and attraction," he said softly against her hair. "There's a lot of things to consider and it'll take some time."

"I've got plenty of time."

"Promise me you won't go away," he asked, slipping his arms around her, and pressing her close against the length of his body.

"I'll stay as long as there is a reason for me to."

"I'll give you as many reasons as I can find. Starting with this." He captured her mouth, and sent the world fading into oblivion.

Chapter Twelve

Sunday morning dawned in picture-perfect spring attire. Bright sunshine, gentle breezes and crystal-clear blue sky. Certainly nothing ominous perched on the horizon to foretell the steady downward trend that was to come.

Thunder had two games scheduled for the afternoon, and Danny had been especially looking forward to them, since they were against the team's archrival, the Jackson Rangers. Thunder walked away with a 4–0 victory in the first encounter. The second game against the older boys was a different situation.

As the team took the field, DeShea stood with Ellen, the wife of Joe, the assistant coach. She felt a rush of pride when Danny assumed his position near the goal. He looked so grown-up, so mature in his uniform she couldn't help but smile. Even his attitude changed when he stepped on the pitch. He became serious, focused, and she began to understand what Nick had tried to tell her.

Danny was dedicated to the sport. He lived it and gave it his entire energy. It was the same attitude she'd seen in Natalie each time she walked into Clotilles. The look that said, "This is what I want and I'm willing to work at it." But where in Natalie it had seemed an obsession, with Daniel it was more like supreme confidence and the willingness to work hard to achieve his goal.

DeShea felt her heart swell with pride that her young nephew had such depth of character at so young an age. What a lucky child he was to have had such a secure and loving upbringing that he was, despite the tragedy in his life, so well adjusted and happy at thirteen.

When the whistle blew to start the game, her eyes went immediately to Danny and the player on the other team he was guarding. That boy wasn't particularly big for his age, but he was solidly built and there was a cockiness to his stance that brought the uneasy feeling back to DeShea's stomach.

As the game progressed, her concern grew. The boy obviously was spoiling for a fight. Twice he tripped Danny, and more than once he rammed an elbow firmly into Danny's midsection. The referee, however, was blind to the blatant fouls. When Danny was shoved to the ground, DeShea decided it was time to speak up. If the comments from the other parents were any indication, she was not alone in her opinion. The game was definitely getting out of hand. When the whistle blew for the half, she started toward Nick, but was forced to hold her tongue while he gathered his team and outlined his plan for the remainder of the game. Finally he dismissed them to get drinks, and DeShea grabbed his arm to claim his attention.

"You've got to take Danny out," she said firmly.

"What?" he said absently, his mind clearly tuned elsewhere.

"That boy is going out of his way to get Danny."

"It's a tough team," he admitted. "They're older, but it's something our guys will have to get used to. Next year they'll move up to under-sixteen and they'll have to learn to play with kids much bigger physically than they are."

"Nick, he's going to get hurt," she persisted.

"Shea, it's okay. I'll agree the ref has lost control. Jackson has always been a very physical team, but Dan will be all right."

"Nick, please. I have a bad feeling about this."

"Shea, not now, okay?" He patted her arm solicitously. "Don't worry. I'll take him out if it gets worse."

"Nick—"

"You're worrying over nothing. I know the situation better than you do." Turning his back, he walked away down the sidelines.

DeShea couldn't decide which emotion was stronger at that moment—her anger at Nick's bullheadedness or her mounting fear for Danny's safety. She felt edgy and nervous, like a tightly wound spring. Overlying everything was a tremendous dread, a sense of impending doom. Was this what being a mother was like? Did you agonize over your child's safety every minute, envision disaster at every turn?

Glancing around, she looked at the other parents. The men were strung out along the sidelines, watching and talking among themselves. Some were obviously unhappy with the officiating, and disappointed that Thunder was behind in the score, but none seemed overly upset. The women were clustered in little groups, some talking, some ignoring the game entirely, others watching, arms crossed in irritation, a few pacing the far ends of the field. One stood off by herself, a study in tension and concern, but none reflected the outright fear DeShea was feeling. Perhaps Nick was right and she was worrying for nothing. Her fears were born of love for Danny coupled with a lack of understanding for the situation. Apparently she'd just have to get used to living with the knowledge that Danny could break an arm or a leg. It happened to boys all the time, and they healed and went on, didn't they?

As the game progressed, DeShea's fears began to subside. Danny seemed to have found a way to handle the other boy's aggressiveness, and Thunder had tied up the score. While the parents cheered the tying goal, DeShea breathed a sigh of relief and walked over to the cooler to get a soft drink. She had turned to speak with one of the mothers when the woman's face paled and she uttered a stunned, "Oh, my Lord."

Turning to look, at first DeShea saw nothing. Then she noticed one of the boys was lying on the ground.

"Who is it?" she asked, but even before she heard the name, she knew. Nick was racing across the field toward the ring of boys. Dr. Martin, father of one of the Thunder players, followed on his heels.

DeShea felt an odd sense of detachment, as if she were watching the whole thing from a great distance. Someone near her asked someone else what had happened, and she strained to catch every word of the answer, unable to take her eyes from the prone figure of her nephew.

"I don't know. He went up to head the ball, turned around, and just dropped to the ground."

Frozen to the spot, DeShea didn't know whether to remain on the sidelines or go to the field. She wasn't aware of making the decision but suddenly found herself in the middle of the field, looking down at Danny. He was lying perfectly still, but was awake and looking at the doctor. Someone slipped an arm around her waist, and she vaguely recognized Ellen.

"He'll be all right," she told DeShea quietly. "They've sent for an ambulance."

While the comment was meant to be reassuring, the words only increased DeShea's fear. Dear God, it was more serious than she'd imagined. Her heart felt cold and her chest constricted. She wanted to go to Danny, hold him. But Nick was already there, holding his hand. The doctor was on the other side, checking his arms, legs and neck.

Time seemed to pass in spurts of activity between long moments of slow motion. When she looked up again, two uniformed men were joining the doctor, kneeling next to the boy and asking him questions that made no sense to De-Shea. Why would they ask him his name and where he was? What difference could it make? But when she heard Danny's reply to the question "Where does it hurt?" she felt a rush of fear that threatened to buckle her knees.

"My back."

All the horror stories about back injuries flooded her mind. She closed her eyes, praying Danny would be all right and that the injury was minor. When she opened them again, she felt as if her prayers were fruitless. The paramedics had slipped a cervical collar around Danny's neck and were securing him to a backboard.

As they carried him toward the ambulance, Nick came to her and squeezed her arm. "He'll be all right, Shea. I'll go with him in the ambulance. Joe, would you bring DeShea to the hospital? I'll see you there."

In a fog of fear, she moved wordlessly with the assistant coach, barely aware of the ride to Baton Rouge General. Inside the emergency entrance, DeShea was told she could not have access to her nephew since she was not his guardian. The next half hour stretched on for an eternity.

Finally a nurse entered the waiting room, searching the faces, until her gaze settled upon DeShea. "Are you Ms. Ballard? Come with me, please."

DeShea followed the nurse down the hall toward the examining room. "Danny's uncle thought you might like to wait with him."

She stepped through the electronic doors in time to see an orderly wheeling Danny's gurney in the opposite direction. The boy looked so frail and helpless that a shaft of panic lanced through her. Fortunately, Nick was at her side instantly with words of reassurance.

"It's okay. They're just taking him to X-ray."

"How is he? What's wrong with him? Is it serious?" She fired the questions at him anxiously.

"They don't know yet. But the doctor doesn't think it's serious. He's awake and lucid, and he can move everything. But they have to take X rays to make sure."

Holding her close to his side, he steered her back into the small examining room to wait. There was only one stool, but DeShea firmly refused Nick's suggestion to sit down.

For a long time neither one spoke, but the silence was more frightening to DeShea than any answers she might hear. So at last she asked, "How was he? Was he awake in the ambulance? Did he talk to you?"

Nick nodded. "Yeah. He was scared, but he talked a little."

"Did you see what happened to him? I looked away for just a moment and then he was on the ground."

"I'm not really sure," he said with a deep sigh. "I didn't see him get hit or tripped. He just headed the ball and started to walk back to his position, then all of a sudden he just collapsed."

"Was he unconscious?" she asked, biting her lip against the moan of fear that threatened to erupt from her throat.

"Yeah." Nick rubbed his eyes. "For a few minutes. He came to right after I got to him."

"Does he know what happened?"

"I don't think so. He said he just got this pain in his back and then..."

DeShea felt her stomach heave at the thought of what serious back pain could mean, and her terror made her speak without thinking. "You should have taken him out. I told you this would happen."

"It was an accident," Nick replied calmly, but his voice was thick with worry and fatigue. "It had nothing to do with that boy."

"Are you sure?"

"He said no one pushed him."

Memories of the fall he'd taken in Dallas pushed Nick's attempts at reassurance out of her mind. "I hate this game. It's too dangerous for someone his size."

Nick was in no mood to pinpoint blame right now. Turning, he walked to the door, looked down the corridor for some sign of Dan, then checked his watch. It had only been ten minutes. Too soon to expect him back.

"I knew something was going to happen." She thought back to another time she'd had this queasiness, the sense that something bad was going to happen. The next day Marette had left.

Nick felt a mounting irritation. He didn't care about DeShea's premonitions at the moment. All he could think about was Daniel. He felt nauseated, and his nerves were pulled as taut as the strings of a tennis racket. He rested his hands on his hips, head bowed a moment before he replied. "No one could have predicted this."

DeShea felt suddenly shaky and weak and sought the comfort of the wheeled stool. It felt good to sit down but did little to alleviate her fierce concern for her nephew.

Nick paced the small room, looking at his watch again. Twenty-five minutes had passed. God, he was scared. Terrified. He tried not to even think of what the X rays might find. His mind kept replaying the sight of Dan being carried off the field on the backboard, the white collar cradling his neck. He refused to let the word *paralysis* settle in his mind. The possibility was too horrible to even consider.

Glancing at DeShea, he saw she was staring at her hands, nervously rubbing one palm with her thumb. He knew she was scared. Her eyes were a dull lavender and wide with fear. He knew he should be offering her comfort and reassurance, but he was too scared himself. He wanted to help her, but he was too burdened with his own fears to reach out to her now.

The hands on the wall clock seemed frozen in place. DeShea had looked at them three times and they'd barely moved. Why didn't the doctor come back? What was taking so long? She'd had X rays before, and they'd never taken forty-five minutes. Had they found something wrong? Something serious? Had they taken him into surgery? Was his back broken? Her heart had squeezed into a compact ball that was barely beating, or so it seemed.

Danny had to be all right. He was too precious, too wonderful a child to be struck down now. He was so energetic, so mobile. The word *paralyzed* seemed to loom over her thoughts like the blade of a guillotine. This couldn't be happening to her again. Danny was the first person in her life who had loved her unconditionally. Why was he being punished for loving her back? She didn't want to believe that she was jinxed, but why else would everyone she loved be taken away? Her eyes stung and she fought back the tears. She shouldn't even think about that until the doctor came back.

"Mr. Couvillion." Nick and DeShea both turned as the doctor came into the room, followed by a gurney bearing the smiling Daniel.

"Nothing to worry about," he announced firmly, smiling down at the boy. "Nothing broken or even out of place. Our soccer star just zigged when he should have zagged and gave himself a nice case of myalgia."

DeShea gasped and reached for Danny's hand.

The doctor grinned and spoke before Nick could. "He pulled a muscle, that's all. He's going to be real sore for a while. But he'll be back on the field in no time."

"When can I play again?" Dan asked.

"I'd stay out for at least a week, maybe ten days, depending on how you feel. Just follow all the instructions I'm going to give you."

"Does that mean he can go home?" Nick asked, ruffling Danny's dark hair affectionately.

"Usually, I'd say yes, but since he was unconscious briefly I'd like to keep him here overnight just for routine observation. You can come and get him tomorrow. I'll send in the nurse and she'll get him admitted." He smiled at his patient. "Take it easy, Pelé. Goodbye."

"Bye," Danny called as the doctor went out the door. Then he smiled over at his aunt and uncle. "He's a pretty cool dude. He told me he played soccer in college."

The thoroughly normal attitude of their young nephew was more reassuring to DeShea and Nick than any medical pronouncement.

It was nearly ten o'clock when they finally returned home. Once Danny was settled into his room, the Thunder team, along with parents and concerned relatives, had created a steady stream of visitors. The nursing staff had finally chased everyone away so the patient could get some rest.

The relief over Dan's condition was beginning to wane, to be replaced by fatigue and the emotional letdown that usually follows a crisis.

Nick and DeShea entered the house in silence. Nick walked directly to the refrigerator and pulled out a soda. "You want one?" he asked. His voice was raspy and strained.

DeShea shook her head, one hand massaging the stiff muscles in her neck. "No, thanks. I think I'd rather have something hot. Would you mind if I made some tea?"

"Help yourself." Nick retreated to the living room, scooped up the remote and punched on the TV. Lounging back on the couch, he stared at the picture, not really caring what was on, merely letting the familiar routine and dull drone ease some of the fragments of worry that clung to him. He felt old and bone tired, but profoundly grateful that Danny was going to be all right.

He didn't even want to think of how his life would have changed if the circumstances had been different. All he wanted at the moment was mindless oblivion, a chance for the terror of the afternoon to subside and the anxiety to dissipate. With any luck, a good night's sleep would put everything back into blessedly normal perspective by tomorrow. But he was still too wired to go to sleep. The vision of Danny in the ambulance, so helpless, his eyes wide and scared, his small frame looking so incredibly fragile, haunted him. He needed a few minutes to unwind, then he would shower and go to bed.

The sound of DeShea in the kitchen penetrated his thoughts, and he sighed inwardly in contentment. As soon as she had her tea, he'd pull her down beside him, and they would unwind together. No hanky-panky tonight, though. They were both too tired for that. But they did need a few moments to be close and take comfort from each other. The thought was so soothing he closed his eyes and imagined she was seated at his side.

DeShea took two sips of her tea and realized she was much too exhausted to finish it. What she really wanted to do was to talk to Nick and get his reassurance that Danny was going to be all right. The doctor and the nurses had all been confident there was nothing to worry about. Even Danny's brief unconsciousness had been dismissed. The overnight stay was strictly precautionary. Still, she felt this gnawing fear that complications might yet arise. It was silly. But Nick's calm presence would ease her troubled mind tremendously.

Draining the teacup into the sink, she sighed heavily with exhaustion. She knew she should go to bed, but she needed a few moments to come down from the emotional Ferris wheel she'd been riding on all afternoon and evening.

As she walked into the living room, she saw him sitting on the couch, eyes closed, TV murmuring softly in the background. He looked tired, his hair mussed from running his hands through it repeatedly. Worry still clung to his slightly slumped shoulders. She could feel his fatigue, his concern, his profound relief.

Her love for him began to swell from deep inside, intense and titanic. It spread throughout her body, filling her chest, clogging her throat, ringing in her ears. It bombarded her senses. She put her hand to her mouth. The magnitude of her love for Nick was terrifying.

How was it possible to love someone more than your own life—to feel his pain and his fear with such clarity that it became your own? This was ten times stronger than her anger in Dallas, her fear in the hospital. It was glorious and ghastly, heaven and hell at the same time. Why hadn't she known she loved Nick this much? She had known she was in love with him, cared for him very deeply but this... This was agony. She didn't think she could stand it. She'd never loved like this before. Not Marette, not Eric.

It hit her then. She'd loved Eric, but he had left her for someone else. She'd loved Marette, but that hadn't kept her sister from leaving.

Love meant loss. It always had. She had thought her love for Danny was the one relationship that was untouched by her past, that it was sacred and invulnerable. But tonight proved that it couldn't be counted on either. Danny could have died. She could have lost him the same way she'd lost Marette.

Nick could leave, too. What would happen when he did? Her stomach heaved at the idea. She couldn't lose anyone else. She couldn't live through that again. There'd been too many—too much heartache, too much pain.

Loving Nick the way she did, she'd never recover from losing him. She knew as surely as she breathed that she couldn't survive that. It would kill her.

She should never have opened her heart, never let go of that final hold on her emotions. She'd broken her rule and given Nick ultimate power over her. Now she'd laid herself open to more agony than she'd ever known.

Surely it would be better to leave now, to cut the ties while she still had the strength, rather than wait and lose him. She wouldn't survive that loss.

He'd find out the truth sooner or later. That she didn't understand love, that anyone who loved her was jinxed. Hadn't Danny's accident proved that? If she stayed here, something would drive Nick away, too.

She had to leave, now. She had to go back where she belonged and let Nick and Danny go on with their lives. It wasn't safe to love, not like this. Not for her.

She started across the room to the stairs and the safety of her room. She felt brittle, like a thin piece of glass. Every breath cut with a strange, painless precision.

As she passed behind the couch, Nick stretched out his arm toward her. She recoiled. She couldn't touch him now. She'd shatter into pieces.

"Shea, come and sit down. Relax a little," he said softly.

Her voice was paralyzed. It was all so achingly normal. The kind of scene she'd envisioned in her dreams every day she'd been in Baton Rouge. Those beautifully mundane moments when two people were so secure, so content that all they needed was each other. But when Nick looked over his shoulder, she retreated behind her shield.

Something in DeShea's eyes scared him. "What is it?"

She forced herself to move, to get away. "I'm . . . tired."

"I know." He smiled sympathetically. "Come here and let me help you relax. I can rub your neck and shoulders, okay?"

She moved toward the stairs.

"Shea, what's wrong?" He got up and came toward her, a feeling of dread starting to coil in his gut. She had her back to him, that stiff perfect posture that always characterized the Ice Princess. His stomach kicked in response. Not now. He needed her tonight. They needed each other. Didn't she understand? He needed comfort and reassurance. He needed her to hold him. Didn't she need it, too?

"DeShea?"

She would never know where she found the strength to face him. Maybe it was habit or training, maybe fear. "I'm going to my room." Whose voice was that? she wondered. Hers? It sounded so odd. "It's been an . . . unpleasant day."

Nick took a step backward, as if he'd been physically struck. Before his eyes, Shea had transformed herself into the Ice Princess. Red, boiling anger filled him. "Unpleasant? That's how you see what happened today?"

Visions of Danny lying on the field swamped DeShea. He had seemed so young, so small. Fear washed over her in waves. Danny had been her one constant, the one person in her life who had loved her without question.

"Damn it, DeShea. Answer me!"

Nick's loud command temporarily brought her back, but when she looked at him she felt the panic start again.

"What's the matter with you? Don't you have any emotions at all?"

Emotion? That was all she was made of now. Fierce, omnipotent scalding emotions. Where was the comfort of isolation? Where was that blissful void she'd lived in most of her life? It was cold and lonely but it didn't wound her like this. "I just want to be alone." She had to get away from him before she lost her mind.

A tidal wave of hurt and anger surged through Nick, leaving a loud ringing in his ears. She was doing it again, retreating behind the marble. It scared the hell out of him. He wanted to hit something. He'd shown her he could understand her fears and concerns if she'd only open up. He'd be damned if he'd fight that battle all over again.

"Shea, don't pull back now. Talk to me."

He felt so vulnerable, his emotions laid bare. He searched her face for some similar feeling, and for a fleeting second he thought he saw pain in her eyes, and he lunged for it. "Shea, don't hide. We need each other to get through this. Tell me what you're feeling. I want to understand but I need your help."

But all she could do was shake her head.

"Please, Shea." There was a tone of desperation in his voice. "Talk to me. Like you did in the car. Remember, huh? You were afraid of your feelings, but you confided in me and I told you it was all right. It was normal and you felt better. Talk to me now. Tell me what you're feeling."

What was she feeling? Love so strong it was like a million tiny knives slowly slicing each nerve. Fear so potent it was eating through her insides like a slow burning acid. She felt everything. She felt... "Nothing." She wasn't even aware she'd spoken the word aloud.

All the old perceptions erupted in his mind. "Damn! Can you really switch your feelings on and off so casually. Can you? Or don't you have any?" He gritted his teeth, and turned around, ramming a fist down on the back of the couch. "I thought I was getting to know you. I thought there was someone warm and exciting inside you and you were too scared to let her out. But maybe not, huh? Maybe all you have to give anyone is a few wild hours between the sheets. That's the only time I ever saw any honest emotions. Is that the big attraction here? I'm a nice little fling, no obligations, no strings attached?"

DeShea's face was an expressionless wall. A barrier he had no hope of breaching. He hurt like hell and there she stood, plunging a knife in his gut, twisting it slowly with her marble-statue appearance. "I don't understand you. You blow hot and cold, on and off, with every shift in the wind. One minute you're all sweetness and light. The next, an Ice Princess. Is there anything normal inside you?"

Normal. The word came at her through a haze. She had no idea what he meant. Normal was something she'd never known.

"Answer me!"

"I'm the way my mother wanted me to be." *Alone,* came the ancient echo from deep within.

Nick's eyes were black with fury and his lips pressed into a hard, thin line. "That's for damned sure. Now you know why Marette left. She didn't want to become what you are. Marette had a heart. All you've got is a block of ice."

Nick suddenly realized what he'd said, and clamped his jaw shut. Dear God, what had come over him? He didn't mean any of the horrible things he was saying. The unreadable mask DeShea had worn shattered for an instant, and he

saw pain lance through the violet eyes. The implications of
his angry words hit him. He was a bastard. All he was doing was making matters worse. All because he was too damn
tired to see straight. His mind was coughing up nothing but
irrational thoughts.

To DeShea, Nick's voice was like an arctic wind slicing
through the room. He was right, her heart had frozen, and
with each word he spoke small icy shards were being chipped
away.

She faced him then. Her head was throbbing, but she
looked him in the eyes and her voice was low and steady
when she spoke. "I am not Marette."

With what little composure she could find, she turned and
walked up the stairs to her room, shutting the door firmly
behind her.

Dazed and unable to grasp her meaning at first, Nick
stared openmouthed for a long moment until he could force
his body to move. But before he could top the stairs, she had
closed the door to her room with a final, silent thud.

Suddenly he was drained, thoroughly exhausted. He felt
one hundred years old. He went over the scene again,
struggling to make sense out of it, to understand why he'd
gotten so angry at her. But he was forced to give up. It would
have to wait. He couldn't think, couldn't focus. He ached
all over. He'd fix it tomorrow when they were both thinking more clearly, when their emotions weren't so distorted.
After they were rested and Dan was home, safe and sound,
everything could be looked at calmly and rationally. There
would be plenty of time tomorrow. Tomorrow.

Chapter Thirteen

DeShea followed the line of deplaning passengers without conscious thought. Her body might be in Atlanta, but her mind was still in Baton Rouge. She went through the motions of a live human being. She walked, talked and breathed, but she felt more like a mechanical doll. It had been like this since last night when Nick compared her to Marette. She'd spent all night packing and making plans. At 1:00 a.m. she called Howard and asked him to make arrangements for her in Galena. Then this morning as soon as Nick had gone to work, she left.

She'd stopped at the hospital to see Danny. He sounded wonderfully normal and much more upbeat than she'd expected. She told him she had to go back to New York but promised to phone and to have him up to visit. He tried to persuade her to stay, but she explained that she had to start earning a living and it would be more practical to do that closer to New York. It wasn't exactly the truth, but she didn't have the strength to tell him the real reason behind her decision.

At the airport she'd purchased a ticket, then made a quick call to Hugh. He'd been a good friend, and he deserved at least a brief explanation. He, too, tried to persuade her to stay, to at least wait and talk things over, but she stubbornly refused.

"Let me talk to Nick, DeeDee," Hugh offered.

"No. It wouldn't change anything."

"It might if you told him how you feel. What have you got to lose?"

"Everything," she answered.

"Then that means you've got everything to gain, too."

He didn't understand. She had to put some distance between herself and Nick. It was the only way to ease this pain.

"Destination?"

The red-jacketed ground attendant interrupted her thoughts, and she dragged her mind back to the present.

"Connecting flight?" the man repeated.

"Albany, New York, flight 563," she said flatly.

"Gate 18C. Have a good flight."

Blindly, DeShea Ballard walked down the concourse toward the plane that would carry her home.

When the dawn began to break, Nick gave up any further attempts at sleep. He'd been tossing all night in remorse, calling himself all kinds of names for letting his temper get out of control.

He'd never meant to hurt DeShea. The flash of pain he'd caused in her eyes haunted him. He would never forgive himself. He realized now she'd been as numb with shock as he was. There'd been a dazed look on her face, and her eyes had been that ominous deep-purple color.

But when the Ice Princess appeared he'd panicked. That glacier she hid behind made him crazy. He couldn't explain it to his satisfaction, but he knew he reared back like a threatened crawfish, claws snapping. The irony was that in the midst of it all he'd realized how much he loved her. How could he tell her he loved her after the way he'd acted? He'd accused her of not having any feelings, of being in his home purely for the sex. Shame inundated him.

He had to fix this, to make her understand that it was the fatigue and the lingering fear over Danny that had gotten control of his better judgment.

The house seemed unnaturally quiet as he climbed the stairs, his stomach churning with anxiety as he approached DeShea's door. Doubt was beginning to seep into his mind.

He stared at her door, listening for some sound from inside that would tell him she was up. It was almost a relief when only silence came back at him.

Seated in his car a few minutes later, he rationalized that it was just as well DeShea was asleep. She needed the rest. When he came home at noon they'd talk and then go pick up Dan at the hospital.

Most important, the delay would give him more time to sort things out in his own mind.

Nick knew the minute he stepped back through his front door that DeShea was gone. There was something stagnant about the air, an emptiness as if someone had sucked all the life out of the house. He didn't have to look in her room to know she'd left. But he did.

There was no note. Nothing left behind to explain her departure.

His immediate impulse was to go after her. He'd said things to her he didn't mean. If he could explain and ask her to forgive him... But he didn't know where she'd gone, and there was no time now to find out. He had to get Dan at the hospital first. Then he would figure out what to do about DeShea.

But as Nick navigated the heavy noon traffic on Airline Highway, hurt and disillusionment began to settle in. He pulled the cloak of righteous indignation around his male pride. How could she just turn her back on him? On

Danny? All the promises—to stay, to work things out—had been a lie. And now he saw why. The reason she didn't say *I love you* wasn't because of fear or insecurity, but because she simply didn't care. It had been easier to cut and run than to face him and admit she had no feelings for him or for anyone.

As he walked through the hospital toward Danny's room, he wondered how he was going to explain this to his nephew? How would he take the news that she was gone for good this time? How could Nick make him understand something he himself didn't?

Danny was unusually subdued when his uncle arrived, discouraging any attempts at conversation. Nick chalked it up to lingering aftereffects of the accident and proceeded to check him out of the hospital. They were barely out of the parking lot when Danny blurted out his complaint. "Why did you make Aunt DeShea leave?" he demanded.

"How did you know she'd left?" Nick shot back curtly.

"She came to say goodbye."

Great. DeShea explained to Daniel but not to him. It only confirmed where he stood in her estimation. "I didn't make her leave, Dan. She wanted to go."

"No, she didn't. She wanted to stay," he stated firmly. "She was going to start her new job. She said Baton Rouge would be a very inspirational place to write her stories."

"What stories?" Nick snapped, a deep frown creasing his forehead.

"You know, the ones that magazine wants to buy."

"What are you talking about? She never mentioned anything to me about writing."

"She told me about it," Danny said haughtily. "She even wrote a story about me and the soccer team. Writing was the only way she could say how she really felt. Her mom never liked her to talk about her feelings and stuff. She thought it was dumb or something."

"When did she tell you all this?" Nick asked, feeling as if he'd just come in to the last half of a movie.

Daniel thought a moment. "The day we were late for practice."

Nick suddenly remembered the day DeShea had told him her future might change. Had that been what she'd meant? That she'd sold her stories, not that she'd just made three million dollars? *Wonderful,* Nick thought to himself. Add another rung to his ladder of guilt.

When they pulled into the drive, Nick sighed in exasperation at the sight of Hugh's sports car. Apparently he wasn't finished making explanations regarding DeShea's sudden departure. His brother would not be satisfied until he had all the gory details. He managed to fend him off until Danny was settled in front of the TV and they could go to Nick's study to talk.

The moment the door was shut, Hugh let loose. "Just what in the hell did you do to DeeDee?" he demanded.

Nick suddenly felt like an outsider in his own home. "Why are y'all ganging up on me? I didn't leave. She did."

"What happened?"

"She left. Like a thief in the night, okay?"

"Why?"

"How the hell should I know?" Nick snapped, then felt instantly contrite. He was being unfair. He sat down in the chair and rubbed his forehead. "I was ragged out after that thing with Dan, and I . . . said some things I didn't mean."

"What did you say?" Hugh persisted.

Nick went over last night in his head, not certain he could explain. "We were both exhausted. I thought we could relax together, but she wouldn't talk to me. She shut that door in my face again, and I got angry." He looked up at Hugh. "Satisfied?"

"No. What door are you talking about?"

"You know, that wall of ice she ducks behind whenever she doesn't want you to know how she feels. *If* she feels at all."

"I've never seen it."

Nick scoffed. "That marble mask, that deep-purple glaze in her eyes. It sends chills up my spine."

Hugh studied his brother. "The only time I've seen her eyes like that is when she's scared or sad. Did you try and talk to her?"

"Yes, and I thought I was getting through." Nick sighed and took a few moments to measure his words before he went on. "Our relationship was just getting started. We'd barely gotten to know each other." Nick's conscience smarted at his own words. They made the relationship seem casual, meaningless. Reduced it to a few nights in bed. That was not how he meant it.

"Do you know where she went?"

"Probably back to Clotilles. It's all she really cares about," Nick acknowledged sourly.

"Maybe you should have tried harder to talk."

"I did. She wouldn't even admit she had feelings for me." Nick looked away, and Hugh shook his head. "Maybe she was telling you only you weren't listening. I know how you can get, big brother. You think you have everything figured out, that you know all the answers. I guess that's our fault for always coming to you with our problems, always looking to you for advice. But I think this time you missed the point entirely."

"The point is, DeShea ran back to New York without a backward glance. Now I don't know what sort of conclusion you draw from that, but it tells me she felt there was nothing here worth staying for."

"You didn't want her to go then?"

"No. I was falling in love with her," Nick admitted. He turned around, trying to sort out his confused emotions. Part of him wanted to find Shea and bring her back. But a stronger part of him was scared to take that step. If she could leave so easily, what sort of chance was there?

Hugh's expression softened. "Did you tell her how you felt?"

"I asked her to stay so we could work things out. What else could I have done?" Hands on his hips, Nick stared ceilingward. "You know that's the real irony. For the first time in my life, I find someone who listens to me, who advises me, someone who never asks for my opinion or advice. I could open up to her. She understood things about me and about my life that no one else ever has. But she couldn't talk to me."

"Maybe that's why," Hugh suggested. "Maybe she was more concerned with how you felt than how she felt. I don't think DeeDee deliberately kept things from you. She had trouble expressing her feelings. But she's a very giving person. She was probably so happy to be sharing your problems that her own were simply put aside. She'd have gotten around to talking about them. Sometimes it's the ones we love the most that we have the most trouble talking to."

Nick looked over at his younger brother. Had Hugh understood Nick's difficulty in talking to his family about personal matters? "If she cared at all she would have opened up to me. I gave her every opportunity. She should have trusted me."

"Maybe she was afraid."

"I've never done anything to make her fear me. Well . . . I've raised my voice a few times."

Hugh grimaced. "Your patriarchal roar, no doubt. Nah, that wouldn't scare anyone. Were you two—uh . . ." He wiggled his fingers and bobbed his eyebrows.

"That's none of your damned business."

"I thought so. Well, if DeShea felt strongly enough to do that, then she trusts you."

"What makes you such an expert?" Nick asked sharply. The thought that Hugh might know more about DeShea than he did didn't sit well with him.

"I wasn't in love with the lady. I'm not looking at her through a haze. I do know that with DeeDee you have to go by what she does."

"What about the words? I need to hear her say it." Running his palms over his scalp, Nick sucked in sharply. The hurt was like nothing he'd ever felt before. God, he must have some masochistic streak in him he'd never realized before. How else could he explain this new ability to inflict pain upon his heart by repeatedly trying to melt an Ice Princess.

"It's that damned deep freeze she retreats to," he growled. "I can stand anything but that. If she would just give me some sort of response, anything. Screaming at the top of her lungs, cussing like a sailor, even throwing things across the room. Good, honest emotions I understand. Tears, I can handle. Even outright disgust or rejection is something I can meet head-on and deal with. But the silence—" he exhaled loudly "—the tight-lipped impassible withdrawal. I can't fight that. How can we work anything out? How can I start to understand her if she shuts me out?"

"What about her actions?" Hugh pointed out angrily. "They should count for something, too."

"She never admitted any feeling for me at all. Even when we made...were alone. She *acted* like she cared, but she could never bring herself to say the words. How am I supposed to handle that?"

"Damn. You beat all, you know that?" Hugh snapped. "For someone who can see other people's problems so clearly, you sure are blind to your own." Hugh watched the play of emotions on his brother's face. "It was obvious from the start that you were the one she was interested in. I made a play for her big-time, but she just laughed it off. All she wanted to know about was you. DeeDee loves you."

"If she loved me she would have stayed and worked it out. She promised but she didn't keep her word."

"Go after her, Nick. Bring her back."

"I'm not sure she'd come."

"Don't you mean you're not sure you want her to?"

"I know that's what you think, but there's more to it than that. It's not only my feelings that are involved here, there's Danny to consider. She doesn't know the first thing about kids. Maybe if it was just the two of us, me and De-Shea..."

"You're crawfishing," Hugh grumbled, perching on the edge of the desk. "DeShea was great with Dan and he took to her right off."

"There's too many obstacles between us. We're all wrong. I can't get a handle on who she really is. One minute she's soft and sweet, like a little girl amazed with life. Sometimes she's more like a friend, sympathetic, thoughtful and wise. But whenever I try to get close she steps into this icy shell and hides, and I can't reach her. I tried everything I know. I can't fight that, Hugh. I've got to have some feedback, some communication. She keeps everything inside." He ran a hand through his hair in irritation.

"Marette was like an open book. She seemed to fit in to the family from the start. DeShea is so remote. She's an enigma. It just doesn't make sense."

"Makes sense to anyone with half a brain. Marette broke free. She found René, and all of us. She had nearly twenty years to adjust. DeShea has been under her mother's thumb for thirty years. But you expect her to learn to change in a month?"

"I don't know what I expected."

Placing a reassuring hand on Nick's shoulder, Hugh offered his advice. "I suggest you track her down and get her back here. You owe it to yourself and her to at least try and work things out."

"I want to," Nick said. "I really do, but I'm not sure it can be worked out."

"Then you're a bigger fool than I ever imagined."

Chapter Fourteen

As the weeks passed, Nick found he could forget neither Hugh's words nor DeShea. He tried to convince himself that it was best she was gone, but life in the house was different now. Nothing seemed as comfortable or as warm as when she was here. Even Danny was giving him the cold-shoulder treatment. At night he tried with little success to keep her from his dreams, and every waking thought centered on DeShea.

He realized he was in serious trouble when he found himself in her room one day, standing there staring like a zombie. Even after the weeks that had passed, the scent of her lingered in the air. But there was no other trace of her presence. The cleaning lady had erased it all. The closet was bare, the bath spotlessly sterile, the bed smooth and untouched.

His eyes came to rest on the nightstand and a silver pen that lay there. He didn't recognize it as one of his own. It must have been DeShea's. The cleaning lady probably didn't know what to do with it after she dusted, and so had just left it out. The sight of the pen brought back too many images, and he picked it up, preparing to drop it in the drawer. When he pulled open the drawer he saw the notebook DeShea frequently had had with her. He'd always assumed it held business notes. He knew now that she had been writing. His fingers trembled as he pulled the thick notebook from the drawer. Then he opened the cover and began to read.

When he finished the last entry he shut his eyes against the realizations that were bombarding his mind. He'd found the missing piece to the puzzle. It was all there. Everything he needed to know about DeShea. All the things she couldn't say aloud had been put down on paper. He'd read about her grief for Marette, her deep affection for Hugh, her devotion to Dan, her fascination with Baton Rouge and the "lively" Couvillion household.

He read about her loneliness, her fear, her uncertainty. He felt her joy when her story sold, her delight in Dallas and her newfound appreciation for soccer. He read about the longing she felt when she saw him and Dan together, how she ached for someone to care that much about her and to look at her with the "eyes of love."

Then he'd read about her love for him. Her desire, her admiration and her agony that she might not be entitled to the happiness she craved but didn't expect to acquire. He saw now that she'd been afraid to say she loved him. Instead she had shown him in every way she could. He'd misunderstood the passion she gave him. He hadn't realized what a precious gift it was.

She hadn't shared with him because he wouldn't share with her. He'd made halfhearted attempts to understand her, but each time she retreated he'd got mad.

The Ice Princess had frightened him, not because she shut him out but because she felt it necessary to protect herself from him. He'd interpreted her marble shield as callous indifference when the truth was, she had been guarding her vulnerability and uncertainty. What a blind fool he'd been.

"DeShea," he said aloud. The sound of her name was like the sun bursting through clouds, clear, warm and glorious. His heart filled with his love for her. He felt as if he'd swallowed the sun and it was lighting him from inside.

He had to go to her, tell her how he felt and convince her she belonged here with him and Dan. But how could he repair the damage he'd done? How could he make her see that if she came back with him he'd never shut her out again?

Reaching for the phone, he sent up a prayer and started dialing. An hour later he was ready to rip the instrument from the wall. DeShea had vanished. He'd called halfway around the world, talked to two dozen people, but no one knew where she was. He was stymied. Out of desperation, he called Hugh, ignoring the pang of jealousy he felt. It still bothered him that his charming younger brother might know more about the woman he loved than he did.

When the gregarious sibling arrived, Nick was seated at his desk, forehead resting on his clasped hands.

"You okay?"

"No. Yes." Nick rubbed his stiff neck. "I will be. Hugh, I've got to find DeShea."

The smile on Hugh's face, as he sat down, was cocky and self-satisfied. "I wondered how long you were going to suffer in silence."

"You were right. I know now that DeShea does love me." Hugh raised an eyebrow at that, but Nick continued. "I found the journal she'd written while she was here."

"I tried to tell you," Hugh reminded him. "Hell, Nick, even Daniel had an inkling how you felt. It was obvious to anyone with two eyes. It's nice to see you've come to your senses at last. I guess you're a normal male after all." Nick frowned, clearly unable to grasp the point, and Hugh went on. "I used to wonder sometimes if you were human. You were always so wise and noble. It got to be real nauseating. Not to mention impossible to live up to. More like a dad than a brother."

Someone else had suggested that to him. Someone with lavender eyes and hair like sunshine. "You trying to tell me I took my role of big brother too much to heart?"

"Something like that, yeah."

Nick leaned back in his chair, his shoulders slumping dejectedly. "I don't feel particularly wise, or fatherly. I feel lost. I need her, Hugh. I didn't really know how deep my feelings went until she was gone. Then I read her journal and saw how she felt about Dan, about being here . . . and about me." He sighed and leaned toward the desk, forearms resting on the hard surface. "I believe this is where you point out what a jerk I've been and offer a heartfelt 'I told you so.'"

"Nah," Hugh drawled. "I hate to hit a big brother when he's finally feeling like the rest of us poor, ordinary slobs. Though it's reassuring to find that you do have some flaws. You know, I think I feel closer to you now than I ever have. Small comfort, I guess." He shrugged.

"I've got to find her, Hugh. But no one knows where she is."

"Where have you tried so far?"

Nick dragged a hand over his face and sighed wearily. "The new owners of Clotilles and the real estate agent in Greenwich, telephone information in Connecticut and New York City."

"Did you look up Howard what's-his-name?" Hugh asked, slouching in the chair.

"Yeah. He's retired to the Bahamas, no number yet. I tried London, her old apartment in New York. Nothing. Where can she be? Do you have any ideas?"

The brothers turned as Daniel strolled noisily in. Nick hadn't realized that it was already time for him to be home from school.

"Can I go to Aunt DeShea's for the summer?" he asked casually, taking a sip of his canned drink.

"You know where she is?" both uncles yelped in unison.

Danny reared back and blinked. "Yes, sir. She calls me a couple times a week."

"You've talked to her? When?"

Danny shrugged and glanced at the floor. "She calls after school, before you get home."

The implications weren't lost on Nick. "Why didn't you tell— Never mind, it's okay, Dan. I need to find her. I need—" he forced himself to stay calm "—to talk to her."

"Are you going to bring her back?"

"I don't know. I'm going to try. But you'll have to help. I don't know where she is or how to find her."

"Do you have a number where we can reach her?" Hugh asked.

Danny nodded. "In my room."

"No, I don't want to do this over the phone," Nick said with a shake of his head. "Do you know what city she's in, Dan? Do you have an address?"

"No, sir. Just the phone number." He reeled off a string of numbers.

Nick consulted the phone book and shook his head. "That's not the area code for either New York City or Connecticut. I thought the house was in Greenwich?"

"That was the mansion thing," Danny informed him. "She's at the old farmhouse in the country."

"That's right," Hugh agreed, sitting up in his chair. "She mentioned that the only thing she had left was an old Victorian house in upstate New York."

"Where? What was the name of the town? Did she ever say?"

"I don't know. Oh, wait," Danny said, his expression hopeful. "She said it was a small town near Albany. I remember because it was the state capital."

Hugh sighed. "There are a hundred little towns around Albany. Anything else you can remember?"

"Hold it," Nick said suddenly, flipping through De-Shea's notebook and scanning the last few pages. "Could it have been Galena?"

"Yeah, that's it," Danny declared.

"Hugh, get me a flight out to Albany," Nick ordered on his way out of the room. "Book it out of New Orleans if you have to. I'm going to pack."

After Nick left, Hugh and Danny exchanged smiles and triumphant high fives.

DeShea stared out the window. The sun was shining, the trees and flowers beginning to bud. Spring was coming to New England. But she still felt the deep biting winter inside her heart.

Where was the blissful oblivion that she'd counted on to protect her? Where was her dependable shield that was supposed to keep all the pain away?

That belonged to another life. She didn't have Clotilles now; the routine, the endless obligations and decisions were gone. The sale had gone through and all she had now was loneliness. A new kind of loneliness. Not the old sad lament that had threaded itself through her life. This was a raw, throbbing ache in her heart that refused to ease even with the passage of time. She missed Danny more than she could stand. And Nick—thoughts of him were best avoided.

She'd just sold two more stories. Her new career was going well. She was grateful that her stockpile of work was extensive. With a little judicious editing and some minor revisions, the abundance of completed work would eliminate for a while the necessity of writing new stories, something she'd found impossible to do since leaving Baton Rouge. For the past month, her literary efforts had leaned sharply toward the depressing side, hardly the kind of work she wanted to submit to her friend.

Her calls to Danny were the only thing keeping her sane, though she was careful to call when Nick was out. She didn't think she could bear hearing his voice yet. Maybe in a few more weeks when she was stronger. She was already improving. Thoughts of Nick only intruded at night now instead of around the clock. Getting settled in her new home had helped fill the long hours and editing her stories had given structure to her days.

But no matter what she tried, nothing would altogether erase the image of Nick from her heart. She knew it was ridiculous to even try. And if she was truthful with herself, she didn't really want him erased. She wanted to keep his memory in a nice, quiet place in her mind. She wanted to file away all the moments, the little details, like the way her name seemed to come from his lips as a cherished whisper, the way his nearness sent her nerves to dancing, and the way his very presence seemed to add strength and purpose to each day.

For now, she couldn't unveil those memories. They were too fresh and much too hurtful. But in time, she would be able to pull them from the back of her mind and remember them as a nice dream, a long-ago love, brief and with no future, but still very dear and special. She'd fallen in love with a wonderful man, but they were not meant for each other. A simple fact of life. But she couldn't help wondering if it was possible these days to die from a broken heart.

Turning off her typewriter, she went downstairs and toward the front door. Outside she slipped her hand into the mailbox and pulled out the few envelopes that had been placed inside. Nothing noteworthy. Bills and some junk mail. Back inside, she started toward the kitchen, only to stop when the doorbell rang. Perhaps the mailman had forgotten to give her an envelope or package. She swung open the door, only it wasn't the mailman.

For an instant she thought she must be hallucinating. Then her heart leaped into her throat. "Nick."

She'd almost forgotten how devastatingly handsome he was, and she filled her eyes with the sight of him. The hair was dark, thicker, more wavy than she remembered, the lips more sensuous, the eyes a warmer brown. During the past six weeks, she'd thought she'd memorized every detail, every slope of the firm jaw, the curve of the strong shoulders, the taut waist. But she realized now that her memories, as vivid as they were, paled drastically in light of the real thing.

"May I come in?" he said as the silence between them lingered.

Dazed, DeShea stepped back, and with a nod ushered him inside. Words failed her. She'd stopped fantasizing that he would find her. She had no idea what to say or how to begin the conversation. To her immense relief, Nick took charge.

"You're a hard person to track down. Galena isn't exactly on the main tourist routes." *Jackass,* Nick cursed mentally. That was not what he wanted to say. He wanted to tell her he loved her, that he needed her, that life without her was barren and cold.

"How did you find me?" she asked, unable to take her greedy eyes from his face.

"Daniel," he said quietly. "He remembered you talking about the old Victorian house you still had."

Danny! Dear God, what was she thinking of? Why else would Nick come all this way? "Something's happened to him, hasn't it?" Her voice filled with panic, and she clutched his arm frantically. "Complications? Another accident? Is he all right?"

Nick shook his head and laid his hand reassuringly upon her small one. "No, Shea, he's fine. Everyone is fine. Except me."

"You?" she asked.

"Shea, we have to talk. *I* have to talk. Please."

The tone of his voice sounded so strange, so unlike the usual deep, rich tone that DeShea felt a twinge of apprehension settle over her. She led the way into the gracious old parlor and sat stiffly on the edge of a chair, steeling herself for the worst.

Nick took up a position on the sofa, staring at his hands for a long moment before speaking. He'd stood outside the yellow Victorian house for nearly thirty minutes before he gathered enough courage to knock on her door. He didn't know what he was going to say, how he would approach her. If he botched this, she might retreat into herself so deep he'd never get her out. He had hurt her. Now he wanted to make it right. But he wasn't at all sure how to do that. His confidence in his ability to solve other people's problems had disappeared when he had to deal with his own.

He looked up at her. She was pale and wan, her dark purple eyes filled with sadness. She was in so much pain and he hadn't seen it. He'd told her he couldn't read any emotion in her eyes. How could he have been so blind? It was all there—the fear, the loneliness, the love. He didn't need the journal. He had only to look in her eyes.

He wanted to crush her against his heart and make love to her until they were both senseless. But first he had to clear up the tangled mess between them, no matter how difficult or painful that might be.

"Shea, that last night in Baton Rouge, I said some things...." He took a deep breath. Why was it so hard to say what was in his heart? "I was tired and I didn't understand...." He rubbed his forehead, searching for the right words. He glanced at DeShea, then rose to his feet. He'd never get this all out if he had to look into those sad purple eyes.

He began to move about the room in nervous anxiety. "Ever since Dad died, I've been the father confessor for the family. I'd sit back smugly in my chair and listen and advise and hand down my pronouncements on what everyone should do and how they should behave. I had explanations and theories for everything. I thought I was a better than average judge of character.

"But then I met you. And I was totally baffled. I felt threatened and confused. I couldn't make sense of you, so I snarled and griped and tried to believe you were just like your mother, even when I knew you weren't. I realized that Ice Princess mask was a protection, but I didn't understand why. Each time you hid behind it I'd panic. Hugh tried to get through to me but I wouldn't listen. I was determined not to fall in love with you. But I did."

DeShea's heart felt the first beat of hope.

"I fell hard, Shea. Totally, and forever. It scared the hell out of me because it didn't feel like I thought it should. I'd been so busy analyzing everyone else's emotions that I'd never looked at my own. I didn't understand the depth involved when you love someone."

"Love hurts," she said softly.

"No, it doesn't, Shea. It feels good. It's the best feeling in the world. But sometimes we can hurt the people we love without meaning to. Shea, I love you. The things I said to you that last night were because I was scared of losing you. I needed you that night, but you hid behind that mask. I hated it when you retreated from me. I was afraid you'd run away one day and I'd never get you back." He rested his hands on his hips and sighed. "It seemed like the closer we got the more you withdrew. It should have been just the opposite."

"I was afraid. I didn't know how to handle all that I was feeling." It cost her to admit that.

"Now I know it was your way of coping with pain, but it kept me outside, separated. And it made me doubt how you felt about me. I wanted to hear you say you loved me. But you wouldn't. So I told myself you didn't really care."

"Words can't make people stay or leave," she said softly.

Nick turned to her, his eyes questioning. How could she explain, she wondered, make him understand? "I tried to tell you, several times, but you didn't understand. It's hard for me to... talk about how I really... feel." If she was going to make this work, then she had to begin facing some of her fears.

Taking a deep breath she continued. "When I was very small, I told my father I loved him. The next day he was gone. I never saw him again. I said it to my mother once, a few days after Marette left. I was feeling so lost, so scared and confused without her. I was afraid Mother would leave, too. She told me I was a fool. That if I had any brains in my head at all I'd realize that no such thing as love existed. Love only undermines a relationship, she said.

"I turned off my feelings that day. Or at least I tried to do so. They still occasionally welled up and betrayed me at the most awkward moments. Marette could always stand up to Mother, but I was too timid. After a while, I got used to keeping things inside and when the need for release became too great, I'd write."

Braving a look at his brown eyes, she was buoyed by the understanding she found there. "I wanted to tell you so many things—about me, and how I felt. But at first you didn't like me, and later... you said we were different, too different to make it work. I tried to say the right words, but it's not an easy thing to learn. And I wasn't sure how you'd react."

"Ah, Shea, I know that now. I know you were trying to show me what you couldn't say. If I'd been paying attention I'd have seen it. But it took this to open my eyes and let me see that you do love me, almost as much as I love you." He pulled out the notebook and saw her eyes widen.

"I thought I'd lost it," she mumbled.

"You left it in your room."

"Did you read... this?"

Nick nodded. "It told me things I should have seen, should have felt, but was too stupid to realize. I'm used to everyone pouring out their souls to me. I couldn't comprehend you not telling me how you felt. So I told myself that those nights we spent together meant nothing to you."

He tried to look into her eyes, but she was staring at her hands, one thumb rubbing her palm. "I'm sorry, Shea," he said. "I've hurt you. But all I want to do now is hold you and take you home where you belong. I want us to be a family, you, me and Danny."

DeShea was filled with panic. He was offering to make her dreams come true and she was terrified. It wasn't as she'd thought. She wasn't filled with contentment and happiness. Instead she was riddled with doubt and insecurities. She stood and walked across the room, widening the distance between them. Looking over her shoulder, she shook her head, her voice faint and trembling. "I can't. I don't understand your world. I don't fit in. All I know is Clotilles and being... alone."

"No, you're not meant to be alone. No one is. And you know a lot more than you think. I've seen you with Dan, with everyone. You belong with us." He held up the journal. "It's in here, Shea. All the answers, remember? Trust your instincts. Trust your feelings for me."

When Nick said it, she almost believed she could do it. "I don't know what I'm supposed to feel. The pain is awful but I'm afraid to give it up. It's familiar. It's the way I'm *supposed* to feel."

"No, Shea, it's not. You had a horrible childhood. Everyone in your life abandoned you. But it wasn't your fault. You had no control over those people. But that's in the past. You don't need to be afraid."

"It's all I know."

"That's your mother talking. Not you. You've been using Natalie's approval or disapproval as a gauge for your life, to measure love." He took a few steps toward her. "Don't you see? She's dead but she's still living in your head, still trying to control you from the grave. Don't let her do that to you, to us."

"How do I stop?" she asked softly.

"You've got to let it go, Shea. That part of your life is over. You've got to realize the difference between what you can change and what you can't. You'll never get the love and support of your mother. I wish I could give you that. I can't. But I can promise to give you all the love and encouragement I have to let you be who you are, who you were meant to be."

God help her, but she was starting to believe him, starting to think it might be real. A shiver of fear and hope coursed through her.

Nick saw her shudder and went toward her, his hands outstretched to take her shoulders. Then he stopped and let them fall to his side. "Shea. I love you. The life you had before is finished. No one in that world loved you. But I want you to share *my* life. *My* world is built on love and there's plenty to go around. We'll surround you with it."

She shook her head. "No. Everyone I love leaves. You will, too."

"No. Not me. Never."

"You could die," she said, glancing at him quickly. "Danny could have died. I've lost so many people. I couldn't stand to lose you, too. It would kill me."

"I've lost people, too. I understand how you feel. But you're wrong, Shea. You're a survivor. That's how you've made it through all this pain and heartache. Even if something should happen to me, my family would be there for you the way they were for Marette."

"It's too risky."

"Life is risky. I can't guarantee you nothing bad will ever happen. René and Marette had twelve wonderful years together. Wouldn't you rather have a short time together than none at all? Do you want to grow old alone and always wonder what it would have been like to be part of my life? I love you. I've waited a long time for you and I'll do my best to make you happy. That's the only guarantee I can give you."

She wanted him, wanted desperately to take what he offered. She weighed the risks against the love, the need against the fear. Tears welled up in her eyes, and she pressed her fingers against her mouth. She looked into his eyes and saw her heart reflected there. He was looking at her with eyes filled with love.

"Come to me, Sunshine," he said, holding out his hand.

"I'm scared."

"I know. Life is scary. That's why you find people to help you through, people like friends, family, husbands. I'll give you everything I have, Shea. I'll cherish you, love you with all my heart.''

She took the first step toward him and placed her hand in his.

He enfolded her in his arms and held her close. "I won't ever let you know loneliness and pain again."

In his arms the fear began to ebb. Hope flowed back into her heart. She felt his strength, his love pouring into her and looked up into his eyes. "Nick—" she took a deep breath and crossed the barrier "—I love you."

The look in his eyes filled her heart. She'd never known three words could put such a look of joy in his eyes. Why hadn't she said it before?

"Ah, Sunshine, that's all I ever wanted to hear." With a moan of desire, he captured her mouth, drowning in the passion that erupted between them, claiming her heart, mind and soul.

Twilight was setting on the yellow Victorian house when Nick and DeShea put aside their physical hunger to talk more about their future. Seated beside her in the creaking porch swing, Nick toyed with the slim fingers that were entwined with his.

"Shea, I've been offered a new job in Memphis. I haven't told anyone about it yet, but maybe I should take it and stop playing patriarch to all the Couvillions."

"Is that what you want to do?" she asked quietly. Knowing how deep his familial roots went, the fact he was considering leaving his hometown was indicative of the change in him.

"I didn't think so. When my regional manager first suggested it, I wasn't even going to consider it. But then on the way here to find you, I began to wonder if it wasn't the perfect opportunity for both of us. I thought about what you said to me that night on the levee, about breaking away." He shifted his position on the slatted swing and looked at her eagerly. "It's still close enough that we could be home in a few hours for visits or holidays. They have a good soccer program there for Dan, much better than Baton Rouge, and the job pays more. Of course, there's more responsibility, but it's a good promotion. We could start over fresh. You and me and Dan. We could build a life that didn't constantly remind us of the past. A life for *us.*"

"Do you think Danny would like that?" she asked cautiously, but her heart was already soaring with hope.

"Yes, I do. He misses you, and he loves you very much." He grinned sheepishly. "He's barely spoken to me since you left. He told me in no uncertain terms that it was entirely my fault."

"Danny asked me to stay, to live in the house with you so we could be like a family."

"He did?" Nick asked in surprise. "When was that?"

"The day his English teacher called."

A smile tilted the corner of Nick's mouth. "He knew right from the beginning that you belonged here. What did you tell him?"

"That it wasn't practical. But that I'd think about it."

"And now?"

"Now, I think I'd like to tell him I'll stay, and maybe add to the family."

Nick turned and looked at her, brown eyes searching the depths of her lavender ones. "What are you saying?"

"That a little brother or sister might be good for Daniel. I'd like to put some of my theories on raising children into practice."

"I'll teach you everything I know," he said, placing a kiss gently on her parted lips.

"About children?" she asked, her voice breathless under his kiss.

"About love," he replied, pulling her closer and beginning a tour of her neck with his lips.

"I'm a slow learner," she whispered.

The faint squeak of the rusty chain on the swing was the only sound in the twilight as Nick and DeShea retreated into the solid comfort of the old Victorian house.

* * * * *

COMING NEXT MONTH

LURING A LADY
Nora Roberts

Sydney Hayward came from a wealthy, privileged background and she wasn't prepared to take over the family corporation or to deal with complications like carpenter Mikhail Stanislaski. They were from different worlds...

OVER EASY
Victoria Pade

Lee Farrell was supposed to be retrieving his Uncle's stolen work, but a white lie had him playing bodyguard to Blythe Coopersmith, the scientist who'd absconded with the goods!

PRODIGAL FATHER
Gina Ferris

Kelsey Campbell's business was making wishes come true. Cole Saxon denied that he dreamt of reuniting with his father but Kelsey was determined that this stubborn man was going to have even his hidden desires satisfied.

Silhouette Special Edition

COMING NEXT MONTH

PRELUDE TO A WEDDING
Patricia McLinn

Bette Wharton's business was to keep Paul
Monroe's business running, which was a nightmare
as he lived only for the moment. Why couldn't he
think about his future – and her role in it?

JOSHUA AND THE COWGIRL
Sherryl Woods

Globe-trotting financial wizard Joshua Ames swore
he'd never go west again after business had made
him visit the uncivilized wilds of Wyoming. But
he couldn't avoid the snowy cattle country or the
maddening, irresistible woman he hadn't been able
to forget.

EMBERS
Mary Kirk

Disaster and fire summoned Anne Marquel home to face
the ghosts of the past. She'd left in silence, confiding in no
one – not even Connor, her girlhood hero. What would Con
think of her after all this time?

4 SILHOUETTE SPECIAL EDITIONS

AND 2 GIFTS ARE YOURS ABSOLUTELY FREE!

The emotional lives of mature, career-minded heroines blend with believable situations, and prove that there is more to love than mere romance. Please accept a lavish FREE offer of 4 books, a cuddly teddy and a special MYSTERY GIFT...without obligation. Then, if you choose, go on to enjoy 6 more exciting Special Editions, each month at £1.75 each. Send the coupon below at once to:

SILHOUETTE READER SERVICE, FREEPOST, PO BOX 236, CROYDON, SURREY CR9 9EL.